OLIVE BLUES

The Edge of Provence, Book 1

Bren Atkinson

REBEL
MAGIC

REBEL
MAGIC

To C and C, with love

Contents

Chapter 1

Shirley

It's one of those days where writing anything good is like pulling teeth. Maybe it's because I'm attempting to produce my own advertising material, which feels odd, or maybe it's because I've been putting it off for too long and it really has to be done.

Dominated by its imposing stone keep, the small town of Crest nestles beside the river Drôme. Close to vineyards and amid mountains, rolling hills and picturesque, unspoiled villages, it is France at its most intimate and charming.

No. Clichéd.

You'd think I could do a better job of this considering the amount of tourist blurb I've written or translated, for countless clients, and for well over three decades.

Crest is just ten kilometres – (or shall I put miles? Or both?) – *from Provence.*

Technically, that's true. In practice, will those ten kilometres put people off? Should I even mention it? Will they think it's not as good, somehow, as real Provence? Is this false advertising, even using the name?

I'm probably over-thinking all this. Nothing new there. *Onwards, woman!*

A wonderful location, offering a wealth of things to do and see, plus a distinct penchant –

Can a town have a penchant for something?

A bed and breakfast with that special –

Special what? Touch? Feel?

Nope, delete that bit.

With its superb views over farmland and forests, airy rooms, a heated pool and a garden with quiet, shady corners or places to soak up the sun, our bed and breakfast – with modern, sober furnishings, wifi –

No again. Sounds like a shopping list.

We offer varied breakfasts, always with home-made bread and delicious preserves. Guests can also enjoy gourmet evening meals featuring home-grown and organic produce, if ordered at breakfast time at the latest.

That's sort of okay, if a bit long-winded.

Should I quote some typical menus? Yes, probably.

And speaking of menus, I'll have to get on with tonight's meal before long. Any moment now I'm going to be disturbed by our current 'guest', who happens to be my mother and who went for a quiet read on the covered terrace after lunch. Not that it isn't normally quiet around here, but a gang of stonemasons and a bulldozer do tend to shatter the peace a little and they're due back any moment now.

Fortunately, Mum doesn't understand French that well, and French obscenities even less. My own command of the language – which is not bad if I say so myself – has improved vastly in terms of the more colourful bits over the last few weeks.

Yes, that's their van returning, so the brief interlude looks like it's over and we'll be back to concrete mixers and raucous banter.

The noise, the mud and the general upheaval haven't really bothered me that much over the last few weeks, because I can see our three new guest rooms taking shape nicely. I've been able to get on with work more or less as normal, grateful that my writing and editing jobs are flexible enough for me to provide tea, coffee, cakes and pastries at regular intervals. This keeps the builders – and thus me – happy.

Until my mother arrived.

The builders are still reaping the benefits of my baking, but my sanity is taking a beating.

This short hour's respite has been a case of escaping Mum for a while on the pretext of having some work to finish. Fortunately, she is not impressed by computers so she can't tell whether I'm working or not. She probably thinks I'm neglecting her all the same.

And here she comes. She's a poem in pastels. Neatly permed white hair, pale blue (or pink, or turquoise) top and skirt. She's remarkably spry for eighty-eight – and as critical as she's always been. She doesn't approve of our B&B project, knows how to put walls up better than the builders, and is probably on the warpath about something right now.

"I don't want to disturb you, but–" she starts.

If I had a Euro for every time that I heard that, we'd probably have enough for a smart meal out every time she leaves. Basically, it means I should drop everything and do whatever she's expecting.

I've had nearly six decades of experience with my mother's character.

This time, she can't find the secateurs because she thinks the geraniums should be dead-headed and I'm clearly too busy to get around to it.

My gut reaction is to tell her that I've done a million other things this week, of which half of them have been interrupted by her finding different tasks for me, so the bloody flowers aren't an issue.

Good sense tells me that if she potters around with the secateurs and a bucket, I can get dinner started in peace. Until she comes back to remind me of something else.

***

This should be delightful – a meal with friends at the end of the day – but instead we're being treated to Mum holding forth on how the wicked French mistreat the poor British calves exported here. Not even the dish of olives, which Mum adores, has softened her diatribe.

I roll my eyes discreetly at Helen and Joe, our friends who are over, and kick myself for saying 'I'll just check on the veal' a few minutes ago. That was her cue.

I should have produced a nice tough chunk of pork, overcooked and with insipid apple sauce.

The whole thing about the poor calves was apparently all over the British press. If I'm not mistaken, though, she's given up newspapers and only watches the television news, because you can never believe all the rubbish that they put in papers these days. We've had that lecture too.

I ask – all innocence – which paper she's reading lately and bingo: she admits she doesn't read one regularly. She knows from discussing things with friends who do.

She also throws me a filthy look.

Steve shoots me a warning glance, but it's at least subtle: my husband usually is, bless him, or at least when it comes to keeping the peace with my mother. I neatly change the subject to the lovely weather we're having, and the fact that we can still have pre-dinner drinks outside in early October.

Before the veal episode, the deepening dusk over the garden, the pool and the hills had almost loosened the constant knot in my stomach that takes up residence every time my mother does. Almost, but not quite. I was still expecting some sort of criticism tonight and sure enough, here we are.

We've seated her with her back to the bulldozer and the heaps of mud in a bid to avoid her gloomy predictions of how builders always let you down, but now she's moving onto that.

I think it's time to eat.

Mum is soon onto her second or third glass of wine. Despite her disdain for 'French drinking habits', probably also learned from the television news, her friends, magazines at the hairdressers, or all three, she can knock it back happily. To her credit, I've never seen her less than sober. I keep hoping a few glasses might mellow her a bit.

Mum isn't a great fan of France. I think she still considers the French are weak-kneed cowards who gave into Hitler.

French cooking comes under regular criticism: in her opinion it's too fancy, and therefore no match for England, particularly South Yorkshire, or more particularly Sheffield, on my sister's table.

What I've made tonight isn't particularly French. As a starter, I've made a cold soup of tiny, fresh courgettes spiked with lemon, basil and garlic and mixed with Greek yoghurt. I've added some oven-crisped flakes of cured ham and a grilled slice of garlic bread.

Joe pronounces it delicious and it is. Mum says it's 'very nice.' From the expression on her face I'm ready for the 'but.'

I'm not disappointed.

According to my mother, my sister Gillian is an excellent cook, perfect wife, and used to be an amazing career woman. She never serves courgettes because they're just so *uninteresting*. That slides into a description of her last meal chez Gillian and Clive, when they had an absolutely *wonderful* starter with a really *generous* portion of smoked salmon. Cold soup as a starter in those tiny little cups is, well, a little too *simple* if I'm going to actually serve meals to *guests*.

My mother always talks in italics when the subject is my sister.

I see Helen raise her eyebrows and my husband shoots me yet another of his looks: he probably sensed me bristling yet again. Thirty years of marriage and three decades of observing the relationship between my mother and I, means he knows when to defuse things.

"Nothing like a bit of Scottish salmon," he says mildly. "Top up your glass, Edna?"

Well done, Steve. It stops me from growling that the idea of the soup and the small portion was because of her often-stated preference for eating light meals in the evening.

Things continue predictably. There's more to come on my sister's culinary prowess and other amazing skills. That segues effortlessly into my sister's former job, her new kitchen, their holidays, their brilliant son, and their new car: the latest model with all the trimmings of course.

The continuation of all that over cheese and dessert, even with Steve's heroic attempt to steer the conversation onto something other than my sister, makes me gulp down too much wine, too fast, and to hell with what she thinks.

It's all par for the course and by the time Helen and Joe get up to leave, I feel like I do every evening when Mum is over. Exhausted and miserable.

To escape for a few minutes, I accompany Helen and Joe outside, and Helen gives my shoulder a squeeze.

"Is there anything your sister can't do?" she says casually. "I nearly asked, but I didn't think it would go down well."

I chuckle.

"She may need a brush-up course in nuclear physics, or in the lesser dialects of Africa," I sigh. "But I did warn you she was a bloody saint. And I'm sorry – that wasn't a very comfortable evening."

"Don't sweat it," Joe says cheerfully. "Wonderful meal, Shirley. How much longer is she staying?"

"Six days. If she lives that long."

"It'll be fine," Helen says. "And Emma's coming tomorrow, right?"

"Yes." The thought of my daughter visiting is a positive one. "At least that. Sorry again, both of you. I'm being a self-pitying idiot."

"No, you're not. Your Mum pushes all your buttons."

"Tell me about it," I grimace.

"Chin up. Give me a call tomorrow if you can escape, and we'll make a date for you to come over. Don't let her get you down, Shirley."

"I'll try," I say, aiming for a grin that I suspect is more a grimace. Having a friend like Helen is a godsend but tonight she's been essential for my sanity.

I head back inside. Steve's probably stacking the dishwasher and getting an earful on how my sister *never* lets Clive help in the kitchen because it's not a man's job. Fortunately, my husband knows that one by heart, so he'll let it pass as he always does.

I'm right. Steve's not only got the machine loaded and running but he's washed the glasses and Mum's drying them.

"Let me do that," I say. "You must be tired."

15

"I was just helping. Gillian doesn't put her glasses in the dishwasher either."

Wow. I'm doing something right.

"But then she does have *really* beautiful crystal glasses, and she says that even though she has an *excellent* dishwasher, it would be a shame to spoil them. She does entertain a lot, you know – but I told you that, didn't I? Silly old woman that I am, I must be repeating myself."

There's really no answer to that.

Give it a few days, I tell myself, and I'll finally tell her I never, ever want to hear the epic of Gillian's kitchen renovations again, or her breath-taking culinary achievements *sans* courgettes.

"Nice couple, Helen and Joe," Mum says, relinquishing the tea towel.

Oh, please no, not a post-mortem. There's bound to be a 'but' in there, too. My mother has been criticising everybody she meets as soon as they're out of earshot since I can remember, whether they were card-playing friends, the people at church, Dad's customers, the neighbours, or our relatives.

Either my hearing was particularly good, the walls of the three-bedroomed semi were too thin, or Mum didn't bother to keep her voice down, but there were many nights when, from my bedroom, I would hear her holding forth downstairs, systematically finding fault with people. When I was still fairly small, I'd actually asked her whether we were really *good* people and everybody else was bad.

She didn't have an answer to that, but for a while she either kept her voice down or chose her moments better.

There are a few exceptions to those deserving criticism. On the Edna Whitlow stamp of approval list, Gillian is number one, closely followed by Clive and their son Kevin.

Emma, her granddaughter, does pretty well too, and her partner Rainer seems acceptable. He's Swiss, dresses well and he's got a great job, which are all points in his favour.

I think she's fond of Steve too, or maybe it's just that she can't find much to criticise apart from the fact he opted out of life as a corporate man in lovely, civilised Switzerland (which is on the list of approved countries) a few years back and now resides in the land of veal-eaters, doing non-manly things like filling dishwashers and chopping veg.

"They're lovely people, Helen and Joe," I say firmly. I nearly add that despite living in two French-speaking countries for the last three decades, we still enjoy speaking English to other people and are happy to have found an English couple who share our sense of humour and love of the area.

Saying so, though, will only lead to more anti-French statements. Most of our other friends are French, but handling Mum *and* playing interpreter *and* trying to curb her anti-French statements over a dinner was more than I could handle.

"And retired early. If only your dad could have done that."

"Joe was in the police, Mum. They get to retire earlier."

"All right for some, isn't it? Your dad was in the war and he didn't have special treatment."

I'm not getting into the whole scenario of Dad, the shop, and his death within six months of retiring. I still miss him, and I'll lose my temper right here and now if she starts on the whole story of how hard they'd worked, how badly life treated her, and how they, and particularly she, had deserved better.

Dad found nothing wrong with being a grocer. He loved his girls, he loved what he did and – I think but I'm never really sure – he loved Mum while constantly wondering how the hell to handle her.

"So, they also like living in the back of beyond?"

She's not going to let it die that easily. That's right, Mum. Make it sound like some sort of distant outpost of society. Crest has 9,000 people. It's not Sheffield, but it's not the Gobi Desert. Valence, graceful and bustling, is half an hour away. It can take that long to get from Mum's semi on the outskirts of Sheffield into the city, and that's on a good day.

"I think they enjoy life here," Steve says cheerfully, handing me the last glass to dry. "Like Shirley and I do."

I nearly applaud.

Mum sniffs.

"Joe needs to watch himself though. Smoking like he does. And I *really* don't mean to be rude but why don't people dress up when they go out to dinner?"

"I really think it's none of our business whether people smoke or not, Mum," I say, trying not to sound snappy.

Mum gave up during my teens after smoking like a chimney for years, before the whole notion of passive smoking was even talked about. Since then, she's given new meaning to the phrase 'there's no prude like a reformed prostitute'.

"And no," I add. "People around here – or at least people we know – don't do heels and skirts when we see each other for a meal."

"It's just common courtesy, that's all," she fires back. Mum has been at war on jeans all her life and these days I tend to live in them. So do Helen and Joe.

Being a coward, I've opted for plain black trousers and a silky shirt tonight and Steve's wearing some rather elderly yet clean linen ones because that's what I shoved into his hands earlier.

"Times change, Mum," I said, attempting to sound more cheerful than I am. "According to Em, it's quite the thing for her generation to get all dressed up in London when they go out, but maybe my generation was born to be scruffy. Now, let me get you a glass of water to take upstairs. It's getting late."

Blessedly, she lets it drop and heads off upstairs.

She must be tired, because we're spared the speech on Gillian *always* dressing up for her guests. That usually comes with the spiel on her cooking and her dinner parties but was omitted tonight in front of Helen and Joe. I'm not sure whether it was out of politeness towards them or whether she just forgot.

How uncharitable of me.

"Oh." She pauses halfway up. "I'm not certain I brought my indigestion tablets with me. And after that rich food –"

***

Ten minutes later, snug in a fleece, nursing a generous brandy by the pool and lighting up a well-deserved cigarette, I take some long, deep breaths.

I've nearly given up the nicotine. Most of the time. The reproachful stares from Mum mean I resort to a sneaky one with the builders during the day, well out of her sight.

"I need this," I say. "It was bloody purgatory tonight."

"The veal was great," Steve says. I can see him smiling in the dim light from the solar lamps. We didn't put the proper outside lights on to avoid any reappearances from Mum, who hates to miss anything. "Poor little calves, though."

"And I went and forgot my evening dress and pearls. But thanks."

"For?"

"Knowing how to handle her."

"Water off a duck's back," he says, taking a long sip. "You really shouldn't let her get to you."

"You've only told me that, what, a dozen times this week? Half a million since you first saw the Shirley and Edna show?"

"Don't," he says gently. "She's just the way she is."

"And that means she's got the right to treat me like…"

"People can only hurt you if you let them. As you used to like telling Em when she got bullied at school."

"I know." I twist my glass around in my hands. "And it worked. At least with the kids in her class."

"Right. And if I could possibly change the subject from your mum, who's held centre stage all night; we need to find a decent carpenter. The masonry people said they have somebody who works with them, who specialises in it, so that could be a plan."

I sigh. We'd chosen a carpentry company, accepted the estimates, and now they seem to have simply dumped us. I've avoided all mention of this in front of Mum, because it would have fuelled the anti-French fires, but it's bothering me. We need to get on with the woodwork and soon.

"We'll remind them tomorrow then, and see if they can give us the name. And we need to check if the tiles arrived. If you're going to pick up the taps, can you call in and give them a nudge, if they haven't?"

"Will do." Steve glances over at the bulldozers. "They should finish the walls within a couple of days and start on the outside patio. Right on schedule."

"Miracles still happen, eh?"

I do hope they do, and glance up at the main house. Despite everything, I smile. It has that effect on me.

When we fell in love with the place four years back, we started talking about what we could do with the outbuilding even before we'd fought our way through French bureaucracy to make the purchase.

It's a lovely Provençal style villa with a sizeable chunk of land, and it's graceful and timeless, despite being only a few years old when we bought it. The style of architecture hasn't changed much in decades, if not centuries, around here, and I hope it never does.

Everywhere you go in southern France, you can't help but notice the terracotta roof tiles, the pale stone or stucco houses with their covered and generous terraces. Ours is no different. It's in a soft pink with wooden shutters on the upstairs windows painted in the typical Provençal blue that I love.

Our original idea was to buy a stone house, but every one we saw within our price range needed so much work doing to bring the electricity and plumbing up to date that we hesitated. We almost lost hope and gave up the search, but when we drove up the hill from the centre of Crest, along a tree-lined lane and into the yellow gravel of the drive here, it felt right.

It still does.

It wouldn't take that much to smarten the additional part up and make it into B&B rooms one day, we'd said optimistically, once we'd taken in the view over the hills, grinning as we discovered one room after the other. Everything was airy, with lots of white walls and a few pale wood beams to give it warmth in the sunny main room. The tiled floors seemed practical, and the open kitchen with a small terrace outside was perfect.

I was already imagining rugs on the floors and adding a few more flower beds when I caught sight of the pool.

I'm a Yorkshire girl. There aren't that many houses with pools on the outskirts of Sheffield, and particularly not in the part I grew up in. This looked like paradise. Nearly all the houses we'd seen had pools, but this one was set below the house, down some shallow steps. It had a wide terrace overlooking the rest of the garden and was edged with a couple of bushes and palm trees to give it privacy. In one corner was a stunning olive tree, blue-green and reflected in the gentle dapples of the pool. A pool that wasn't a plain old rectangle but had softly curving edges.

The tree, and the idea of basking in water and gazing out over the hills, were the icing on the cake.

We underestimated the work it would need for the B&B project, but tackled it all anyway. It's taking a small army of builders, an architect, and a million details to worry about, but we've been fortunate with everybody involved so far. Having read some horror stories about French builders (I didn't admit that to my mother), we'd expected a long series of catastrophes.

The builders roll up on time and enjoy what they do, and they're bang on schedule. And there's the added bonus of my steadily increasing repertoire of French profanities.

Steve, who still puts in a few hours of work a week helping small foreign companies set up in business among the nightmare of French or Swiss bureaucracy, is far happier with a power tool or a garden fork in his hand than he ever seemed to be with corporate budgets for a multinational in Switzerland. His inheritance gave us a chance to take a new direction, and that's exactly what we're doing. He had the opportunity to take early retirement and snatched it, and we moved to France only months after that.

I should count my blessings. At the grand age of fifty-eight, Shirley Sandford, née Whitlow (and once upon a time dubbed Witless by the school bullies) is going to have fun and do what she damned well wants to. I am not going to let my mother make me feel guilty or inadequate about this project. So there.

I grab Steve's hand, although it's getting chillier now. There's still a whiff of honeysuckle, and a couple of bats swoop low, drinking from the pool.

"Stonemasons and noise at eight," Steve says eventually. "Better make a move, Mrs Sandford."

"Indeed, Mr Sandford," I nod. "You know what's good, though? Despite everything, the words "boarding house" never passed her ladyship's lips once tonight."

"See? She's getting used to the idea. And you're thinking positive."

"Now we just need to find a carpenter, right?"

"Right. Or we'll send for Gillian" Steve chuckles. "Considering how good she is at everything else, maybe she could just pop over with a load of two-by-fours?"

Chapter 2

Emma

Emma Sandford glanced at the clock, waking for the third time. Six thirty. She could manage another hour in bed yet.

They hadn't got to bed too late after a few drinks with the gang and a hastily grabbed takeaway, but she'd had trouble getting to sleep. Rainer, of course, hadn't.

The evening's conversation – if you could call it that – had been one of those 'aren't we wonderful' ones. Jakey, loudmouth that he was, had been showing off about his skills with computer networks as he always did. Somebody else had been sharing his extensive knowledge of corporate politics, which had been so boring Emma had just switched off. Rainer, however, had seemed fascinated by it all and particularly impressed by Jakey.

Maybe she should give in and get going, Emma thought. Rainer always seemed to take it badly if she didn't get up and get the coffee machine on before he emerged. His first shot of caffeine was sacred, although he called in at a Starbucks before work as well. Or was it a Costa now? One was apparently more acceptable than the other with the in-crowd, but she forgot which.

A police car went past, sirens wailing. Strangely enough, she'd almost welcomed the sound of those when she first came to London. They were different to the high-pitched French ones that used to fly past her window so often, and particularly when she was a student living in a horrible dump of a place in Lyon.

This morning, though, they were a damned nuisance, just like the upstairs neighbours who apparently wore clogs and danced jigs before they went to bed. Or the Chinese restaurant up the road. Had it always given off the smell of stale prawn crackers? And something sickly. Maybe the pork with caramel she'd been such a fan of when they first moved in?

She wouldn't criticise London, though. She *loved* London and said so over and over – in different ways – on Facebook, on Twitter, and to her old friends in Lyon.

Besides, London wasn't the problem. London was fun, it was exciting and that hadn't worn off a bit in the year she'd been there. The hardest part was the poky flat, and the increasingly boring job wasn't helping.

And Rainer, a little, or at least recently, she thought, but then bit her lip.

No, Rainer wasn't a problem. They were a modern couple. They had agreed to take a positive attitude to the whole relationship. They worked things out, listened to each other, and had bad patches. Didn't everybody?

At least they didn't act like her parents had – her mother's martyred silence, her father's capacity to focus on his job and little else and never talk about his feelings. Things had frequently been dodgy during all those years he'd worked and worked. It felt like her mother had been constantly worried, because he worked crazy hours, because he was exhausted, because he was in his own world of finance, budgets, and deadlines. And yet, they adored each other. They were happier now, and that was good to see.

Emma had vowed never to be a worrier or a martyr, and mostly, she wasn't. A workaholic, though – yes, she took after her father in that but that was how you got ahead.

She turned the alarm clock away, not wanting to see it and not wanting to wake Rainer too early, which always made him grumpy and led to arguments.

Rainer usually started the arguments because he was so critical, she thought, but she shouted back. Then they made up over furiously wonderful sex and ridiculously greasy takeaways.

Recently there'd been few rows and even fewer takeaways. Rainer was on a health kick and had joined another new gym. Besides, his latest rise at the bank had meant they went to restaurants more often: funky, modern places where everybody took photos of the food for their Facebook and Twitter accounts. She'd started doing it too.

Rainer had embraced social media with a bang, and she was curiously addicted too. So, they had that in common.

Nothing serious was wrong between the two of them, she decided. Even if he'd said the results of her latest online clothes-shopping spree looked 'a bit cheap' a couple of days ago, he didn't mean tarty cheap, surely?

She'd wear it all anyway. A girl needed fun clothes and accessories, and she enjoyed trying new, unusual things. The Swiss weren't quite as adventurous. Even when she'd moved to Lyon to study, she found the French students chic but lacking in fantasy. In London, it was 'anything goes' and she liked that even though Rainer was less enthusiastic about anything he considered too showy.

Lots of misunderstandings came from him being Swiss – the German-speaking variety –so she cut him a bit of slack. His English was fine, but he hadn't had her advantage of growing up bilingual. They always spoke in English, so Rainer was at a disadvantage, as he pointed out from time to time.

At least he never suggested they speak German, she thought with a wry smile. She'd disliked the language from the moment she'd had it forced on her at school in the French-speaking part of Switzerland, but she understood it well enough.

If they had children, she was most definitely going to speak to them in French, but that topic wasn't on the programme for another year or two. They'd already decided to live a little first. People had kids over thirty now, didn't they? At twenty-eight, she had a few years to go. Her biological clock was ticking away so quietly she didn't notice it much.

Her parents weren't putting her under any pressure, although she suspected they'd love the idea. Being grandparents was fun according to Gran's take on it: spoil them a little, and you can always give them back to their parents when you've had enough.

Gran could be remarkably down to earth about some things, although her mother never seemed to accept that.

Emma stirred restlessly and considered reaching for her tablet to see what her online friends were up to, but that might wake Rainer. She didn't feel like getting out of bed and going into the kitchen that always felt chilly, even in summer.

Her mother raved about the sunshine in France, but Emma would retort that she didn't mind English weather. She was living her dream in London and the weather wasn't going to make any difference to that.

All it needed right now was for her and Rainer to regroup a bit. They'd have to have some quality discussion and soon. The last few weeks had been so busy they'd hardly had any real time together. Maybe that was what was niggling at her even more than the job and the flat.

When she got back from France, she'd suggest it. They could spend a whole weekend in pyjamas, eat junk food, play video games, and snuggle up to talk about what came next – including finding somewhere nicer to live.

That made her smile and she looked affectionately at the short, spiky hair – soon to be tamed into submission for the day ahead. A banker's lot included suits, short haircuts, increasing overtime, and problems with new projects.

"What time is it?" Rainer turned over, seeing her awake. "You turned the clock around earlier." It sounded reproachful.

"Nearly seven. Sorry, did I wake you?"

"Yes. Doesn't matter, I'll make an early start. We have a review of the new project this morning."

He still said 'rewiew'. And, for that matter, he still had trouble with the 'w' sound. As in "Wery vell." It was part of his charm.

"I'll get coffee then? And how about I make us a proper breakfast and you skip the coffee house? As I'm leaving today?"

Dammit, she thought, she was doing the whole making every phrase into a question thing again, which he hated. But he didn't seem to notice, and instead was digging around for his phone.

"Why isn't it charged?" he said, looking at it and frowning. *Vy.*

"Maybe because you forgot to charge it? Plug it in now and it'll be OK for the bus. Pancakes?"

"No pancakes. Just coffee. And where are all the *fucking* cables? Don't you put *anything* in its place?"

"And good morning to you too, Mr Grumpy," she said. "Your charger is beside your laptop."

"Probably buried under your papers."

She wasn't going to take the bait. Some of their arguments were because she was untidy. Shouting right now could be interesting if it could eventually lead to a little fun making up under the duvet, but Rainer had never been one for sex on weekday mornings. Teutonic discipline, she often teased him. Just like his firm belief that the pill was a good thing, but the pill plus condoms were even better. More hygienic.

By the time the coffee was brewed, he emerged dressed and still frowning as he perched at the minuscule breakfast bar and dropped three cubes of sugar into his cup. Emma made herself tea, and enjoyed the warmth of the mug as she clasped it.

"So, how's work?" he asked, stirring. *Verk*

"Work work or course work?" Rainer wasn't given to either asking about her work or making idle chit-chat before the first shot of caffeine, but this was good, wasn't it?

"Both."

"Work work… same old, same old," she said ruefully, not wanting to complain too much because he told her regularly that she was lucky to have a job, much as it was starting to seem like a dead end. "The course work's fine. I've made a start on my dissertation, and thought I'd focus on –"

He wasn't listening, she realised. Too busy checking mail on his tablet, which fortunately was charged.

"The sex life of hamsters," she said calmly.

No response.

Rainer wasn't keen on her doing the certification course on digital media marketing, saying it would be too hard on her with a full-time job and she had her MBA anyway. Emma tried not to think it was because he preferred her to spend more time on housework.

The place was messy, she realised, looking at the kitchen. They hadn't cooked anything for a week, but the dishes from the last time they'd done so were still piled up on the drainer, and the sink was full of dirty cups and glasses.

The silence continued until he stowed his phone in his suit pocket and picked up his briefcase.

When had he started wearing sober blue ties instead of the ones with Deputy Dawg or rows of flying pigs on them? She'd liked those. She'd bought most of them.

The bank had probably sent out a memo on excessive flamboyancy.

"So," she attempted an upbeat tone. "I'll see you Tuesday night. I'll give your love to Mum and Dad and tell them you'd have been far happier drinking their wine and helping them lay tiles than earning a living, shall I?"

"Of course."

Oh, come *on* Rainer, she thought. At least say you'll miss me?

He didn't, but he wasn't the effusive type.

"Want me to bring anything back?"

"French food? I think not."

Rainer shared Gran's low opinion of French anything.

"We'll go out when you get back," he added. "Alex told me about a really great sushi place –we should try it out, get Jakey and his new girlfriend to join us."

Emma blinked. Rainer didn't like sushi, or not usually, but then Alex was his new boss so they would, of course, try it out. Maybe she'd eventually meet this person whose name cropped up now and then. Not that they socialised much with his work colleagues, though, and the bank didn't really go in for 'bring your partner' events.

"Fine. Cross your fingers the Eurostar's on time then. French trains and all that."

"Call me," he nodded, and left.

The tea had gone cold, and the sight of the kitchen wasn't helping her mood. The living room was even worse than the kitchen. Maybe she'd give it a quick tidy before she went to St Pancras – there was plenty of time. She could get on with her dissertation on the train.

She flicked on her tablet, raising her eyebrows at a tweet from Alex, cursing about bad service in a restaurant. All the woman ever seemed to do was to pick fault with things. Why did Emma even follow her?

Because Rainer had suggested it, and because it was Rainer's boss and he said that she, like them, enjoyed the bar and restaurant scene.

Sometimes, Emma admitted to herself, Alex's impressions of places were amusing: her profile said she was 'A Swiss discovering the best and worst bits of London', and nearly all her photos were of meals and monuments. Her profile photo showed a skinny blonde woman on the deck of a yacht. She was no spring chicken and probably a boring Swiss banker.

Oops. They weren't all boring, she reminded herself.

Her mother had tweeted the previous afternoon for the first time in days. *Damned carpenter gone AWOL. On quest for new one.* The 'damned' was quite uncharacteristic of her posts, but then Gran was in residence.

She imagined her parents, sitting outside on the terrace drinking disgustingly strong coffee. Some Provençal sunshine and her mum's cooking wouldn't go amiss, and nor would somewhere tidy. Emma liked tidy, but she just wasn't good at it.

Should she do the dishes? Maybe later. Or maybe not at all. The kitchen was hardly functional anyway, and as grim as the rest of the place.

Rainer had chosen the flat, and she'd never liked it. It was furnished, not attractively, but it had been temporary and an easy bus ride to the bank. Moving was difficult in London because of the property prices and the lack of decent places, and every time they'd looked around, they'd given up. Emma decided it was now essential. They'd make time for it somehow.

Rainer had added a few extras, such as the sophisticated coffee machine, because he'd moved there first, a few months before she did. Her own furniture and kitchen equipment were in storage in Lyon, but she wondered if they'd meet with Rainer's approval.

The icily elegant Frau Feldmann would be horrified by this place. The Feldmanns lived in a huge old house in Bern, where she was certain nothing was ever out of place. Emma and Rainer had visited last Christmas and it was glamorous to the extreme. Designer tree, designer ornaments, and everything so organised and expensive she'd been frightened to even move a chair.

Rainer's father was fun. Round-faced and constantly cheerful, he seemed unimpressed by his wife's airs and graces and ignored the pursed lips and looks of disapproval. Emma had been told to call him Markus and been regaled with stories about his love of France.

Markus was a great person to talk to about anything at all. When he came to London on business, she could discuss anything with him: business, wine, travel.

Emma suspected the Feldmanns didn't have a happy marriage, because Markus seemed to come alive once he got away from the stifling atmosphere at home. If he and his wife were a total mismatch, which was how it looked, they must be together for a reason, but what? Maybe Frau Feldmann liked his money? Maybe they'd been happier once?

Relationships, Emma decided, were a minefield. But Rainer wouldn't turn out like his mother, would he?

Reaching for the washing up liquid, she found the bottle empty, which called for a quick text.

"Pls buy washing up liquid. Love you xxx".

She decided to pop to a supermarket and buy some oatcakes and lemon curd – things her mother found hard to find in France and among the precious few things she still missed after three decades of living away from England.

She'd bought a book for Gran, and checked that it had no sex in it, which was apparently essential – it was a brand-new historical romance, set in Yorkshire. Plus some ridiculously expensive *Liberty* chocolates, although Gran would say she still preferred Thornton's, made in Sheffield.

It was going to be strange meeting up with Gran in France. Emma made the effort to visit her in Sheffield now and then, often just for a day to take her out for a meal in a local pub. Once, Rainer had gone too. They'd driven up in his car and taken her to an unpleasant, pseudo-funky place in Derbyshire that he'd found on Yelp.

Rainer had quickly decided that he hated Sheffield, disliked Derbyshire, and loathed Gran's house and its distinctly fussy décor, but he'd been a gentleman and admired the fact that it was immaculate. *Wery* immaculate.

What more could anybody ask of a guy who was ambitious, good-looking, good in bed, and polite to his girlfriend's grandmother?

Emma went into the bedroom and reached for a suitcase, throwing some casual clothes in. She loved travelling and had inherited that from her parents. There had been superb family holidays in Morocco and Kenya when she'd been a teenager, followed by backpacking to Italy as a student, or a cheap and rather horrible all-inclusive week in Tunisia during her Masters. Part of the thrill was the journey itself. The change of pace during a journey appealed to her whether it was a few hours on the Eurostar or flying to the other side of the world.

Her job was supposed to include travel, which was why she'd taken it, but trips any further afield than a dreary trip to Wales hadn't materialised and there didn't seem to be any more on the horizon. At least her job in Lyon, where she'd done both her degree and her MBA, had included trips to London and Amsterdam.

Marketing was exciting. Emma had known that early on in her studies and had dreamed of being sent all over the world on projects. The job in London wasn't bad; she liked her boss, and had decided to stay for couple of years to get ahead because it was a promising company. Now, she was less sure.

Maybe it was time to think about changing that as well, with her new qualifications under her belt.

Feeling cheerful, Emma took time over her makeup. She loved cosmetics, and a new mascara or a bottle of bath oil were instant cheerer-uppers. She grinned at her latest indulgence, which was a particularly good eyeliner brush, and congratulated herself on her smoky-eye skills.

Life was what you made it. She was going to enjoy Crest and being with the family, write an outstanding dissertation, find the perfect flat in the ideal location for an affordable rent, and her dream job would fall into her lap.

Chapter 3

It's just getting light as we let the cats out and follow them through the French doors.

I'm praying the coffee machine hasn't woken Mum. She flatly refuses to go to bed before we do, despite napping on the couch after dinner. Then she's up and at it the moment she hears movement in the morning. It's as though she can't bear to think of us having a few minutes' peace.

Once she appears, it's action all the way. Breakfast is expected immediately because she's taken her pills and she's supposed to eat straight away. Taking them once she's downstairs and I've hauled out the toaster would be way too easy.

Her regular breakfast used to be toast and Marmite – but not toasted baguettes, which are too tough or too thick. Then it was Special K. Then it was Weetabix. Now it's toast and marmalade, but not brown toast, thank you.

I found some Seville oranges last January and made some marmalade from scratch, and she's making inroads on it, even if it's not as good as Gillian's – who cuts it finer, or thicker, I forget which. The other day, she thought some All-Bran might be a good idea, because foreign food tends to, you know, slow your digestion down. The last time, it gave her the runs.

I'm not going to let it all get to me. I'll listen to the daily blow-by-blow account of her night and her bowel movements and smile.

What will it be today? A bit loose, all that rich food? A bit of a restless night, again because of the food? Or a wonderful night's sleep and it was so lovely that Felix came to visit?

Felix, our largest and most sociable cat, adores visitors of any kind. I've already made a mental note to put guests with allergies in the new wing and never in the two upstairs rooms. He's rather fond of scrambling up over the porch and landing with a thud on the roof, or seeing open shutters as a challenge. Having a large, furry body leap into the bedroom could be a bit off-putting. I hope the windows in the new rooms are just a bit too high off the ground for him. All the same, I mentally add that to my list of minor worries.

The major worry is the carpenter. The windows and doors need fitting as quickly as possible now, before the October and November weather, and there's the flooring to do as well.

"Ready for action?" Steve asks as the shutters in Mum's room close with a squeak, which means she's getting dressed.

"As I'll ever be," I sigh, picking up my cup and hiding the pack of cigarettes. "Don't fix that noisy shutter yet – it's my early warning system."

***

Things grind into action, and I'm more or less in control. The three masons are their usual cheerful selves. The little Romanian guy seems blissfully happy with the bag of croissants and *pains au chocolat* Steve picked up from the bakery, and the big guy with the shaved head is whistling what sounds suspiciously like Hayley Westenra. I had him down as a hard rock type.

I make a quick batch of scones for this afternoon and get out the makings for tonight's *boeuf bourguignon*.

Mum emerges from the bathroom and comes downstairs with a book. I glance at the cover, hoping it's one of those I've put in a pile in her room, after doing the usual check on whether it includes sex scenes. I've learned the hard way, after a number of outraged lectures on today's morals when I was younger. Once upon a time, she found me with Thomas Hardy. I had assured her that *Far from the Madding Crowd* was school reading and pretty tame, but she retorted that he'd also written *The Virgin and the Gypsy*, which was shocking.

I wonder if she knew that from reading it, or whether the title put her off?

I learned to hide my reading material better after that.

I mostly read on a Kindle these days, which means she can't see what I'm reading and can't offer an opinion. She disapproves of Kindles, because 'everything has to have a plug on it or a battery in it these days.' Explaining that it only needs recharging every few weeks is just wasting my own battery.

"Toast, Mum?"

"Are there any cereals? I fancy a change. I buy Tesco's own brand, you know."

No, I didn't know, but manage not to tell her so, or to make some comment about it being a long way to pop out for some. I offer some with fruit and fibre, which meets with approval. So far, so good.

"Now," she says, "can I do anything to help?"

I weigh up whether I prefer her to act offended if I say no and suggest she relaxes with her book, or whether to have a monologue on Gillian's recipes while she takes forever to chop vegetables.

"That would be great. Can you do the carrots for tonight? In batons?"

"Why on earth cut them into sticks? You're just making stew, aren't you?"

I grit my teeth.

"OK then, slices are fine."

I blanch the tiny onions so I can slip them from their skins more easily and manage not to argue when I'm told that those silly little ones are more trouble than they're worth. Soon everything's in the pot and cooking gently.

Gillian doesn't put wine in her stews. Or bay leaves.

Next up is to peel and core a huge bag of downy, golden quinces that Helen brought me from their tree, which I've decided to use for jam.

"You can't make jam with quinces," Mum says almost pityingly. "You make jelly."

"You can," I say, aiming for breezy.

"Never heard of it. Are you sure? I know making jelly is difficult, of course. Gillian makes a lovely crab apple one."

I'm not rising to the bait.

"Certain. I add lemon and almonds and it's gorgeous. I think it's a Greek recipe. I've made jelly in the past too, but we love this."

That gets a sniff. Greek jam is clearly beyond the pale. She does, however, peel and core some of the fruit for me.

By lunchtime, I'm in full-on defensive mode but we have half a dozen jars of wonderful-smelling jam on the counter. While stirring it, I got a run-down on proper ways of making jams and jellies and why on earth would people add stuff like vanilla to apricot jam, or a slug of brandy to damsons. She's obviously been reading the labels on my jars.

I could use a slug of something strong.

Out of spite, I serve up boiled eggs with plain white bread and butter for lunch, deciding that at least Gillian can't do *that* better or differently. Except three of them crack. I give her the whole ones. She doesn't like the vinaigrette with the salad but manfully eats her greens and says she can't understand why France has never discovered salad cream.

Steve is cheerful enough. He volunteers to pick up Emma at the high-speed train station in Valence, and to pick up the taps and check with the tile company at the same time. And to take Mum with him.

The man is a saint.

I say I'll get on with some of the publicity stuff I'm working on, get a short translation out of the way, and have dinner ready for when they get back, jumping for joy at a couple of hours off duty. I can even steal a couple of cigarettes with the masons when I serve up their afternoon *goûter*. And I can keep an eye on my "stew" and cross my fingers that the famous carpenter is available.

***

Emma

Emma stretched luxuriously and smiled as she woke up to cheerful purring. Felix had decided to be liberal with his favours and keep her company during her first night in France.

Slivers of light trickled through the edges of the shutter, and the lack of sirens and a faint smell of warm bread increased her feeling of wellbeing.

"Morning, fatso."

The cat turned a pair of placid, golden eyes on her and decided a little stomach kneading was in order.

"No need for that, thanks. Don't you have any lizards to catch or something?"

He gave a cat shrug and stalked off. He'd soon be back demanding treats. Her parents had always loved cats and always spoiled them.

Rainer wasn't fond of them and had said their flat was no place for one. The hair, the litter box, were just not very appropriate. *Wery.*

Rainer. She reached over for her phone, wondering if he'd messaged her after her last quick text with a goodnight kiss. He hadn't, but he'd sent one earlier in the evening to say he was going out for a couple of drinks after working late.

Still in the old, comfortable pyjamas she'd left at her parents' place, she pulled her hair into a loose ponytail and padded to the bathroom.

Staring at herself and wondering if she should suggest her mother add a decent magnifying mirror to the guest bathrooms, she remembered that rural France was hardly the place people would go to apply careful makeup. In fact, it was good not to reach for the foundation and mascara wand before she'd even woken up properly. Her family, and Crest, could survive without her appearing in a full paint job.

Gran was finishing her breakfast as Emma arrived in the kitchen and was 'off to get ready' although she didn't wear makeup and was already in her usual pastels. Her mother would never do pastels and pearls when she got older, Emma thought. She'd just go on wearing semi-ethnic, flowing things in deep, rich colours, when it wasn't jeans. Her mother wasn't the flamboyant type, but she still looked attractive, with a trim figure and plenty of laugh lines.

Emma brewed some tea, toasted half a baguette, spread it liberally with butter and some quince and lemon jam and headed off to the small terrace that always caught the morning sunshine. It was chilly even so, but adding a cardigan solved that. Being outside was lovely, and even the sounds of the masons and their machinery didn't bother her as they were at the other side of the building.

She leaned back, watching the pool ripple and wondering if the water was really too cold for a swim later. Her parents had turned the heat pump off the week before, during a colder spell, and declared the swimming season over, but it looked tempting.

Taking a bite of the baguette and contemplating a few extra spoons of jam she saw a UPS van pull up. The driver hauled out a package and her father appeared, beaming. New blades for the tiller, he told her as he took it. Emma wasn't sure what a tiller was.

Five minutes later, the postman arrived. This time her mother rushed out. Her French was fluent and she had adopted all the hand-waving that went with it.

She came over, with an armful of what looked like brochures for bedding. She was off to the garden centre with Gran, she said cheerfully. Did Emma want to come?

Emma didn't. With a little luck, she could have a quiet morning to get on with her dissertation. In the meantime, she turned her tablet on and dripped jam onto it.

She was still wiping that off when the next van appeared. It had the builders' logo on the side, and two men got out. Emma pointed them towards the new wing, barely looking up as she scrubbed at the screen with her sleeve.

"All action here this morning," her grandmother said, emerging from somewhere with her cardigan buttoned up and handbag ready. "Mind, it always is. Where's your mum? She said we'd be off by ten. And did you see that man with a ponytail?"

"She's probably on her way, Gran. And which man was that?" Emma hadn't noticed, being more interested in her breakfast than haircuts.

"One that just arrived. I always think men with long hair look daft."

Emma let that one slide. It was too early in the morning to try and change her grandmother's view on anything.

"He's the carpenter. I wonder if I need a thicker jacket. Aren't you cold?"

"Nope. I'm made of tough stuff."

"It's those Yorkshire genes."

Emma chuckled and noticed that she'd still got jam on her pyjamas.

"Damn. Better sponge that off and get a refill for my tea. You want a cup, Gran? I made a pot."

"Better not. Makes me wee, and you never know if these foreign garden centres have toilets. Just tell your mum I'm ready, will you?"

Her mother appeared on the terrace, glancing at her watch, before she had time to go inside.

"Sorry I'm late, but the good news is that we have a carpenter."

"With a ponytail," Emma and her grandmother answered in unison.

"He speaks good English, too. He says his mother is from England, and his uncle is a partner in the masonry firm."

"Good grief, Mum. You've already given him the third degree?"

"I was just looking at that bit of wall they were working on yesterday while I was waiting for you. I thought they'd have finished it by now. They're probably standing around talking too much," Edna proclaimed.

Emma saw her mother's eyes widen slightly and she half-expected a tart comment on who exactly had been 'standing around talking' to the builders just before but it didn't come. Good.

"Right then. Let's be off," Shirley Sandford said. "I hope they have some decent roses."

"It's the wrong time of year to plant roses."

Emma hoped they wouldn't come to blows before they reached the garden centre.

***

The following day, Emma admired her gran for navigating Crest's cobblestones and the Saturday market in general. She seemed interested in everything, from the array of local cheeses to piles of olives. She was intrigued by the old guy who sat outside his upholstery shop, re-covering a beautiful antique chair in fabric that looked like graffiti. Emma fell in love with its quirkiness but could already imagine Rainer's reaction if she got it back to London.

"Right." Her mother, also part of the expedition, gently put a selection of fresh goat cheeses into her big market bag and swerved expertly around a couple of camera-carrying tourists. "I need to go and talk to the lady who stocks locally made soaps and other nice smellies for the bathrooms.

"How about me and Gran having a coffee while you do that?"

"That's a good idea," her grandmother nodded with what looked like relief. They'd been browsing for a while, and even Emma's feet were aching despite low heels. "I don't know why you have to provide toiletries anyway. I always take my own when I go away."

"It's all about the little touches," Emma said firmly, getting a word in before her mother did. It was one more example of how one or the other of them would say something and the other was bound to take it badly.

"Exactly," her mother nodded. "I won't be long."

Emma volunteered to guard her mother's market bag and steered her gran to a table on the little square near the town hall, waving to the waiter.

"Glass of wine, Gran? Seems a bit more interesting than coffee."

"I don't mind if I do. When in Rome."

"Pavement cafés and sunshine are always a good thing, right? I love all this." Emma waved an arm to take in the bustling street, the stalls, the people. "Lyon was good for markets, but this is lovely."

Her grandmother nodded, watching people stroll past, gathering in little knots and chatting.

"It's a far cry from Sheffield."

"And Mum and Dad are – what's the phrase you use up there? Like pigs in dirt?"

"Muck."

"Muck, then. And I'm delighted for them. I know you are as well."

"I just wonder if they know what they're doing, Emma."

"They do," Emma said firmly, even though she'd wondered now and then if the whole B&B plan was some sort of mid-life crisis. "Look how happy they are? And if anybody knows how to budget things, it's Dad."

"I suppose so. It's just all so *foreign.*"

"Come on, Gran. How many times did you visit us in Switzerland? Last I heard that was just as foreign."

"But maybe a bit more civilised."

"And what's civilised?" Emma said, as the waiter brought their wine. "I think wine at eleven in the morning, sitting outside in autumn, is pretty civilised, myself."

"You're probably right. I'm just a silly old woman."

"Silly, nope. Old? Well… pretty old," Emma chuckled. "But I think you're wearing pretty well, which is what you were hoping I was going to say. Admit it."

"Cheeky madam. I should be grateful I can still get around. How's London? Are you happy? You haven't talked about it much since you arrived."

That was true, Emma realised. Her grandmother was more perceptive than her own daughter gave her credit for.

"It's okay. Not much to report really. The job's a bit disappointing lately, but I'll look around."

"And the rest?"

"Rainer? He's…" Emma hesitated. "He's still very Swiss."

"That's a good thing, isn't it? Hard-working, serious…"

And sometimes self-centred and hyper-critical, Emma thought to herself but was ashamed that had come to mind. She was also a little irritated that he'd hardly been in touch but there was no way she was going to admit that.

"He's probably a good influence on me. I'm messy and a bit frivolous for his taste. But we're doing fine."

Did she sound defensive?

The pale eyes were studying her carefully.

"Don't worry, Gran. I suppose I'll have to be a real adult one of these days and be a bit more serious myself. And what about you?"

Her grandmother took another large sip of wine and Emma grinned to herself, waving at the waiter for refills.

"Oh, you know. It's a quiet life. I see Gillian. Do a few things at church."

"And get to visit France and let your hair down now and then. I'm glad you came."

"Really?" The surprise looked genuine.

"Well of course. I bet Mum has been worrying herself silly about whether you approve of all they're doing. It makes her a bit on edge."

"I suppose so."

"I think kids always want their parents' approval," Emma said, making inroads into her second glass of wine.

"You could be right. I just find it a bit strange, all these changes when your dad has had such an impressive career."

"He wanted it as well, Gran. I think they're following a dream and we should be proud of them."

"Maybe we should," her grandmother said thoughtfully, and seemed about to say something else when her mother came back, winding her way between tables.

"All done. It all worked out wonderfully. And what's this? Wine?"

"Wine," Emma said cheerfully. "Shall I get you one?"

"Well…"

"Live dangerously, Mum. Gran and I are already on our second."

Her grandmother turned pink and her mother stared at them both.

"I can't leave you two alone for ten minutes, can I?"

Emma rolled her eyes.

"Mum, please. We've been putting the world to rights, and saying how amazing your project is, and how well it's going."

"Really?" Shirley Sandford sank onto an empty chair. "Well thank you, ladies. I just need to decide between verbena and lavender for the shower gel and soap now."

"Verbena," Emma said.

"Lavender."

"Toss up?" Emma laughed.

"No. I'll give it some more thought. Maybe we could go with the verbena shower gel and lavender soap."

"That reminds me of Jim. He never did understand colours. Or perfume." Her grandmother drained her glass. "Make your mind up."

"Verbena then. Unless... well, lavender could be nice too. More typically Provençal."

"But verbena would be fresher, Shirley."

Emma rolled her eyes at them both, called the waiter over and asked for another carafe.

"Then there's a sort of herby one... rosemary and something."

"Definitely not, Shirley. You don't want people smelling like a leg of lamb."

"We need to smell them, I think," Emma said firmly. "Did you bring samples?"

"I didn't, and I should have done. You'd better come with me and we'll get a few on the way back to the car. But not until I've caught up with you old soaks a bit."

"Charming," Emma said, as the wine arrived. "This is not the way to treat your experts, Mum. So, we'll let you pay. Right, Gran?"

"Right. You think they have any peanuts?"

"Nope," Emma said. "But we can do better." She fished into the market bag and broke off a large chunk of fresh, crusty *baguette*, tore it into three, and solemnly handed pieces over. "There you go, Gran. France has a few things going for it, and that includes wine and decent bread."

Her grandmother hesitated, and then nibbled a bit.

"You might just be right. You couldn't do this at home."

"Then it's all the more fun to do it here," Emma said, chewing blissfully. "A bit more, Gran?"

***

Shirley

I feel the tears start the moment Steve drives out of the airport. He reaches over and squeezes my knee. We've been here before, every time my mother goes home.

It's relief, mixed with frustration and anger. Two weeks of my mum are a lifetime, and by the time she leaves I'm wrung out, irritable, and I want my life back.

I scrabble in my bag for a cigarette. Usually, smoking in the car is a big no-no, but I deserve it. Sensibly, Steve says nothing.

"Sorry," I mutter. "I'll be all right in a minute."

I sniffle a bit more and get another knee-squeeze.

"Particularly," I say, "if we get to stop off for lunch somewhere nice?"

"That's my girl," Steve says cheerfully. "And it wasn't *that* bad this time, was it?"

"Don't ask me to answer that," I mutter. "Em did help, though."

"Emma seemed to enjoy herself, including being with your mum," he says thoughtfully. "And she's looking great. I much prefer to see her without all the war paint."

That makes two of us. He's right about the makeup, and he's right that she seems to be a good influence on her grandmother, too. Steve has a habit of being right.

Emma takes after her father in many ways, including in her ability to just get on and deal with things. She's tall, with a mop of glossy dark, wavy hair and blue eyes. I've always been glad she didn't inherit my mousy brown hair and eyes although everybody wants to have whatever they don't have. I've been jealous of my sister's blonde curls for decades.

You couldn't call Emma skinny, but she's well-proportioned and long-legged. I think she's lost a bit of weight, in fact, although judging from the past few days she still loves her food. And fresh *baguettes*.

"I don't know if she's eating properly in London," I say, remembering their tiny kitchen.

"I don't think there's much chance of her starving," Steve chuckles. "Are you short of something to worry about?"

"Mother's privilege," I say. And the word "mother" suddenly conjures up visions of Christmas in Sheffield with mine. We promised to go – or rather Steve promised to go. I very nearly start crying all over again.

"Why did you have to say we'd to go England?" I sigh. "What I'd really like to do this Christmas is to bugger off to Marrakesh for a few days, forget the whole commercial circus, and be waited on hand and foot. Emma's going to Bern and I rather liked the idea of just you and me and a few bottles of Moroccan rosé."

"I thought it was either suggest we went over or see you go into meltdown when she started on about the lamb last night. Besides, she'd been dropping hints that Gillian and Clive would be going away somewhere and how much they deserved it after working so hard all those years, so she'd be all alone. We *could* have invited her back here?"

"No way."

"Well then."

"She was odious about the lamb," I almost shout. "*Gillian* doesn't half-cook it because it shouldn't be pink inside. And she doesn't muck around with herb crust or an endive *tarte tatin,* she does the Great British Roast and Three Veg. *Gillian* makes fabulous trifles and isn't *crème brûlée* with Grand Marnier just tarted-up egg custard?"

"Stop it," Steve says, but he says it gently. "We can go for a couple of days and then lie through our teeth and say we're invited to see some friends on Boxing Day. And then we can hole up in some little B&B in Derbyshire for a night or two."

"And watch it rain, knowing our luck," I say, but a bit more cheerfully.

"In that case we can stuff ourselves with Bakewell pudding and venison sausages and do the navigation by pub thing you do so well."

My husband is fond of small country pubs. Despite my parents' rather conservative views on drink, I'd discovered a fair few in Derbyshire with a couple of boyfriends, assuring my parents I stuck to Britvic orange like a good girl. I'm not sure they believed me, but I'd had the good sense never to come home the slightest bit tipsy.

Dad, I remembered, got garrulous after two glasses of wine and fell asleep after three. Mum always put it down to his Methodist upbringing, which he'd been forced to abandon in favour of the Church of England she frequented sporadically. On that issue, I'd have trouble with any religion that frowned on alcohol, so for once I'm on her side.

"And then," Steve says, sounding pleased with himself, suddenly, "we could probably run to a few days in Marrakesh for New Year. Maybe even see if Em and Rainer want to join us after Bern?"

Let's hand it to Mr Steve Sandford, husband *extraordinaire*. Both of us love Morocco and have had a soft spot for Marrakesh since we first visited, many years ago, with Emma. We all love poking around the souks, which gives me an idea.

"We can get some bits and bobs for the guest rooms," I say, completely forgetting the tears and worries for a few minutes and thinking fondly of Moroccan fabrics, pottery and other treasures.

"As long as you remember the baggage allowance. One day your luck will run out when you sweet-talk the people at check-in counters to let you get on the plane with a dirty great lamp under your arm. Or what was it? Twelve plates?"

"Ten," I correct him, stuffing my handkerchief back in my bag and settling back into my seat. "And they do ship stuff."

"You do remember that table that arrived in two halves?"

I also remember the exorbitant customs charges for a rug we had shipped that seemed like such a steal at the time.

"I'll be reasonable then," I reassure him but not completely honestly, and lean back in my seat.

That train of thought leads to something else to worry about. I'm not sure if Rainer would take to Morocco, and particularly Marrakesh. Somehow, I think he's more of a luxury hotel with a spa and high-speed wifi person than somebody who would fall in love with our little *riad* in the *medina,* the old town. It does have wifi, of the pedalling rats variety, but the décor is more quirky than smart.

I could be wrong, of course. I'll see what Em thinks. She didn't talk about him much this time, except to say he's doing well at the bank.

Em was wonderful company. She had the builders wrapped around her little finger after just a day of handing out tea and cakes, and joined in with the wine and snacks in the evening when we'd held a mini-celebration with the masons, who had finished off the walls in record time.

She chatted about her job after they all left and Mum had nodded off on the couch, probably after a fair amount of wine. She seems frustrated by it at the moment, but she's enjoying studying again.

All through her school days, she sailed through her homework with music playing, frequent breaks to play video games, and while texting half her classmates. I'd left her to her own devices as long as she didn't start getting bad reports, which she hadn't. They were all glowing, except for the odd comment about being boisterous or argumentative.

It was all a very far cry, and intentionally so, from my school years in Sheffield. Homework had to be done downstairs. Ostensibly it was because the bedrooms were not heated but I suspect it was more to make sure I didn't listen to that awful pop music on my little yellow transistor radio – a present from Dad.

Sitting down with a book was a Bad Thing. Books – from the library, mainly – were always inspected in case they contained anything smutty, particularly after the Thomas Hardy episode. Fortunately, most of them passed muster.

Later, I got my hands on Gillian's sickly romantic novels and read them in secret, disappointed the characters never did more than chaste kissing. Then I found Mum and Dad's stash of James Bond books and read those, carefully putting them back in the cupboard under the stairs in the morning after a wicked, but enjoyable dose of 007 under my blankets with my Girl Guide torch. ('I need more batteries, Mum – these ones are rubbish, and you know how Brown Owl is very strict about checking all our material works.')

More lies, but that one was in service of my education. A girl can learn a lot from James Bond.

Gillian had been hopeless every time I'd asked her what sex was all about. I started to wonder if she even knew, but then she and Clive had produced the dreadful Kevin, so I presumed she'd found out. Eventually, I'd found out myself, thanks to a very solemn, horribly awkward lecture at school.

I'm surprised to be reminiscing about Sheffield, and family life, with fondness. I've slid into the habit of finding everything about it negative. Plenty of things were fun: doing the washing up with Dad and talking about anything that came to mind. Or watching Star Trek and eating toasted sandwiches in our fingers with trays on our knees. That was a special treat on Saturdays.

"Shirley?"

I blink, surprised to see we're already off the motorway and heading down to the Drôme.

"Sorry. I was miles away."

"Still want to stop somewhere for lunch?"

"Is the Pope Catholic? How about that place that does *foie gras?* And *pintade?"*

"A woman after my own heart," he beams. "We can be there in twenty minutes. And no lectures on the poor little ducks or the guinea fowl."

"Definitely not". I laugh out loud. "She's *gone.* Well, until Christmas."

"Oh, come on. Sainsbury's turkey roast, lots of bloody sprouts and instant gravy. What's not to love?"

"We can have Christmas pud, though," I say. "Admit you adore that."

"I do. See? You're being positive."

"Doing my best. Thanks for being a bastion of sanity and reason for two weeks."

Steve grins, and I reach over and squeeze his hand on the gear lever. I feel relaxed, and it's nice.

"Or quail," I mutter. "They sometimes have quail. I thought about doing quail fillet for mum but thought better of it."

"Poor little birds," we suddenly chorus.

Chapter 4

Emma

Emma wondered how in hell anybody could get enthusiastic about coat hangers.

Mr Reginald Small – *call me Reg* – could.

Where was her company going if it was now working on marketing strategies for coat hanger manufacturers? When they'd taken her on, they'd been getting interesting clients – anything from the video games industry to big-name luxury goods companies, but things were going downhill, and rapidly.

According to Myles, Emma's boss, *Reg* was a magnate of the industry. They produced millions of the things. 'From wire to wood with exciting new lines', their current – awful – brochure gushed.

The brochures were only a tiny part of the mess, which had been an ongoing struggle from the get-go.

She'd dutifully studied the subject. Wire for dry cleaners, plastic for clothes shops, wood or plastic for hotels, standard ones for supermarkets and the slightly more attractive-looking ones that had inspired the company to actually look at its strategy.

"So, Mr Small. Reg. I've looked at your current clients and your capacity, and your idea of getting into designer coat hangers," she started. "And it's a great idea, although I've been looking at some of the competition, and –"

"Where? You have to look in the right place, you know." The broad Birmingham accent grated.

"We use open source information. The internet, mainly, but also the specialised press."

Mr Small gave a tiny sigh of exasperation. "You've got to *feel* a good coat hanger, you know."

"I'm sure," Emma said politely. Considering the way he constantly leered at her neckline, he'd probably like to feel a few other things too. "So, it would be very useful if I could have a few more figures to work with, on your manufacturing costs, and then I'd suggest we start on some possible approaches, to see –"

"Now, Emma," he shook his head. "As I've told you, I can't release figures. And I'm no great fan of these fancy new approaches. You know, all this SWOT and balancing act rubbish – I've looked into them all. As I told your boss, we just want a quick makeover of the brochures and maybe some input from your outfit on possible new markets with big margins."

"We can find you graphic artists and copywriters, certainly – your photographs are a little outdated and the texts are a bit bland. But I understood you wanted to re-think your strategy as a whole. Which new markets you should focus on to start with."

"Like I told you, darling. We need places where we can get big margins. I mean just look at this beauty." Reg Small dug into his desk drawer and brought out a twig-shaped rod of aluminium. "Go on, feel it. Nice and long and hard, eh?"

Emma swallowed, and ignored that. Myles, her boss, wanted the client.

"Very nice, Reg. And this would be the kind of thing you want to sell in décor shops or to big designers?"

"Oh definitely. I've got it all planned out. Bleached wood version for those ethnic-type places. Stainless – that's the top of the range, for yer *haute couture* (pronounced hoat kerchure – Emma tried not to chuckle) and modern design shops, and I thought in fluorescent plastic for, you know, sexy gear. You should know where to find that sort of place, right?"

She was not going to blush. Or slap him. She wished, though, that she'd worn a longer skirt. Or trousers. And a shirt buttoned right to the neck. Or a burqa.

Reg Small was leaning back, smiling broadly. Paunchy and balding and probably in his early fifties, he had pale blue, rheumy eyes. Maybe he'd been handsome once, if you went for blokes with hairy hands and a habit of licking their lips. Right now, he had a bad case of nose hair, and could use the name of a good deodorant, looking at the underarms of his too-tight black shirt. The gold necklace would have done Tom Jones proud, but there was no wedding ring.

He was also expecting an answer, and she struggled for one.

"That... shape. Is it, um, going to be popular? It might make clothes look a bit lopsided?"

"See, darling, this is where you should leave things to the experts. It might *look* a little off-kilter but in fact it's just modern. Perfectly balanced. Sensuous. Want to feel it again?"

Emma picked it up, trying not to handle it in any way that could possibly be interpreted as sensuous.

"See? And we can make millions of them. Sexy as all get out, they are. Don't you think so? I thought we could even do some – you know – daring advertising. A bit kinky, even. Like a pair of lips kissing them? Or sliding them up a leg wearing fishnets."

"That would be... different."

"I could even get you to help, you know? Nice young lady like yourself – I'm sure we could do some brainstorming together."

"I think–", Emma didn't know what to think. Basically, she wanted him to stick the damned thing where the sun didn't shine. "I think I'd better get back to you with some suggestions. And some figures for your capacity really would help."

"Capacity's no problem. Got plenty of Chinks and nig-nogs on the job. Like I always say, the sky's the limit."

Chinks and nig-nogs? Emma felt her jaw drop.

"Impressive, eh? How about a spot of lunch to discuss the fine points of our future campaign together? Somewhere nice and intimate?"

Over my dead body, Emma thought.

"I'm afraid I have another appointment," she lied crisply. "But thank you so much for your time."

"The pleasure's all mine, darling. And make sure you're free afterwards next time we meet. There's a lovely little club I know where we could get some inspiration."

"I'll do my best," she said, instantly regretting it, but she was a professional and she'd handle him somehow.

"Oh, and I'm reconsidering that idea for an interactive website," he added smoothly.

That was good news. Or was it?

"We could slip in some videos, right? You know?" He actually winked.

"Maybe," Emma said weakly, stuffing her papers into her briefcase and feeling sick.

"Fancy yourself as a video star, do you? You know, you could probably save us all some money and be a model."

"I think not," Emma said firmly. "It's – well – against company rules."

Not a very good lie, but it seemed to work, or at least temporarily.

"Well, I'll have a word with your boss about it, maybe. But as a special treat," Reg Small said. "I'm going to give you your very own stainless-steel version to play with. Just enjoy those lovely rounded edges and that smoothness. That could be a good catchphrase, right?"

She took it and slid it into her case as well, rapidly, touching it as little as possible.

***

It wouldn't take much, Emma decided as she waited for the tube, for her to tell Myles she'd rather fry in hell than see the revolting *Reg* again. In fact, she'd gather her wits a bit and talk to him seriously about dealing with that particular client himself.

Myles did sympathise over difficult clients, though. The last tricky one – who hadn't been after a grope but had finally refused the offer because, he'd said, he "felt the young lady was not sufficiently experienced" – had opted for another, far cheaper consulting company. She'd got wind of that through her contacts, and bravely told Myles. He'd been philosophical about it and appreciated that she'd come clean and told him.

As bosses went, he was pleasant, although probably too much so. Somewhere, deep down, she wanted him to be more critical and less *nice*. Nice didn't seem to be bringing in decent contracts.

She could call it a day now. It was nearly five, and she'd write up a report of the meeting. on their couch, preferably with a very large glass of wine. Maybe tease Rainer a bit more. He'd asked her if she'd been flirting in France when she'd got back, and she'd assured him that she had. Lots of nice beefy builders, including a toothless Romanian, a big bald guy with pierced ears and tattoos, and a long-haired carpenter who was, according to her mother, an artist as well. All of them beyond the pale in Rainer's world.

Her mood improved by the time she opened their door. Rainer had texted that he'd be home in good time, and the place still looked as spotless as it had when she'd got home from France a few days before. Rugs vacuumed, dishes washed and put away, washing likewise. There were even clean sheets on the bed. He'd obviously missed her, which was a good thing.

Better still, he'd agreed to leave the bar early the night she'd got back. They'd met up with some friends near St Pancras for a couple of pints and then gone home. She'd been so impressed with the look of the place that she'd forgotten she was starving, and even more impressed when they'd tested the clean sheets thoroughly.

In bed, Rainer was most definitely an expert.

There were times that she found him too much of an expert – as though it was another facet of the Swiss efficiency that he prided himself on. That was being unkind. Rainer was proud of giving her exactly what she liked.

She did wish that he was more spontaneous about it. Spontaneous sex rarely happened any more – they'd slid into a routine of a couple of times during the week and sometimes on Sunday afternoons.

Then there was the condom issue. It was time they gave those up, in Emma's opinion. Hygiene be damned. She'd always believed that when she finally had a long-term relationship, the pill would be enough.

She sent off a quick text: *Eat in or shall we order pizza and be self-indulgent?* and then, reluctantly, pulled out her papers and the horrific coat hanger of doom and looked at it. Maybe she could turn that into a game?

Healthy stir fry – can you buy please meat and veg? came back.

Sensible man, if a little grammar-challenged, but pizza was much more what she craved after a pot of soup the night before and a pre-packed salad from the food court for lunch.

Half an hour later, she dumped two bags on the counter, and pulled out a bottle of wine and a tube of Pringles, pleased to note that Rainer was already home and probably in the shower, judging from the briefcase by the door.

Where was the damned corkscrew, anyway? Considering the kitchen was tidy, it should be in the drawer, and it wasn't. Nor was it anywhere else that Rainer might have thought it belonged.

"Rainer?" She pushed open the bedroom door to see him on the phone, speaking in Swiss German. His mother, maybe. She waved the bottle at him, pointing at the cork.

With a brief flash of irritation, he cut the conversation short. She caught a couple of words, much as it didn't much resemble the normal High German she'd learned in school. Something about "see you soon".

"Your mother?" Emma asked, following him back into the kitchen.

"No, a colleague," he said shortly and opened the drawer that should have contained the corkscrew. "Damage control at work. As always."

That was one of his favourite phrases. Damage control. Or sometimes contingency plans. At least neither phrase had a "v" or a "w" in it.

"When did we last have wine? I always put the corkscrew back in the drawer."

"You do? What a miracle," he said, frowning. "I don't want wine anyway, or only a glass – I had some at lunch."

"Lucky you," she said tartly. "I didn't. Are you on some sort of diet, suddenly, with this one-glass-only business?"

"Not a diet but being…"

"Swiss and reasonable," she teased. "But as I'd like a glass, where's that famous Swiss army knife of yours? That has a corkscrew, doesn't it?"

Rainer sighed and looked around, and then headed for the bedroom – emerging, surprisingly, with their normal corkscrew.

"What the hell was it doing in the bedroom?"

"Knowing you, it was the last place you put it," he shot back. "I remember seeing it there last night."

Weird. But she'd done weirder, like putting a pair of his clean socks into her briefcase, or a jar of mustard on top of the washing machine.

Glass in hand, she pulled out some spring onions, carrots and broccoli and started chopping. An argument about her being distracted at times didn't seem worth it.

"About Christmas," Rainer perched by the counter. "My mother called while you were away. They're having a big reception on Christmas eve."

Emma inwardly groaned. Swiss Germans *en masse* were a little intimidating, from past experience when she'd lived in Switzerland, and the ever-so-chic ones his parents were bound to invite would probably be even more so.

"Nice," she said, hoping to inject a little enthusiasm into her voice. At least his father would be there and make it more or less tolerable.

"It will be formal. Maybe you should buy a cocktail dress."

A *cocktail* dress? The whole little black number thing?

"Okay," she said carefully.

"Not your usual style, though," Rainer said bluntly. "Something sophisticated will be necessary."

"Are you seriously telling me what to wear? *Again?*"

"Emma," his tone was half-wheedling but with a definite streak of bossiness. "You cannot attend a formal reception in things like that blue dress with the many stars."

"A galaxy," she corrected out of spite. The dress he was referring to was glorious, sexy, flowing, and absolutely *her.* "And why not? Is that *cheap,* too? For your information, it wasn't."

"It's – interesting. But not appropriate."

"I see." Emma continued chopping, savagely. "Then how about you paying for me to go and choose something *appropriate* at Chanel."

"Let's not be ridiculous."

"Ridiculous is you being ashamed of me. Or your mother dictating what I wear. Or *you* dictating what I wear. She can take me as I am or I'll…"

"It's important. Very important, Emma." *Wery.*

"Why?" Dear God, was he going to pop the question or something? Emma gaped at him, not even sure what to think.

"Because of my parents' social status, if I have to spell it out for you. My father moves in political circles. They are expecting me to… have an appropriate partner."

"One who doesn't wear dresses with many stars, apparently" she said waspishly, and threw the sliced chicken and vegetables into the wok with just slightly more force than necessary. Oil spattered over the cooker. She poured herself more wine and dug into the Pringles.

"My father really likes you," Rainer said suddenly.

"Good," she snapped.

Emma liked him too, and somehow thought that Markus wouldn't judge her on her clothes. Frau Feldmann, however, probably would.

Over the meal, eaten in virtual silence, she had another two glasses, thinking about the Feldmanns. The possibility of talking to Rainer's father was the only thing that could make Christmas in Bern halfway acceptable. She always left conversations with him feeling there was so much more to say.

"I'll do my best," Emma said eventually, resigned to the idea. "For the damned party."

"I knew you'd be sensible," Rainer said. "It will be an interesting evening."

Later, in bed, Rainer seemed to thaw a little and even started to caress her. Emma was, if she was honest, hardly in the mood for sex and still angry with him – and not at all convinced she could please Frau Feldmann whether dressed in Chanel or anything else.

She didn't pull away, though, and he took her rapidly, harder than usual, the moment he'd rolled the condom on with his usual efficiency.

That didn't make things any better and it was painful at first. Gradually, though, she found herself responding, losing herself in it and getting closer, although somehow it all seemed mechanical.

"Come for me," he said eventually, as he always did, but somehow it felt like an order.

She faked it, for the first time ever, and was glad when he finished and rolled away.

So much for her initial idea of a heart-to heart about condoms.

What was going wrong?

Chapter 5

Shirley

Making bread is one of the most remarkably cathartic things. Just like pruning – all that snip, snip, snip can calm me down rapidly, but thumping dough around is just as good.

Both activities also produce excellent results.

Today, it's malted rye. I'll fold chopped olives into half of it and make some dinner rolls – lovely with cheese – and some mini-loaves. Cut thinly, olive bread is great with pâté, with some fig chutney on the side.

I don't particularly need catharsis, though, even if the miraculously problem-free project has been springing a couple of leaks lately, and one literally. Nothing serious, fortunately, but there have been a few irritations like a cracked pipe in the kitchen and a lake on the floor, and a massive crop of what looks like alfalfa in the new flower bed we've made beside the guest rooms.

That will teach me to cheerfully accept a huge load of earth for free, courtesy of one of the departing masons. When we told him that we'd be creating a rockery and a path, he'd called a friend who had rolled up with a truckload of earth and some massive boulders that were 'lying around'. The new lavender and rock plants are now half lost amid a carpet of cattle fodder. Weeding it is challenging, but with patience it's sorting itself out.

Emma's been a bit grumpy. I've had a couple of terse text messages, but she has at least been giving me good advice on polishing up the website. She sounds miserable about her job, and Rainer is on some big project and either working late or travelling a lot.

I pull the last few rolls into shape, cover them with a cloth, and go outside to admire the building work. The new wing blends beautifully into the house and doesn't look as though it was just tacked on, or even that it was originally a row of garages and an outhouse.

Luc Theyroux is doing an excellent job on the woodwork, and a couple of guys from the masonry company who also do woodwork are helping out, so we're still on schedule. He's proving handy with other jobs too: he told me yesterday that he's looking forward to helping with the tiling. Steve is pretty good on many things but admits openly that French wiring and plumbing can be beyond him and tiling isn't exactly a speciality.

We've had electricians and plumbers in for the heavy work but the fact that Luc and Steve can do a lot of the fiddly things together is good. Luc is happy to work as and when needed so he can work on his wood block engraving the rest of the time. It's a technique I knew nothing about, but it involved carving a picture into the smooth face of a block and then printing the design onto paper, using a press. He's obviously passionate about it.

He's not a huge talker, which means he doesn't get on Steve's nerves, but his wry sense of humour is nice. He lives alone and he's said cooking for one isn't his thing, so he's stayed for a meal several times. I'm pleased to have a guinea pig to test out some of the things I want to make for guests, and so far, they hit the spot.

Maybe I'll dig out a few frozen *mirabelles* – tiny, yellow plums from the garden that I've pitted and frozen – and make a crumble. The end of October has brought cooler weather, and it's heading towards comfort food time.

The phone rings as I'm peering into the freezer and I answer it breathlessly, juggling a bag of fruit and a canister of rice.

"Allo oui?"

"Oh, you are there, then."

More dough may require thumping. It's Mum.

"Sure I am. I was just making bread, as a matter of fact. How are you?"

"I was starting to wonder if you were all right. It's so long since you called."

It's only been a week, but I don't say so. Gillian calls her every day.

"We're fine, thanks. Nothing to report – everything's going fine."

Find a new adjective as a variation from 'fine', Shirley. But I'm damned if I'll admit to the glitches we've had lately.

"Well I'm glad it is for you. My blood pressure's up again. Probably worrying about you and that boarding house of yours."

"Maybe we should use that as its name, Mum," I say evilly. "Guesthouse or B&B really do sound better, though. And sorry to hear about your blood pressure."

"Yes, well. I've got some new pills. This awful weather's not helping with my rheumatism either. I've been stuck in all week."

"Shame," I say, trying to be sympathetic. I only hope she's not angling for another visit. "Didn't you go up to Gillian's for dinner this week, then?"

Oh well done, Shirley. Now we'll be onto Gillian again, but I do feel for Mum if she's been on her own for days on end. Usually she goes to church, to the seniors' club, has a chinwag with neighbours, and goes into town for a look around. Mum loves a good browse around department stores in search of appropriate pastels.

"I did go up there, and to church, but they called off the day trip to the seaside because of the weather. And I'd have got soaked getting to the bus stop, so I didn't get into town."

"Shame," I repeat myself. "So…"

71

"Gillian and Clive are going on another cruise," she says, changing tack – this is clearly what she's called about. "A *luxury* cruise."

Well of course. They like cruises. They've never been to France to see us, or even Switzerland when we lived there before that, but that's probably because a normal house or even a B&B isn't quite like one of those monstrous ships full of two thousand happy holidaymakers, which is what they always opt for.

Oh Shirley, how mean of you. I wouldn't say no to a real luxury cruise myself now and then, but on a small sailing ship and without the booze, bingo and general jollity.

What a snob.

"That's great. Where to this time?"

"The Azores," Mum says. "Apparently it's still warm there at this time of year. Nice for some, eh?"

"Definitely."

"It's their wedding anniversary, you know. Gillian says she's always wanted to go there, and Clive just rolled up with the tickets."

"Fantastic," I say dutifully. "Actually, we may pop over to Morocco for New Year, after we've seen you."

"Oh? Can't see what you see in that place. All those Arabs. They're nothing but troublemakers, you know. I was reading about how they force women to cover their faces the other week at the hairdressers. They aren't even allowed to drive."

"Not in Morocco, Mum. Maybe that was Saudi Arabia?"

"I'm not senile, thank you very much. It was definitely Morocco. Gillian was saying they wouldn't go to those places in a month of

Sundays. The travel agency definitely recommended they stay away."

"There aren't many cruises to Marrakesh, or up in the Atlas or down in the Sahara," I say, knowing I sound irritable now. "Tangiers maybe, but I agree that's a bit dicey."

"I wasn't born yesterday. I do know where Marrakech is. And Tangiers."

"I know Mum, sorry."

I haven't broken my record. I always swear I'll have one phone conversation with Mum, one day, where I don't end up apologising, but it hasn't happened yet.

"Well, I'm obviously disturbing you."

Not many conversations take place without that little phrase cropping up, either.

"No, of course not. Although I should go and get Steve some lunch."

"You're lucky to have somebody to cook for. It's better than being on your own all the time."

Thanks for the emotional blackmail, Mum.

"Well, it'll soon be Christmas and you can cook for us. Steve only talked about your Christmas pudding the other day."

"Did he?" That seems to appease her a little. "Well, I'll make a Christmas cake as well, and some mince pies."

"That'd be great. So…"

"I'll let you go then. And please don't leave it so long before calling again. I get worried if I don't hear."

"You're right. Sorry. Bye Mum."

There I go again.

I go back and look for the pruning shears. There has to be something in the garden that calls for a nice cathartic snipping session.

***

Emma

Myles looked half angry and half exhausted. Emma, however, was simply furious after her second visit to the creepy coat hanger king, as she thought of him.

"Emma, Reg Small is worth millions. He particularly wants you on this project, or he'll go elsewhere. You're putting me in an impossible situation. Can't you just be flattered that he finds you attractive? I did tell him the idea of including you in his videos was out of the question."

"Basically," Emma snapped, "I suspect he'll give you the contract if I let him fuck me. Which is pretty much like working for a pimp, not a serious company. The man actually backed me up against a filing cabinet and he was virtually pawing me, Myles. If his secretary hadn't started hammering on the door because his 'Chinks' had a problem, he could quite well have assaulted me. And *don't* give me that 'but you're a big girl' thing. Or *dare* to suggest I turned him on. *Look* at me…"

Emma glared at him. Not even loose-fitting, maximum coverage clothes and flat shoes had made any difference.

"He's just horrible," she faltered, the anger giving way to disgust.

"I believe you," Myles seemed to have deflated a little, too. "I'm sorry."

"So am I," she said. "I know you need him. But it's really throwing me to the lions and it's not fair. Look – I know we need jobs, but can't you take it over? I'll gladly take over on the lawn products one you said was nearly in the bag. Or anything else. Everything I've been working on is pretty well wrapped up now, I know."

"We lost the lawn products as well." Myles seemed to shrink into his chair.

"Oh." This was not good news. "So –"

"I can see your point, Emma. It's just that we're not doing well. I know it's partly my fault, letting the place get too big too fast."

She stared at him, starting to feel sorry for him. Myles wasn't a bad guy, but as she'd thought before, he just didn't have the drive it took for the job.

"Meaning it's time to get smaller, rather than get Mr Small."

"You're way too perceptive for your own good, Emma. I never could pull the wool over your eyes, could I?" Myles seemed too tired to appreciate the quip that seemed inevitable.

"Not much, no. So, I'm fired?"

"I don't have much choice but to let you go – I'm hardly firing you. You'll get everything due to you. I'll make damned sure of that. And people will snap you up, you know."

"You think?" Emma said bitterly, realising her heart was pounding.

"I'll give you an excellent reference as well. Put feelers out to see if anybody's looking for somebody of your calibre. I do know how good you are, Emma."

"As long as they don't expect me to get excited about coat hangers."

"Glad to see you keep your sense of humour," he said quietly. "I really am sorry. If it helps, you don't have to come in during your notice period. I'll put that in writing. It'll give you time to look around."

"Gee thanks," she said wryly. "You know, I've never been unemployed before. It'll be a whole new experience. Can't wait."

"Emma, what do you want me to do? Grovel any more than I'm doing already? You're bright, dynamic, young, you have a steady partner…"

"I'm little miss perfect," she said dully. "Do I have to sign anything?"

"I'll send you an official letter, and then there'll be a few bits of paperwork, yes. Maybe we can do all that next week when you're feeling less… more…"

"Like jumping off Tower Bridge," she said. "Only joking. I'm attempting to be dignified. Thanks, Myles. Is it okay if I go home now? Lick my wounds and all that?"

"It's fine." Myles took a long, deep breath. "If you want the truth, it's the first time I've let anybody go."

"You'll be fine," Emma said, suddenly sliding into sympathy too. "We both will be. One day we'll laugh about coat hangers, maybe?"

***

Fired. Let go. Made redundant. Terminated. Dismissed.

She'd kept remarkably calm in front of Myles, but it hadn't been easy. Now, it was hitting her.

She kept walking once she left the office, feeling the tears run down her face and not caring if people noticed. At least, she thought, she was wearing Reg-repellent footwear rather than her usual high heels.

Eventually, almost without realising it, she found herself by the river. Tourists milled around, pointing at the Shard, at the boats on the river, but her usual feeling of being a local rather than one of them seemed out of place now. Did she really belong? Had London just spat her out? Had she failed like so many people who moved there, full of hope?

It felt like it.

Bright, she certainly was, she argued with herself. Myles was right about that. She'd find something. She was also the resilient, solid type like her father – her mother had said that often enough, and she wasn't wrong.

The steady partner bit was not quite as steady as she'd have liked. Ever since the evening they'd argued over the damned cocktail dress a week before, Rainer had been criticising everything, even though she'd made huge efforts to keep the place tidy and do all the jobs on 'her' list. She'd even taken to wearing plainer, boring clothes which quite frankly just made her miserable. Emma's idea of dressing was to use colours, to use her curves to their advantage, and she most definitely didn't find the way she looked to be cheap.

Sinking onto a bench, she sat and stared out over the water, ignoring the fact that it was starting to rain – in England it always was, unless it was stopping, only to start again later. Or probably sooner.

What now? How would Rainer react? She'd talked about her first experience with Reg Small, trying to make it funny, but it had fallen on stony ground. He'd told her that work was work (*verk is verk, Emma*). That at least her job wasn't too demanding, with the subtext being that *his* job was demanding, and she could 'enjoy herself with the extra certification course'.

She supposed he was right because it was enjoyable and challenging. She just had to get the final dissertation done and she'd have another string to her bow. A graduate certification in digital marketing would definitely be an asset, and six months ago – a century ago – Myles had been all in favour of it and even paid the fees.

The dissertation wasn't anywhere near finished. She needed to include a couple of case studies. One should be for a big company, and that she could do based on some of the better clients she'd handled. She'd even made a start on that part. The other, for a smaller one, was a bit harder. She'd toyed with the idea of using her parents' B&B as a subject, but somehow that seemed too close to home. Her mother was as stubborn as a mule and had her own ideas about the website and the advertising in general. Emma had the impression it would end up as a battle of wills.

Maybe she wouldn't have much choice now.

The thought of admitting to her parents that she was out of a job suddenly hit her, and the tears started again.

What had her mum always said when she was hurt, either mentally or physically? *It'll be fine.*

And usually – mostly – it had been.

They'd be sympathetic, but her pride hurt.

She'd give it a couple of days before she even mentioned it, and by that time she'd have got her act together. Right now, if she called them, she'd just blubber and whine, and she *hated* that.

A good, comforting cuddle with Rainer would be exactly the thing. Until recently, he'd always been so thoughtful and attentive, so surely he'd come through for her now? The way things had been lately was probably mostly her fault for being so miserable and frustrated about work. A new job – a better one – might be exactly what she needed.

Why were there two Japanese tourists hovering in front of her?

They stepped closer, obviously hesitating. Emma took in the neatly pressed clothes, sneakers, cameras, and rain hats.

"Excuse me?" He said politely. "Please excuse my poor English but are you lost? We have map. We have iPhone app. Help you?"

Suddenly, amid the tears, she wanted to reach out and hug him. His wife – tiny but dressed almost identically – offered a pristine mini-pack of Kleenex with a shy smile.

"You are so kind," she said, taking one to replace the soggy little ball of paper in her hand. "Really so kind. Please – I'm fine."

They were still hovering. Weren't the Japanese supposed to be inscrutable and insular, rather than stopping to comfort a red-faced, weeping woman?

"You are? No need map?"

"No, I don't need a map. Thank you." From somewhere, she raked up a smile. "Just, you know, a small problem."

"Small problem." They both nodded.

"Thank you again."

Why didn't they go?

"Are you from Japan?" Emma asked. She might be dealing with major trauma, she told herself, but she was still extremely nosy. They nodded enthusiastically.

"From Nagoya. Nice City. London, very nice city also. We are on vacation. Please have nice day. We go to Tower, see historical sights now."

"Enjoy." This time her warmth was genuine. Kindness still existed, even in a world of Reg Smalls.

Finally, they walked off briskly, turning to wave goodbye. She got to her feet and headed for a bus stop, feeling a bit better. It was all about positive thinking.

She'd go home, start brushing up her CV and then be cheerful and brave when Rainer got home. That cuddle was still highly necessary, and could, of course, lead to a long, long evening of lovemaking – preferably with a bit more passion than she'd raked up last time.

She'd cope. Definitely.

***

Clutching a bottle of wine, two steaks, and some frozen spinach, she opened the door, put everything on the counter, and then froze.

Later, the few seconds that followed would be imprinted on her mind, in perfect detail.

First, she heard voices.

Second, she realised that there was music playing as well.

Third, one of the voices was Rainer's. It was coming from the bedroom, and he was laughing.

She put the bottle down quietly. Hearing the clink of glasses, she now knew why the corkscrew had been in the bedroom.

When she opened the door, she didn't fling it open and she didn't shout. She took a long, careful look, and registered the surprise, the shock, the horror on two faces. Both of them grabbed at the sheet.

"You will get out. Now," Emma said, with complete, eerie calm. "Both of you."

"Emma –"

"Out. Now."

She turned on her heel and went back into the kitchen closing the door quietly. When it opened, only seconds later, she was perched on a stool, leafing through the newspaper.

"Emma –"

"What don't you understand about 'get out', Rainer?"

"We have to talk."

He looked pale.

"Not now. Not even tonight. Just go."

"Rainer?" The woman was edging towards the door. She was blonde, skinny, but didn't look particularly freaked out after that first reaction. Elegant in a dark business suit with high heels, she had to be forty at least. In fact, if anything, she looked slightly amused.

"Ich komme gleich, Alex."

Alex. Alex, his boss. His boss the 'older woman'. That explained the calls in Swiss German. The special projects. Everything.

"Go," she said again quietly. Later, she'd wish she'd managed some really witty remark about toy boys.

The calm lasted until the door closed. It even lasted until she'd walked over to the bed, picked up the corkscrew, opened the bottle she'd bought, and drank half a glassful.

Weirder still, and despite her hands finally starting to shake, it still lasted while she decided what to do next.

What *did* people do next after that ridiculously clichéd scenario of finding your lover in your own bed with another woman, at one in the afternoon?

One thing, of course, was to get gloriously drunk. Another one was to call her girlfriends, but she only got as far as scrolling through her contact list. Hearing their shocked reactions would just make her spin out of control. They were fun people, but she wasn't close enough to them. It would just be the latest scandal to tweet about.

No, definitely not.

Calling her mother would be even worse. Her mum would probably go dashing off to get on a train or a plane to London, and she didn't want that either. Her mum tried to be nice about the flat, despite its pokiness, but it was not even Emma's place. Not anymore. She paid half the rent, but it was in Rainer's name. Stupid, stupid, stupid. But then you trusted Swiss bankers, didn't you?

So, logically, she couldn't really throw him out permanently, and there was no way she could afford the rent alone even if he agreed to let her take it over.

Taking a razor blade and making confetti of Rainer's suits seemed attractive. Maybe later.

The important thing, she decided over the second glass of wine, was not to cry. She didn't even feel like crying. She didn't feel like breaking things. She didn't even feel like drinking any more. She felt like revenge.

Taking a deep breath, she started pacing. Passing the bedroom door, she saw the damned corkscrew and Rainer's tablet beside it.

It was still on.

A few minutes later, she turned it off and decided it was time to get moving.

Chapter 6

Shirley

This is not a good day. I woke up with a dozen things on my mind, and it's been going downhill since then.

Steve's away, up in Switzerland seeing a client. This in itself isn't bad, because the money's good and he enjoys it. A couple of days apart usually does us good too, now he's not away so much. But me being me, I start worrying about whether he'll crash the car – unlikely – or whether he'll fall instantly in love with some devastatingly beautiful woman – also unlikely.

Steve is not like that. We might have had some ups and downs when his work seemed to come before me, Emma, or anything else, but I'd bet anything I have that he's never strayed.

Steve's been there and been supportive so often, when it really matters, and particularly since he stopped working so much. He doesn't care that I'm not skinny, that I'm hopeless with numbers, or that my relationship with my mother reduces me to a quivering wreck all too often, even via telephone.

Well, that's not entirely true. He's said a couple of times lately that I'm obsessed about her. In his opinion, I should have things out with her once and for all. Everything about Gillian, about our 'boarding house', and her constant criticism.

I've reminded him that on the rare occasions I've tried to broach the subject while she's been over here, it's ended up with her going all dramatic and pitiful: the whole 'you don't want me here, I'm obviously a nuisance' thing starts before I've even said more than 'why are you so critical, Mum?'

When we're in England I'm rarely on my own with her so it's hard to start that sort of conversation. A couple of times, I've asked her not to constantly compare me unfavourably with Gillian, but she always denies it flatly and changes the subject.

I've never had the courage to take it any further. One of these days, I know, I should take Steve's advice and thrash things out.

As though my mother is reading my thoughts, the phone rings and sure enough the caller ID tells me it's her. I'm tempted not to answer but that's just putting things off.

It starts with Mum telling me that Gillian has lost a *huge* amount of weight, in preparation for the famous cruise. The next thing will be that she doesn't want to offend me, but I should maybe think of doing the same.

Bingo.

The truth hurts, at times, but then I don't need a fancy new cruise wardrobe in a whole size smaller, thanks. My clothes fit me, I've stayed at the same weight for years now, and dammit I love cooking and I love wine. I would look better with a few kilos less, but it would be bloody purgatory achieving it.

I tell her that, as politely as possible. So, she changes tack and talks about cooking, because she's been doing some thinking, having consulted with 'people who know about all that'. I suspect that means Gillian, plus possibly a couple of the elderly ladies at the church club.

I'm doing it all wrong, you see. People will expect *properly* served meals, with tureens of vegetables to help themselves and a nice silver platter for the roast. A proper gravy boat. Not stuff already 'slapped on their plate'.

That leaves me speechless for a couple of seconds. I really love the whole presentation part of serving meals and using attractive crockery. For most things I cook, I'm happier putting hot food onto hot plates and serving it up like that than messing around passing things while everything goes cold. There are exceptions though: I like to serve *tagines* in the dish, and people all dig in and then mop up the juices with their triangles of bread.

Needless to say, it's not worth trying to explain any of that. The one *tagine* I tried on Mum – lamb with artichokes, peas and preserved lemons – was another 'glorified stew'.

I say something about plating meals being what I prefer.

She hasn't finished. Her experts have also agreed that what people want is not to feel rationed. Silly little bits on plates just look mean.

I take a couple of deep breaths and say that perhaps the people who said that were not necessarily representative of those who go to a B&B in France.

That gets a snappy comment about how I never listen to advice, so it's hardly surprising people find me odd.

Which people would that be, I ask? Odd how?

She ignores the 'who' but tells me it's the way I dress for a start, and particularly for a woman of my age. Some of the things I like are just not what people expect in Craghill Road. The jeans. That weird cape thing.

The weird cape thing is in fact a superb, cashmere piece I bought in Morocco. Extremely sober, it's fine with anything from jeans to a business suit. It wasn't exactly what you could get at John Lewis but I adore it. Emma borrows it when she gets half a chance, too.

So, I retort, I don't fit in with the inhabitants of Craghill Road. Tough. If I was really such an embarrassment, maybe it would be better if I stayed away from there rather than upsetting her neighbours, or whoever it was who saw fit to pass judgement on her daughter.

No, no, it wasn't that. She often wished I was just more... conventional.

I just can't take any more of this. I say I'm quite happy being odd and end up trying to sound sort of jokey but appeasing. Same old, same old. I even ask her how she's feeling.

Excellent, she says, sounding a little less crabby-tempered at last. The new pills are doing wonders and her doctor and everybody else never stop telling how marvellous she is for her age.

I assure her she is, which seems to go down well.

She'll give my love to Gillian and Clive, shall she? And she sends hers to Steve and Emma.

Phew.

I set about some work on the B&B's website to put my mother out of my mind.

We haven't made a final decision on what to call the place yet, so I ponder that for a bit before getting hopelessly entangled in the formatting, and then end up daydreaming about the décor.

I send Em a quick text about the website, asking her to call me later to help out her non-geeky mum, and then abandon ship to go down to town for some extra eggs. I've got so many walnuts off the tree this week that a couple of date and walnut loaves wouldn't go amiss, and Steve loves them.

I set off towards town feeling much better. It's barely looking like autumn, the sky's blue, and the stone keep on the hill looks majestic.

There's a big flea market in one of the villages this weekend, and Steve's back tomorrow so we can go and stroll around. We both love poking around them and coming back with a few treasures, and after all, I've got three rooms to decorate and another two to freshen.

My improved temper is short-lived. By the time I hit the traffic lights at the bottom of our lane, less than half a mile from home, something smells hot. I groan inwardly. My car – an elderly Renault in what can only be called bright yellow – has been developing all kinds of little problems recently. Affectionately dubbed Tweetie, it's not used that much but it had been cheap considering its low mileage. The colour could have had something to do with that but it's easy to find in car parks. Our bigger car is plain dark blue and resembles half the cars in France. Steve has no problem remembering which row he's parked in. Steve is the sensible one. I'm the weirdo who can't remember things like that and can't have a civil conversation with her mother.

Tweetie is not a car that would be acceptable on Craghill Road, but we wouldn't trust it as far as England anyway. I wouldn't trust it as far as the garage at this moment, because it's coughing and spluttering. It must be… I don't know. Spark plugs? Carburettor? I know nothing about cars.

I turn around and persuade it to limp back up the road. Steve may or may not know what's the matter with it. Otherwise, he can run me to the garage on Monday, staying close behind in case it gives up and dies.

Back home, relieved I've got this far, I glance at the clock. Nope, another two hours before I can sensibly think about a very large gin and tonic.

All it needs now is for something major to go wrong with the building work, I think, seeing Luc heading my way through the French windows.

"Don't bring me any bad news," I tell him. "I'm not up for it today."

"No bad news," he shakes his head. "Very good news. I just called about the tiles again and they're finally there. I even persuaded them to deliver them for free and they'll be here tomorrow, so I could get a start on that before Steve gets back?"

"You are a god," I tell him. "Tea?"

"Please. I've done all I can on the shower stalls until the tiles are here anyway. How's the website?"

"Don't ask. You don't happen to know anything about all that, do you?"

"I wish I did," he sighs. "I'm IT-challenged, big time. It's not helping me get known either. I'll probably use some of what you're paying me to get somebody to help. I can work on digital photos, and I can do email, but anything to do with websites is Greek to me. I hate the bloody social media thing. And don't even get me on texting. I think at my age I must be the only bloke who doesn't get it."

"Emma helps me a bit," I admit, pulling out the teapot. "I use Twitter but not often. I only have an account because Emma wants me to link it to the B&B website. She's really good at all that."

"Sounds like she's good at everything she puts her mind to," he says thoughtfully. "Like her parents."

"Just being a proud mother," I tell him. "And flattery gets you everywhere, including some of yesterday's apple tart, if you want it?"

"Love some." He smiles and sits down. The more I see of this young man, the more I like him.

The other day, I'd caught him sketching just after lunch. With a few simple strokes he'd captured our graceful olive tree and I couldn't help but admire the results. He wanted to turn it into a wood block engraving, he said, and it gave me an idea. We'd asked to see some of his work when he'd talked about it, and the following day he'd brought along a small portfolio of superb, intricate work.

There was one of sunflowers, another of the famous keep in town, some more contemporary designs for book plates, and a few illustrations for a book. They were stunning.

We've been thinking he could design a logo for the B&B, but it would help if we could decide on a name. That was among my early-morning issues and it needs to be resolved.

"How's the engraving?" I ask as he makes short work of the large wedge of apple tart on his plate. "Is the idea to give up carpentry eventually?"

"I don't know," he says. "First, I'm a nobody on the artistic scene, and second, it's hard on the eyes. I know a couple of older engravers who get constant migraines. Besides, I like the building work and it puts money in the bank. My uncle wants me to sign a contract, but then I wouldn't have the flexibility, so I'd rather carry on like this for the time being. I'll have to make my mind up one of these days though. Not everybody makes it as easy to combine two jobs as you and Steve seem to be doing, but there's not that much money in art."

"That would be such a shame, if you gave up that side."

"It's difficult," he frowns. "Getting a reputation. I've only been engraving for a few years. It was one of those things that felt perfectly right."

"You were a carpenter full time before that?"

He hesitates a little, and I realise I'm really giving him the third degree. I apologise immediately and cut him another slice.

"I spent a few years in New Zealand as a carpenter," he says, and doesn't elaborate on it but changes the subject back to the tiles and some of my ideas for the décor. I confess I get bogged down in details at times and start overthinking things like what sort of taps to get for the washbasins.

"I think you're a natural at it," he grins. "But then I'm a bloke. A bathroom is pretty much a bathroom to me."

I chuckle, but at the same time his quick sketches are more proof that he has talent and I'd welcome his advice on all sorts of design aspects.

Luc interests me, although not in the toy boy sense.

He is in his early thirties, but the mass of wavy hair makes him look younger. He's obviously educated, and well brought up as well. I find myself wondering what he'd look like with a short back and sides, and then imagine Emma telling me I'm being old-fashioned.

There's something reserved about him. He doesn't laugh that often. Maybe he's just the quiet type, or maybe he's on the rebound from some awful relationship, as he says he lives alone.

Oh, stop it, Shirley. You can't be a translator and editor, a bathroom designer, a cook and whatever else this project is going to require and start thinking you're a psychologist as well.

The phone rings as Luc attacks his second slice of tart. He admits to having a 'healthy appetite' and he's so skinny I'm more than happy to feed him up.

"Emma," I smile. She must have got my message about the website.

"Surprise, Mum. Can you pick me up at Valence TGV station tonight? At ten to ten?"

I'm amazed. This wasn't planned at all. I'm lost for words for a second.

"You're coming today? Tonight?" I manage finally.

"Yes. Before you ask Mum, I'm fine. I had some time, so I thought I'd come down."

Her voice is flat, controlled, which makes me uneasy.

"Emma, what's going on?"

"Can't talk now, Mum. The reception's patchy but seriously, everything's fine. Can you pick me up?"

"Dammit," I curse suddenly. "Dad's away until tomorrow and there's something horribly wrong with Tweetie."

"Oh."

"Let me call Helen, or one of the neighbours –"

I'm thinking frantically. The station is out in the middle of nowhere, as is often the case with TGV lines, and the connections to Crest by local train and bus are terrible.

"No, don't worry. I'll get a bus or something." Her voice is even flatter, now.

"Emma you know as well as I do that getting here from Valence at ten at night isn't funny. Maybe –"

Luc's trying to get my attention.

"I'll pick her up," he mouths at me. "No problem."

I could hug him.

"Luc's here," I tell her. "You remember Luc? The carpenter? He's right beside me and says he can come to meet you."

"Okay," she says. "Yes, the carpenter. Tell him thanks. See you later."

She cuts the connection, and I take a deep breath.

"Are you sure, Luc?"

"Certain. But there's not really room for three."

I hadn't thought of that. He drives an elderly pickup.

"I'll make a sign with her name on. She probably won't recognise me."

"Thanks."

"You're worried, right?" he asks.

"She said she was fine," I say, trying to reassure myself but it's not working. Is she pregnant? Has she had a big argument with Rainer? Has she quit her job? What on earth is going on?

"Probably just needs to let off steam about something to you and Steve, and by Monday she'll be back on the train." Luc says, obviously trying for positive. "Now and then I go up to Lyon and see my parents just out of the blue as well."

"You could be right."

He could be indeed, but I'm not convinced.

In the past, she had sometimes come rushing back from Lyon for exactly that sort of reason, and usually because she was furious with the boyfriend of the moment. And there were plenty of those.

When Emma's angry it's a thing to behold, but she didn't sound angry. She didn't sound tearful or heartbroken either, and it's always been one or the other when it came to boys.

The next few hours are going to be long. It's just after five, and they won't be back until ten-thirty at least.

"I need a drink," I mutter to Luc "You?"

"Driving," he says. "I'll head off home, take a shower, and make sure she calls you as soon as I pick her up. I'll take my phone with me anyway. You've got the number. What time did she say?"

"Ten to ten. And you're a godsend." I'm already texting Emma: *Sure you are fine?* Almost immediately, as Luc's closing the door, she texts back. *Really fine don't worry sorry battery low later xx.*

I go and find a bottle of Viognier and decide that if I'm not going to pace around for five hours and drink a lot of wine, there's only one thing for it. I need company. I pick up the phone and blurt it all out to Helen.

"I'll be right over," she says. "Kids, eh?"

Half an hour later she's here and allows herself one glass of wine. I'm not really hungry but I haul out some mini-quiches from the freezer to soak up the two glasses I've already had, and in preparation for the next one. That, plus some frozen yoghurt with lime and ginger, cheers me up a bit.

Helen, from a big family and with two kids a little older than Emma, is rarely fazed by the unexpected. We chat idly, and time crawls.

"Does it ever get any better?" I ask her at one point. "Worrying about kids?"

"No," she says cheerfully. "Your mother probably still worries about you."

"Sure," I snort. "Don't get me started on her. Steve thinks I'm obsessing about it all."

"And are you?"

"A bit," I admit. "But when we go up at Christmas, I'm going to sort it all out once and for all. God, Helen, it scares me sometimes. What if Emma ends up loathing me, and I end up criticising everything she does?"

"Don't be daft," Helen rolls her eyes. "She adores you both. She's probably just having a few doubts about that man of hers, or her job, and wants to talk about it."

"I hope you're right," I say and pour myself half a glass. "Better not be tipsy when she gets here, though."

Chapter 7

Emma

Emma had read Cosmo, Marie-Claire, and made inroads into Gala.

'Read' was not quite true but she'd leafed through them endlessly. On one level, her mind was busy comparing the similarities and differences in their customer approach. Work had always been a comforter when things were bad, so keeping her mind busy was essential.

On another level, she still felt completely numb. She'd blocked messages and calls from Rainer before the train had left St Pancras. Before that, she'd packed with remarkable speed, but at this moment had no idea what she'd stuffed inside the biggest suitcase she found – Rainer's – and her own, mammoth rucksack.

In Lille, she'd bought a sandwich and a can of Coke. She wasn't hungry, but her stomach was growling constantly so it seemed wise to fill it. Most of it ended up in the bin beside her seat, the white paper slowly growing translucent as the butter soaked into it.

Mechanically, she hauled her bags onto the platform and headed for the exit, expecting to see her mother and the carpenter somewhere upstairs.

A man on the platform headed towards her. A man with a ponytail and holding a sign that said 'Emma'.

"Hi," he said, reaching for her case. Considering its size, she wondered if he'd make any comment on her not travelling light, but he didn't.

His pickup looked as though it had lived a bit, but there was plenty of room for her case and the rucksack in the back.

"Thanks," she said, climbing in. She just hoped he didn't want to make conversation.

"Can you just call your mum?"

"I bet she's worrying. My battery's nearly out but I can try." That wasn't an excuse – there hadn't been time to charge it before she'd rushed off to the station and she'd forgotten the French adaptor, meaning she couldn't even plug it in on the train. "No, really dead now."

"Take mine," he said, passing it over. She took it, and vaguely registered the smiling woman on the screen. His wife, probably.

"I'm sorry about this," she said. "I'm sure you'd rather be at home with your wife than coming out here so late."

He glanced across as he started the engine and saw her looking at the screen.

"My sister. I'm not married."

"Sorry," she said quietly and dialled. Her mother was doing her utmost to be breezy, so Emma made a token effort too, but she felt exhausted. All she wanted now was silence: to go home, curl up in bed, and sleep for hours and hours. There would have to be explanations, but please God not tonight.

Tilting her head back against the headrest, she let out a long sigh and closed her eyes. If she played sleepy, maybe he wouldn't talk to her.

"Bad day, eh? I'll leave you in peace."

"Pretty bad," she nodded, realising that she was fighting back a sob.

No, not now. Not yet. She gritted her teeth, realising her stomach was roiling too, and dangerously.

Oh no.

"Stop. Please. I have to…"

He glanced across and braked, just in time for her to fling open the door and vomit onto the grass.

Finally, she got her head up to see him standing there, looking concerned.

"Station sandwiches," she muttered, taking the Kleenex he held out. "Sorry."

"Don't be. Just take a few deep breaths."

She did. Slowly, her stomach settled a bit and she stood up, pushing away his arm when he tried to help.

"It's okay. I'm not pregnant or dying," she said, almost snappily.

"Right," he said. "At least that then. You good to go now?"

She nodded and headed back to the pickup, feeling guilty for being so rude to him.

"I really am so sorry."

"You said that already," he said lightly. "Are sure you're all right, Emma?" His voice was gentle, concerned, and suddenly words tumbled out.

"As all right as you can be when a client nearly rapes you, your boss fires you, and you get home to find your boyfriend in bed with another woman, all in the space of four hours."

There, she'd said it. Why on earth she'd said it now, to a virtual stranger, she had no idea, but the tears started flowing. Too many of them, held back for too long.

She was sobbing like she'd never done before; huge, racking sobs.

His arms were around her, and her head was on his shoulder.

After a while – how long she didn't know – it eased, and she lifted her head to see a pair of eyes that looked like they had tears in them too.

"Sorry."

"You said that about five times already," he said, giving her arm a squeeze as he released her. "And you have absolutely nothing to apologise for. I'm the one who's sorry, Emma, asking too many questions."

"You don't have to be. I'm acting like a stupid…"

"No, you're not. Did he hurt you? Your client?"

"Only my pride," she said, with a hollow chuckle. "You could say it's been seriously dented in the few hours."

"More like somebody took a sledgehammer to it. A few days at home'll help."

"Once Mum stops freaking out."

"Your mum's no drama queen," he said matter-of-factly. "But you need her right now. Shall we get going?"

"Yeah. Look –"

"I know, you're sorry. Can we take that as read now?"

"I suppose so. Can you not tell Mum about, you know, just now?"

"The throwing up part or you telling her carpenter about it?"

"Just me freaking out. We're not a freaking out family – not even Mum, you're right. I had my moments when I was a kid, but we just don't, normally."

"My family don't either," Luc said. "Sometimes I wonder if we should, a bit more often. You know, have a major bust up and scream and shout and break things."

"You think?" She watched him, hands on the wheel, his face serene now. She must have been imagining the tears in the dark.

"Maybe. I've thrown a few tantrums in my time. And my dad's got a temper – he's French after all so that's probably where I get it from – but my mother? She never even raises her voice. She's a very proper sort of Englishwoman, deep down."

"My mum's not proper enough for my grandmother," Emma smiled faintly. "Or so she thinks. Me, I think Gran's just a frustrated free spirit. I think she's as jealous as hell of Mum, for actually doing what she wants."

"Sounds like you've got them all figured out."

"Not really. They've just been hopeless at talking to each other as long as I can remember, those two. At least I can talk to Mum. Well, mostly. She's still going to go ballistic, though. I think she approved of Rainer."

Tears threatened to come again, and Emma bit her lip.

"She'll go off him fast enough, I think," Luc said firmly.

"True."

Emma settled back in the seat and closed her eyes.

"It'll be fine," Luc said, warmth in his voice. "You'll see. It'll just take a bit of time."

She nodded, in the dark, too tired to even reply. Only the sound of the tyres on the gravel of their driveway woke her.

***

Shirley

I'm trying to be calming without being too obviously sympathetic. In the past, Emma's told me that just makes it worse. Apart from an untypical threat about cutting Rainer's balls off when I emailed him in the middle of the night, Steve is being natural and matter of fact, which is another of my husband's qualities. I was relieved when he arrived home by mid-afternoon. With Swiss chocolate.

I've not dared ask what Emma's plans are, because asking questions is apparently also irritating. She's said that if it's okay she'll stay a while and work on her dissertation, look around for jobs, and 'breathe a bit'.

Of course it's all right.

She even offers to come to a flea market with us on the Sunday and I admit I'd decided not to go, thinking she might need company. That gets me an abrasive comment about not needing me on a suicide watch.

So far, it's the usual post-break-up scenario. The bad temper is always part of it all, and usually alternates with bouts of weeping. I'm not sure which is worse.

This time it's more serious than her usual break-ups, but on the whole she's being very stoic. As for myself, I'd quite like Rainer's balls on a platter too, with those of the coat hanger client as an additional bonus.

Steve and I go to the flea market in the end. Emma decides not to after all, and she's still being prickly.

I don't enjoy it much at first, wrapped up in thoughts of my daughter. A dozen crystal water glasses for ten euros cheer me up, and I even persuade Steve to haul a massive bird bath back to the car.

In the evening, Emma's browsing on her tablet while I make dinner, and I notice she's brushing tears away. Then she excuses herself from dinner and goes up to her room. I know she's feeling bad if she passes up *gratin dauphinois* and a very rare steak.

In the end, I can't stand it any longer and get to my feet. Steve looks a bit doubtful when I say I'm going to see her, but he's upset by it all too.

"Em?" I tap on the door lightly, remembering when she'd first required that of us. It was in her early teens, when she'd first gone on internet chat rooms. I'd been worried sick about all the dangers involved, and we'd had serious heart-to-heart talks about them. Emma had assured us she wanted to practice her written English, and that was all.

I'm pretty sure that's what she did, obviously with a bit of flirting thrown in too, which I also found normal. Despite being tempted to go to her room unexpectedly, I never did.

I think that was because nothing at home had ever been private. Like all kids, I expect, I'd kept a diary, and poured out my anguish over school, my mother, and the incredibly gorgeous boy on the bus who never noticed me. My mother had found it and told me that my comments about her were 'frankly wicked', and those about my failed attempts at seduction were 'disgusting' because I'd said he was 'sexy-looking.' I'd learned to hide my innermost thoughts better after that.

"Come in, Mum" Emma says. Her eyes are red-rimmed, but she looks calm enough. "Sorry about dinner, and sorry about that comment this morning. I'm honestly not suicidal."

"I didn't think you were. I just wondered if you'd be all right on your own at the moment."

"I was. I really don't get flea markets, you know?"

"I know. Or garden centres. We did try to vary things when you were younger, when we went out."

She chuckles – almost a real chuckle. "It took a lot of garden centres and flea markets for that weekend at Euro Disney as compensation, Mum."

"Cheek," I retort. "I also took you to skating lessons and nearly died of frostbite."

"I know that as well – and I was only kidding. I'm not going to claim I had a miserable childhood Mum, don't worry."

But I do worry. I probably look a bit upset because I very rarely manage to say much positive about my own early years, except for times I spent with my dad.

"I suppose it's easier to remember the bad things when something or somebody hurt you," I say quietly.

"Oh yeah," she says with feeling. "Don't expect me to remember anything positive about that bastard for a very long time."

"But don't let it last as long as my bad feelings for my mother," I surprise myself saying.

"That's different. That's a case of neither of you understanding each other."

I stare at her, angry suddenly. "You have no idea what it was like. Or what it's still like."

"Maybe not, but she's still your mum. And would you mind if we left Gran out of this right now?"

She's right, and I apologise, without mentioning that in over fifty years, my mother has never apologised to me *once,* although by the law of averages I've always felt that I must have been right at least some of the time.

There's an awkward silence for a minute, and I look over at her laptop, open on the desk.

"Is he pestering you?"

"A bit. But I've blocked him on my phone, Twitter, Facebook and the rest. I've just emailed him to tell him I'll go back and pick up the rest of my stuff in a week or two, and that he should arrange to be out. He emailed me earlier with all sorts of apologies because I'd forgotten to block my old work address and they haven't cancelled it yet. All that's what got to me a bit."

"Does he honestly think he could get you back?" I'm outraged at the thought he might.

"He probably did. But I'm not buying what he said, including the part about how the bloody woman seduced him just the once. I know for a fact it's been going on for a while."

"Oh?"

"Long story, but let's say he should have been more careful. Anyway, I've not left him in much doubt about how I feel, and I've told him not to pester me, Mum."

"Good. But what happens if you do decide to forgive him and make up at some point?"

I'm hoping to hell this doesn't happen, but I've been caught out before, so I'm going for realistic. I've admitted to being less than impressed by her boyfriends after they've broken up in the past, only for the two of them to make up and for me to feel like a fool.

"Not a chance in hell. It's not like in the past, Mum. You're free to admit you didn't like him, although I think you did."

"He seemed… responsible and steady," I say carefully.

"Which made a change, right? I do remember what you thought about Simon of the shaved head and dressed all in black, for example."

I do. That was Emma's Goth period, which included black nail varnish and extravagant use of eyeliner. I was really glad when that was over and not least when she'd stopped using dark red henna – all part of the look – and leaving the bathroom like a blood bath.

"He was seriously weird, Em."

"He was. And he was a wimp and a mummy's boy. You got all upset about his tattoos, and the fact he was a vegan, remember?"

"The vegan bit turned out harder to handle than the tattoos," I tease. "Do you remember him only informing us of that when you invited him round and I made pizza because you thought he'd like it?"

"Pizza without cheese and with tofu cubes, maybe." Emma actually giggles. "But to get back to Rainer, you have absolutely no need to worry. Somebody responsible and steady doesn't screw his boss and tell me I look cheap."

"*Cheap?*"

Nobody tells my daughter she looks cheap and gets away with it. "I've got a good mind to –"

"No, Mum. Just leave it. If he does try to call here, I'm not going to talk to him, and I'd prefer you didn't get into a discussion with him either. And if you don't mind, can you also block him on your email and Twitter? I don't want him bothering you."

"If I knew how," I confess. "Email, I think I can do."

"I'll show you tomorrow," she says. "We'll sort out your website and stuff as well, next week. Might as well make myself useful. Start on Tuesday? I'll start putting out feelers for jobs, as well, but I'm paid for two months and I suppose I do have a roof over my head while I look?"

"You do, and that would be fantastic", I say, sitting on the edge of her bed. "It all gets a bit daunting at times, this whole project."

"It'll be fabulous when it's finished. Have you decided on a name yet?"

"No. Other than "Le boarding-'ouse"."

Emma laughs.

"Well, it has a certain ring to it."

"Don't go there," I warn her. "But again, that would be really great."

"In return," she says sternly, "there may be requests for pizza, or chips. I'm allowed comfort food, right? Also, is there any of that *gratin* left?"

She's recovering. I give her a quick, impulsive hug. She hugs me back, and we both head downstairs smiling.

***

By Tuesday morning, Emma's still upbeat, if a bit quiet. She's pottered around on the internet and watched some old French films between job hunting, and she's eaten everything I've put in front of her. I'm ridiculously proud of her, and still furious with Rainer, but he doesn't call the house.

We're still drinking coffee when Luc appears in front of the kitchen window. I beckon him in.

He looks diffident but comes in anyway: today marks the start of the big tiling and flooring work, so he's going to be busy. Steve, who wanted to help him, has a lot of work from his Swiss clients and is acting like a kid with his toys taken away.

Emma is still in pyjamas, and she grins at Luc. He doesn't refuse a plate, the basket of bread, or the jam.

"I'll go and put clothes on and then put Mum to work," Emma says. "Thanks again for picking me up on last week."

"It was a pleasure," he says, reaching for the butter. "Nice to be here?"

"Definitely," she says, heading for the stairs. "Okay, Mum. In half an hour, you'll need to gather your wits. Have more of that coffee."

"Wait," I say weakly. "I still have to get Tweetie back from the garage."

"We can do that first. I can take the other car, and we'll be back in half an hour. You're not getting off that easily."

"My daughter is bossy," Steve says amiably. "Just like her mother."

"That," I warn them, "is dangerous talk. So dangerous that it's jeopardising your chances of a pizza lunch. You and Luc both."

"No, not that" Steve groans dramatically. "We are working men."

"We are the hunter-gatherers," Luc adds. "We need our strength."

"Number-crunching doesn't burn many calories," I say to Steve sweetly. "And unlike Luc, you need to watch your waistline."

"See what I have to put up with?" Steve moans. "Surrounded by women as I am."

"Rubbish. Two of the cats are males."

"Logical. It's easier to chop their balls off than the whole rigmarole with female cats."

I glance across to our single female cat, who is altogether too precious for words and waiting hopefully in case the bread and jam metamorphose into a slice of meat.

"See?" I tell her. "Misogyny is alive and well and living in Crest." She decides to wash a bit of fur rather than do the female solidarity thing.

"Women," Steve sighs. "Have some more bread, Luc. Make the most of it, because we may have to go and kill a wild boar for supper."

I leave them to it.

Chapter 8

Emma

Emma admired her mother's habit of flitting from one train of thought to another and one task to another. The only time she ever stayed in one place was when she was translating or writing, but even then she managed to juggle various subjects in one day and then do washing, pull up a few weeds, or start preparing a meal in the middle of her coffee breaks.

It was multi-tasking on speed, and both she and her mum thrived on it. At the moment, though, it was taking its toll. Her mother was in her late fifties now and she almost looked it. She'd muttered the long list of things to be done that day, that week, and wandered off onto the subject of taps and shower heads, bedding, menus, and the blurb for the website within the space of ten minutes, before finally letting out a long sigh.

"You tired, Mum?" Emma asked, as they headed for the garage.

"Not so much tired as feeling life's just a bit too complicated. But it'll be fine, and particularly if you give me a hand with setting up the website."

Her mother grimaced at the dashboard of the big Peugeot. She wasn't used to driving it and wasn't enjoying it much. Tweetie the Renault – which she was fond of despite its age and shortcomings – had needed a lot of work according to the garage.

"Sorry, I suppose your daughter having a major crisis isn't helping" Emma said. "And don't go all 'I'll be fine'. You and Dad could use a bit of a break. You didn't get away all summer."

"We have a lot to think about. We knew we would in the run-up to opening. We're going to Marrakesh for New Year, though."

"Mmmm fabulous. Can I come too?"

"Absolutely. I must do the booking soon – they fill up so quickly. It's a reward for going up to Gran's at Christmas as well."

"I was only joking about Morocco, Mum."

"Well why not? You love the place."

"I also need a job. Let's see how that goes first. Anyway, at least I won't have to go to Bern. That would have been purgatory."

"That bad?" her mother asked.

"That bad and worse. But to get back to the subject of you –"

"I'm the one who's supposed to do the mother hen thing, Emma." Her mother's expression was stubborn.

"And I love you for it. But you need a haircut and your roots done."

"Right, and to lose ten kilos and dress better." That was said snappily, meaning Emma was on dangerous ground.

"I love the way you dress, and I don't see why you need to be skinny," Emma said evenly. "Come on, Mum, lighten up. Hairdressers are amazing things for the morale. I thought we could both make an appointment for this week. Sit and read trashy magazines, go and have lunch in town afterwards. Cheap therapy, you know? Cheaper than London at least."

Her mother laughed.

"Sounds like a plan. There's no reason why not. I suppose Dad and Luc can fend for themselves for once."

"Does he often eat with you?"

"If he's here on his own, yes. He only takes a short break so he can go and do some engraving. He's a nice kid."

"Your age is showing. He's probably well over thirty, Mum."

"Probably, but I like him. He's quiet, polite…"

"So was Rainer," Emma said curtly. "Remember?"

"But as far as I know, Luc hasn't cheated on his girlfriend or called her cheap," her mother shot back. "I don't even know if he has a girlfriend for that matter. I get the impression he's a bit lost. Lonely."

"Lost?" Emma remembered the night she'd arrived. Lost wasn't the impression she had of him, and as for the girlfriend situation, what guy had a picture of his sister on his phone if he did?

"Oh, it's just the mother hen thing again. But he's trying to get known for his engraving work and he admits he's computer challenged."

"Those hints you're dropping? Bit like a ton of bricks?" Emma said lightly. "What does he want? A website? Marketing advice?"

There she went again. Making a question of every sentence.

"Both, I think, but he was intending to find somebody and pay for it."

"Very heavy bricks, Mum. Did you already tell him I'd help out?"

"Of course not!" Her mother stared around at her instead of the road. "Seriously, Em – the last thing on my mind is pushing the two of you together."

"I believe you. Because the last thing on *my* mind is getting involved with anybody for an extremely long time."

"Sounds like a good idea to me," her mother nodded.

"As it happens, though," Emma said thoughtfully, "I need a case study for my dissertation about helping out a small firm or individual with marketing. I did think of you and Dad, but something less close to home would be better and *Mum* please look at the road."

Shirley Sandford clipped the kerb and swore softly but eloquently.

"Good thing Gran didn't hear that," Emma chuckled. "How's she doing?"

"True to form. You want me to tell her about Rainer, or do you want to do it?"

"I'll give her a call in a day or two. I've got a whole lot of people to contact. About jobs, but I want to catch up with some friends in Lyon as well. I expect Rainer's already working on damage control with the people we knew in London."

Emma grimaced as she spoke. She half-suspected Rainer would love to be portraying her as the impetuous, temperamental bitch who'd walked out on him, but he wouldn't dare, would he? In any case, she'd been wondering who of their circle to contact, to keep in touch with, and came up with an extremely short list. Maybe she was still too angry to be reasonable, but most of them seemed superficial. As long as they had people to go to chic restaurants or bars with, neatly paired off, she wasn't sure they cared who Rainer was with. She'd met them through Rainer anyway, for the most part – and it had occurred to her even at the time that he'd probably been half of another couple not so long before that. Not that Rainer ever wished to discuss it – he had told her right from the beginning that he never discussed past girlfriends. That saved her from having to discuss her ex-boyfriends either.

Sophie, who was French and funny and the one girl she'd been friendly with, who had walked out on Jakey the wannabe hacker a few months before, was probably the exception. Jakey was an arrogant, self-centred show-off, with his nose-tapping and winking when he talked about his IT skills. He'd never admitted to hacking because he probably wasn't that stupid, but she was pretty sure he meddled where he shouldn't. He'd rapidly replaced Sophie with a heavily made-up but otherwise forgettable girl.

With a pang of guilt, Emma realised she'd never asked how Sophie was doing. She'd put that right later that day.

Her real friends were those from business school and her years working in Lyon, and from school in Switzerland. She still emailed them from time to time, catching up on news and where they all were, but probably not often enough.

"Emma?" her mother was glancing over at her again.

"Eyes on the road, Mum. I was doing the positive thinking thing – and I've got to admit I feel better than I expected."

"Thank goodness for that." The car swept into the entrance to the garage, missing the concrete gatepost by a couple of millimetres.

***

Shirley

The new haircut has cheered me up, and I let Emma persuade me to do some clothes shopping in Valence as well. I love the place: it's an elegant town with a fabulous old quarter full of everything from smart boutiques to gourmet food shops. I had a ball, and did considerable damage to my credit card, but I'm glad I did. Retail therapy has its moments.

Emma seems fine and seems to be doing half a dozen things at once. Considering she accuses me of a butterfly mind, her days seem to be a whirl of writing her dissertation, working with me on the website, being bossy about bathroom appliances, contacting friends, and looking around for jobs.

Evidence of my daughter is everywhere – every available surface is used for cables, papers and anything from hand cream to empty mugs of tea.

I try not to grumble, and Emma occasionally rushes round to gather everything up, only to redistribute it later.

Today, I push an assortment of hair clips, nail polish and her phone charger to one side and sit down to check over some catalogues. I've moved on from taps and toilet seats to bedlinen and towels and I'm enjoying looking at the options.

Emma is over in the new rooms at the moment, where Luc is installing the last shower unit and she took him a cup of tea. They seem to get on well although she's a little irritated by his failure to work up much enthusiasm for his marketing campaign. He's decided to give it some thought once the bathrooms are finished. Knowing Emma, she's prodding him a bit more today, as I know she's worked out a few ideas already.

Steve, liberated from his Swiss clients, is taking advantage of some late October sunshine to work on the flowerbeds, so it's delightfully peaceful. The trees are slowly turning golden, and a late crop of rapeseed on the hill is an almost luminous green in the afternoon light. I even caught myself kicking fallen leaves around on the drive earlier and even jumped in them for the hell of it.

I start leafing through the shiny, attractive pages and start a list. If I use all earthy, neutral creams and beiges for the sheets, pillows and curtains, I can rotate those easily and just use splashes of colour for the duvet covers, cushions and accessories. One room, I decide, should be all navy with a little green – lime, probably, another in lighter blues and beige, and the third, I'm not sure.

I'm toying with the merits of bright yellow or burnt orange, or maybe teal. Or would it be better to have mainly blues (real blues, not turquoise) everywhere? The two existing spare rooms have blue as the base colour, and that would simplify things if I get behind with the washing and need to do quick swaps.

I wonder if I should ask Steve's opinion, or Emma's, but neither is particularly fascinated by colour schemes and even less by sheets and towels. Steve once called me a décor bore, and I retorted that he's an Excel bore.

When the phone rings I immediately do a quick mental calculation in case it's Mum, who is one of the rare people to use it. It must be nearly a week since I called her. She took the news about Em and Rainer very calmly, and apart from a grumble about public transport and news of Gillian's rapidly-approaching cruise, it all went suspiciously well.

No, it's Mrs Cruise herself, which is a surprise. We speak rarely, and it's been like that for twenty years.

"Mum's in hospital," she says, and I immediately feel a flutter of shock. "In the Northern General. But don't panic – she's okay."

Gillian's not being particularly clear, but it's something about her getting breathless and dizzy, so they took her in for tests. She might be there for a couple of days, or longer. They don't *think* it's serious.

"Can I call her?" I ask.

"Well yes," Gillian says. "She did say you hardly ever called so she didn't want to bother you."

Charming. Now I'm starting to remember why we don't have sisterly chats that often. I think all Gillian hears about is my shortcomings.

"I called her a few days ago," I snap, but Gillian repeats exactly what she just told before. Another reason we don't talk often – we never seem to find anything to talk about.

Then it hits me. It's Thursday and they're supposed to leave on Saturday.

"Are you worried about going away?" I ask.

"Well of course we are. Obviously, I said to Clive we should cancel. I mean we can't just leave her up there. What if she's in for a week?"

Gillian and Clive do act as her chauffeur for her weekly shop and have her over for a meal afterwards.

"And nobody at church could help out if she can go home?"

There's a silence. I'm being a mean, cold-hearted bitch and I know it.

"Well," Gillian says, "I suppose we could work something out because like I said to Mum, you'd be too busy to even consider coming over to help out."

I'm not the only bitch, I think.

"I'll look into trains and get there Saturday," I say. "Can you organise a key to Mum's place for me?"

I'm speaking carefully. Neutrally. Not giving her the slightest chance of telling Mum I sounded reluctant to do the right thing.

"Well only if you're sure. I mean, if she gets out within a couple of days –"

"Then she'll have to put up with me at Craghill Road." And, I add mentally, I'll be the one wearing all the wrong things just to upset her neighbours.

"I'll talk to Clive, then. And tell Mum. Shall I get you some groceries in?"

"That would be nice, thanks. I'm not hiring a car – too rusty at driving on the wrong side of the road. If she gets out of hospital while I'm there I'll organise a taxi. The other shopping, I can do on foot, or get a bus."

"Right then," she says. I thought she'd sound relieved – I'm hardly expecting gratitude – but she just repeats the stuff about breathless and dizzy again. I put it down to her being worried.

She gives me the number to call at the hospital and I promise to call Mum, and her, as soon as I've booked the train.

***

The Eurostar's on time, but the train up to Sheffield isn't. With a bit of luck, I'll still get there during Mum's visiting hours.

The day's been endless, and it's cold, grey and raining as the train rattles its way north.

The last news from the hospital is good – Mum's being discharged tomorrow and is doing fine. She sounded chirpy when I called to confirm I'd be arriving. Her first words were "I'm not dying, you know".

Fortunately, the hospital staff pass muster, although they are 'mostly Pakistani and a few Poles'. Mum is not known for her appreciation of Sheffield's large population of immigrants. The food is wonderful, however, and Gillian is *absolutely* wonderful.

I feel anything but wonderful. Steve volunteered to come with me and I'd have given anything to accept the offer but he's trying to get the garden finished before it gets much colder and wetter, and his Swiss clients are keeping him fairly busy again too. Also, he loathes Sheffield if trips into Derbyshire aren't on the menu. At this time of the year, and given the circumstances, they probably aren't.

I loathe Sheffield too, and this surprises me every time I admit it to myself. Much as it's where I grew up and where my roots are supposed to be, every time I go back, I dislike it more. The town centre is full of cheap shops – there's a rash of greeting card places, plus the big chains, the discount places, and a fair amount of shops that are empty, windows covered with ripped posters.

For that, it's not that much different to Crest, where small, independent shops come and go rapidly. The economic crisis that hit Sheffield when the steel industry died in favour of Japan and then Korea is still very much in evidence, just as for a tiny, rural French town, the more recent global financial crisis shows too.

Comparisons, I tell myself, are odious – the two places have absolutely nothing common except finding the economy tough. Much more and I'll be acting like Mum constantly comparing me to Gillian.

A cart rattles through the train and I pay a ridiculous amount of money for a small bottle of mediocre wine and a 'gourmet continental sandwich' that features rubbery mozzarella and a sliver of chewy dried tomato. I wish I'd bought two bottles of wine but try to make the glassful last.

Feeling philosophical, I continue thinking about 'home', although Sheffield hasn't been that since I left for university. As I'd told Emma, you remember the bad things when they're related to things that hurt, so maybe I'm letting all the accumulated frustration cloud my judgement of Sheffield.

So, what were the good things? Dad. I remember holidays at the beach when I was small, and paddling in the biting chill of the North Sea, near Whitby. There are memories of him falling flat on his face during the parents' sack race at the school sports day, and laughing so much that everybody laughed with him.

Girl Guides was fun. Tennis was fun too. My friends on Craghill Road were good to play with but they didn't like books much and sometimes I preferred reading to playing with dolls and changing their clothes. I never got into Barbie or the UK equivalent, Sindy, and they all adored that kind of thing.

Where was Mum in all this? I don't remember her at the beach, although she must have been there. I remember her at a school concert in a very smart teal suit and being furious because one of the other mothers was wearing an identical one. She was even more furious because I found it funny. Diplomacy wasn't my strong point then – and probably still isn't.

I also remember her deciding that the kid I liked most on Craghill Road was 'common' and being dissuaded from seeing her. That was a shame – she was the one into climbing trees.

The thing I don't have any memories of is being close to Mum. Doing anything for fun. Shopping for clothes with her was purgatory because I wasn't slim like my sister, and she constantly despaired – aloud – of nothing looking good on me. She was right, too. One day, when I was about ten, I fell in love with a silly, frivolous dress which by some miracle actually fit and I begged and begged to have it – and by another miracle I got my way.

By the time I got home and tried it on again I realised just how absurd it looked on me. I didn't have a waist, so I looked like a barrel wearing rows of frills, and the colour made me look pasty. I was made to wear it, and every time I did, I felt terrible and my mother reminded me how expensive it was.

My memories blur into one another. I'm so drowsy I'm virtually asleep but the images keep crowding in. Mum jubilantly creating sparkly dresses for Gillian, who had a superb figure and was heavily into ballroom dancing when she was in her late teens and I was a dumpy eight or so. Mum talking endlessly about the dancing competitions, about Gillian's popularity with the boys. Mum telling the hairdresser to cut my hair short – pudding-bowl short – because it was so thick and unruly, unlike Gillian's often-permed, constantly lacquered blonde curls.

Stop it, I tell myself, patting the new hairdo Emma persuaded me into getting, and which I like. I'm making myself out to be bloody Cinderella, and I hardly went without shoes or food.

At last the train heaves and groans into Sheffield Midland. The platforms are wet, so I get my umbrella out and head for a taxi rank. I'll call home – home in Crest, as in where my heart definitely is – once I've seen my mum.

119

I give myself a good mental pep talk as the chirpy, chatty taxi driver wends his way up to the mammoth hospital complex. Mum doesn't like it much because it's not in the smart part of town. When Dad was ill, she complained about having to go all that way instead of him being admitted to the smaller one in a posher area closer to Craghill Road. She was certain the care 'over there' couldn't be any better just because it was bigger, could it?

The driver cheers me up. His accent makes me smile too – it's pure Sheffield, despite his obviously Asian origins. I'm impressed when he finds the right section, wing, ward or whatever it is, as dictated by Gillian.

Right, I tell myself. Here we go. I'm going to be helpful and upbeat. I can do this.

I find the right door, smile back at the nursing staff, and knock lightly.

Gillian opens it. Gillian should be on a cruise ship.

I stand there gaping at her, completely lost for words, and for a split second, wonder if something dramatic happened while I was on the train, but no, Mum is sitting up in bed smiling beatifically.

"Well look who's finally here," she says. "We expected you over an hour ago."

I feel like turning around and walking out but I force my lips into a smile.

"The train was late. And why are you here, Gillian?"

"We cancelled," she says, looking half-smug with overtones of poor little me. "I just couldn't leave Mum, you know. And we did get the money back, or rather we can postpone. The cruise line was just wonderful."

I don't know who I want to yell at most: Mum, who doesn't look particularly thrilled to see me (I'm dressed in the famous black non-Craghill Road approved cape) or Gillian, for not letting me know.

"I would have called," Gillian says, "but Mum said to leave it as a surprise. She was just telling the doctor before how wonderful it would be to have us both here."

"I see." I go over to Mum's bed and give her a light kiss on the cheek. She's looking fine and is surrounded with flowers and cards. One is a huge glittery affair from Gillian – I can see the signature from here. Why on earth people give cards to people they actually see face to face daily is something I just don't get, but then neither Switzerland nor France are big on the greeting card experience and I'm obviously infected by weird continental habits.

"I had lots of cards," Mum says.

"I sent flowers," I say, defensiveness rearing its ugly head. "And as I came before the post would have arrived, I'm afraid there's no card."

"Oh yes, thank you," she smiles graciously. "It's that little bunch over there."

My fingers itch again. I expect the massive sheaf of pink and cream roses is from Gillian and Clive, but then they don't have to pay stupid *Interflora* charges. I still feel mean though, and humiliated.

Great. Two minutes in and I'm already a breath away from losing my temper or running away.

"So," I say levelly. "How are you?"

"Much, much better," Mum says. "Gillian's been wonderful."

As far as I know, Gillian isn't her doctor or her nurse, who may have been a bit more responsible for the improvement than my sister, but hell, I'm too tired to argue. I'm royally pissed off, and I'd rather be anywhere else than here.

***

Two hours later, I'm sitting in Mum's living room cradling a tiny measure of brandy. I'm not a brandy fan, but I loathe sherry even more and that's all there is. I daren't even finish the half-inch left in the brandy bottle because it's probably reserved for special occasions.

Gillian did invite me for dinner, but I pleaded tired and said I'd prefer just getting some sleep. Clive appeared at the end of visiting hours and drove me to Craghill Road, saying little. Clive never says very much and never has done since she first started going out with him. I don't know whether he's shy or he hates my guts, but since I've had remarkably little to do with him since then, I can't bring myself to care one way or the other. Gillian isn't particularly chatty either, apart from saying they'll pick up Mum tomorrow and bring her here once she's discharged. Then, on Monday, they'll pick us up in the evening to have dinner at their place.

I can't wait.

Upstairs, my room looks like it did when I left England, nearly three decades ago. The same yellow and tan synthetic carpet that makes sparks when you walk on it, the same yellow nylon covers on the twin beds, the same yellow and tan nylon curtains with swirly patterns. Mum not being a fan of ironing, I'm hardly surprised to see the primrose polyester sheets that Gillian has placed in a pile on my bed, and I'm mean enough to think she could have actually made the bed up but then she was probably busy reorganising her cruise.

I'm being horrible and judgemental, but I don't care. The room is clean and tidy and there's no reason for Mum to keep up with the times. When we moved to Craghill Road from living behind the shop when I was seven, Gillian and I were allowed to choose our colours, so we must have been fans of yellow. No wonder I'm not fond of it now.

This really is a *very* small brandy. I'll nip to the shops early tomorrow and get a new bottle, plus some wine. I'm going to need it. Off-licences are open on Sundays, aren't they? They'd better be. I'm too tired to hike half a mile to see if the nearest one is also open this late at night.

I should eat, I decide, tipping the last tiny measure into my glass.

There are a few things in the fridge: a packet of ham, some eggs, and some cheese slices plus a couple of jars of jam. In the vegetable compartment there are a few potatoes, two tomatoes and one courgette. The freezer yields several small boxes labelled *chicken stew* or *beef stew* in Mum's neat writing, some ready-frozen meals and some frozen veg. The bread bin contains half of what looks like a *Wonderloaf*.

Gillian must have been feeling a bit less than creative with the grocery shopping.

After finding there's no secret wine stash, I pull out a tin of soup and then leave it on the kitchen counter and pull out my mobile.

I am *not* going to cry. I pick up my packet of cigarettes and head into the garage, which is cavernous and empty and cold. Mum never learned to drive, which meant that she didn't see why either of her daughters should. Fortunately, Dad overruled her on that with both his daughters.

I've barely put the phone down, feeling a bit better after a long chat to Steve and Emma, when it rings.

"You were on the phone," Gillian says. It probably isn't accusing, but in my present state it feels like it. To be fair to her, Gillian is not generally a hostile sort of person. She's definitely less abrasive than I am in general, which could be a euphemism for bland, but that's unkind.

"I called home on my mobile and they called me back," I say snappishly. "So I'm not running up Mum's phone bills."

"Oh. Well I just wanted to say that I forgot to buy fruit in for Mum, with all the stress. Can you pick some up, because she does love it? Apples and bananas? We won't be there too early."

"No problem."

"She looked well, don't you think?" Gillian says, almost tentatively. We both talked to one of the doctors and they seem to be fairly pleased with her and think it's just a case of sorting out her blood pressure medication.

"Yes, she did."

"She was tired when she got back from your place though. I thought I'd just mention that because I didn't want to bring it up in front of her."

Ah. So that's the real reason she called.

"Really? I thought she looked great when she left."

"Well, we do worry about her, taking planes at her age."

"Gillian, she gets dropped off at the airport, gets assistance right up to the plane and once she gets off it, and we pick her up. She's never mentioned it being stressful – I think she enjoys it."

"Maybe," she says doubtfully. "But we're not sure she should be doing it. If it's not the journey, I don't know what it is then."

"I only make her do half the gardening, the ironing and the cleaning," I say, aiming for funny. I'm trying to convince myself that Gillian's intentions are good, though.

"Well she did say she'd been helping with the cooking. I always let her relax when she comes up here."

"Gillian," I snap, suddenly furious. "In two weeks, I think she cut up two fucking carrots and peeled half a dozen potatoes and some quinces. That's not exactly hard labour is it?"

"I suppose not. Maybe the food doesn't agree with her."

I've really had it with this conversation.

"You can think what you like. She eats like a horse, just out of interest. And if you don't mind, I don't think I want to discuss this any longer. I've been up since the crack of dawn and I'm not functioning on all cylinders tonight."

"I was just trying to clear a few things up," she says testily. "But obviously you're not interested."

"That's not even true, Gillian. But think what you like. Good night."

I put the phone down, very gently, and then scream out an expletive. Then I decide that much as I loathe sherry, that bottle is calling to me.

By the time I slide into my hastily made bed, I've finished the inch or two that was left and most of my cigarettes. I also discover that tears on polyester pillows make them scratchy and unpleasant.

Chapter 9

Emma

Emma arrived in one of the new guest rooms with a cup of tea, and admired Luc's tiling.

"Working on weekends is definitely a contribution to the cause, as long as Dad's paying you overtime. But it looks great."

"Thanks. But your mum and dad also work around me and my engraving work."

"They told me a bit about it. Including about how you need a website."

"So you said when you first offered to help. Did they also tell you that I'm not a great internet fan?"

"Something like that. But these days it's pretty much a necessary evil. Says the marketing person."

"I just don't like the idea of having my name plastered all over the place without having any control over who sees it," Luc said a little shortly.

Emma bit back a sigh. He hadn't seemed enthusiastic when she'd first mentioned it and didn't seem to have changed his opinion. It would probably be better to bite the bullet and use the B&B as a case study.

She chatted on a little about how useful it was to have an internet presence, ever hopeful, and he listened. At least that.

In the end, he didn't give her a categorical 'no' but then he was French and 'no' was often just a way to get negotiations going.

Rather than push it, Emma let the conversation stray onto Crest and the area. It was not exactly a popular tourist spot for much, she said bluntly, except green tourism, kayak fans and lovers of authentic local markets. It did have room for a few more B&Bs, however.

Luc agreed but pointed out it had been a mecca for the hippie movement decades ago, and that the arts and crafts scene was thriving.

"Is that why you live here?" she asked.

"No, I came because there was work here – with my uncle – and rents were cheap. And I like it here. I was brought up in Lyon, and studied there."

"I studied in Lyon too. I love the place. You studied as a carpenter?"

"Art history. My parents thought that wasn't necessarily going to get me a job, so I learned carpentry during the holidays with my uncle's company in Crest."

"Sounds sensible. And you took it up permanently?"

"More or less. There really isn't a lot of work around for art historians or artists in general, and there's plenty for carpenters. I painted a bit on the side. Then I spent a couple of years in New Zealand with my other uncle. He has a carpentry firm there – it's a bit of a family thing. I discovered wood block engraving while I was over."

Emma wondered what had attracted him to move to the other side of the world, but she'd also moved away from home. Maybe he just wanted a change. She decided not to ask, and instead brought the conversation back to engraving, which was clearly close to Luc's heart.

"Wood is beautiful," he said. "It's so unique, every single piece. Then there's the printing, the inks..."

Emma listened to him, watching his eyes light up as he spoke. Eventually, she asked why he'd come back.

"I missed my parents. And sometimes even France, with all its warts. And how about you? Do you miss the place, now you're in London?"

Emma gave that some thought and admitted that she'd fallen in love with London – its sheer vibrancy, its feel. It felt wonderfully exotic after a childhood in Switzerland and studies in Lyon, but then she missed Lyon too, even if at first she'd been glad to leave and discover England.

After that, they swapped stories of Lyon until she'd started to feel really nostalgic.

"Crest is maybe just a bit out of the way," she said lightly. "Yes, it's pretty but not for me – I couldn't find work here and no way could I ever order sushi or go and see a good band. And as for the shopping…"

"Shopping," Luc told her, "is part of a women's genetic makeup."

"You bet it is," she said cheerfully. "I'm part of the materialistic generation."

"The connected generation," he said, teasing.

"Something like that. But right now, this place is doing me good."

"Me too," Luc had nodded. "Near enough to my family to be handy, and far enough away to be comfortable."

Steve Sandford poked his head in, praised the work and then looked at his watch, muttering about needing to check something before lunch.

"And that was a subtle hint about being hungry," she chuckled. "My beloved father can cook – or at least anything you can put in a frying pan but prefers to have somebody else do it. Right, Dad?"

"Not a new man, then?" Luc had asked.

"Cheek." Her father disappeared again.

"I'll go and make him something. Want to stay?"

"I think a shower would be a better idea, and then I need to do a couple of emails to paper suppliers. But thanks."

"So, email doesn't fall within the curse of the dreaded internet?"

"Necessary evil, as you put it before. But for a change of air and to remind you that there's life outside the media, want to go for a walk this afternoon? You ever been to the keep?"

"I'm ashamed to say I haven't. But sure, why not?"

***

The view was worth the strenuous climb up the hillside and endless flights of worn stone steps.

From the top gallery of the keep, Emma could see the entire town, the river, and the mountains beyond. Much as she wasn't a fan of scenery and countryside, it was stunning.

"Wow," she said to Luc, standing beside her. "It was worth it – thanks."

"I like being on top of things," he said, and then chuckled. "Sorry, that sounds suggestive and seriously corny."

Emma chuckled, but didn't comment, even though she nearly came back with something snappy like women liking to be on top of things too.

Not a good idea.

She looked over at him, his hair escaping a bit from the band he'd tied it with. He looked out over the valley of the Drôme, lost in thought.

"Penny for them?"

"Haven't heard that expression for years." He turned to her. "I was thinking about being here. And Lyon. Your parents and their dreams. Things I want to engrave. Family."

"All that at once?"

"Women might be better at multi-tasking, but I'm the arty type, remember? It's allowed for us."

"So, because I did business school, I'm not allowed to be arty, if arty is thinking about ten things at once? I do, if you want to know."

"Penny for all ten things you're probably thinking about, then?"

Emma paused for a moment, gathering her thoughts.

"London, and Rainer – my ex. My future. My dissertation. Lyon – I still have friends there. And Mum. She called last night and she's really miserable in Sheffield. Did I tell you that her sister ended up cancelling her cruise, after Mum going over so she didn't have to? And didn't even tell her?"

"Weird. But then people are. Your mum is great, though. She really is focused on this B&B."

"And she's pretty much obsessed by the fact that she and Gran don't get on."

"Obsessed is a hard word."

Emma thought about that, staring out over the tiled roofs of the town. Talking to Luc was so easy, with both of them lapsing into French when they couldn't find the right one in English. She'd spent her life doing that with her parents, but in London she couldn't.

"You might be right. She always feels as though Gran compares her unfavourably to her sister – she feels Gillian was always the favourite."

"You're an only child, Emma. Maybe you just can't understand that."

"Maybe. It does make me wonder if parents can't help having favourites, however much they try to be fair. There'll always be one that seems, I don't know, better in some way? Nicer, more intelligent, less of a rebel."

"I think you probably have to be parents to work that one out, but maybe some of them really do love their kids the same, however they turn out," Luc said thoughtfully. "Pop psychology, eh?"

She laughed, enjoying the wind in her hair and Luc's company. She pulled herself up, though, shaking her head at the idea of this turning into anything. The timing was wrong to start with, and life wasn't like cheesy romantic novels for women.

"Another penny?" Luc asked her.

"You don't want to know. So, your parents don't have favourites? I saw your sister on your phone, remember."

"No, I don't think they did. Marie was the brilliant one and I was the big older brother. We got along fine."

"Past tense?" Emma said it without thinking.

Luc turned his head away abruptly.

"She died," he said, his words almost lost in the wind. "Six years ago."

Emma shivered, horrified at her clumsiness.

"I'm so sorry, Luc. I'm too nosy for my own good and about as subtle as a brick."

"It's okay. But I'd rather not go into it."

"Of course not. Look, I really am sorry."

"You say that a lot." Luc half-smiled. "Remember?"

She remembered. That night in his pickup wasn't something she wanted to revisit, so she took a deep breath and decided it was time for a radical change of tack.

"I had an idea last night, after I'd talked to my mum. I have to go over to London to sign some papers for work and sort out some things I left at the flat. Maybe I can get Gran to store them for me, so I'll go up north and see about that while I'm there – take some of the heat off Mum. I told her last night she doesn't have to hold out for a week if Gillian's there. I'll stay a couple of days or so, I think."

Why she was babbling on about her plans she didn't know, but it was the first thing that came to mind.

"Have you decided what to do next? After that, I mean."

"Come back and finish this wretched dissertation. Find a job." It all sounded so simple, said like that.

"In London?"

"I don't even know. I'm putting out feelers everywhere, but I may be filling supermarket shelves before long. Or applying to McDonalds."

"Somehow I doubt that," Luc chuckled. "Not with all your contacts. I suppose there have to be some advantages to all this social media stuff you keep pushing."

"Some," she acknowledged. "When I get back, though, I'll start pestering you about a website again."

"Why am I not surprised? And if you do have time to help and I decide to go with it, I'll pay you."

"Don't be ridiculous. I'm not a professional web designer."

"Don't *you* be ridiculous. It has to be better than frying hamburgers."

"I don't need money yet. I'm still paid for weeks."

"You want to argue about this?"

"Possibly."

"Then we'll argue about it over a meal when you get back. I'll cook. I'll explain a bit more about what wood block engraving is, and then we'll see."

"I'm supposed to be the bossy one," Emma said, letting this idea sink in and rather liking it. "But why not? Although it definitely won't be a date, right?"

"Wouldn't dream of it," Luc said, and with such conviction she was slightly taken aback. She wasn't disappointed, of course. Or was she?

No, she wasn't, she reasoned. It was good to have somebody of her own generation to talk to. Luc was offering friendship, and that was welcome.

"So," she said, turning away from the wall. "I could murder sushi."

"I'm hardly up to Japanese cuisine."

"No, I didn't mean when you cook. I meant right now. A nice little sushi bar at the foot of the keep. And a cold beer."

"Somehow I don't think a sushi bar would be very successful in the depths of rural France, but knowing you, you'd make it work with the right business plan."

Was that a compliment? Yes, definitely.

"Why stop at one? I could set up an entire chain. Franchises. Branches throughout the world. You could design the logo and be my artistic advisor."

"How kind. And I do know where to find a cold beer."

"Lead on."

Emma followed him, feeling cheerful. Watching Luc tackle the stairs with easy grace was pleasing to the eye as well. Maybe she was getting over Rainer even better and faster than she'd thought, despite waking up at times and expecting to see his head on the pillow next to hers.

Her mind was processing information and that soon took over from the bout of nostalgia. She was tough, after all, and Luc had realised that. Tough stopped you getting hurt, or at least helped you get over it fast.

His sister had died – how and why? He wanted to cook for her? Why? He admired her business sense but didn't seem to have much of his own. Why? Wasn't he ambitious at all?

Why, why, why. Well, it could be interesting to find out.

***

Shirley

I wake up from a restless sleep to hear the phone ringing and bolt downstairs. By the time I hang up, I feel a million times better, thanks to Emma. She sounds cheerful, and her 'master plan' as she puts it is brilliant. I get scolded for not having 3G, whatever that is, so I could get my emails on my phone but retort that it's already quite something that I've learned to do it using normal wifi.

Getting dressed to go out, I give my black cape a swirl, hoping that everybody living on Craghill Road watches me leave Mum's house just so they can confirm her suspicions that it's definitely the wrong thing to wear. Considering it's cold and grey, it's actually perfect.

Reaching the shops, I feel a pang of regret to see our old grocery now turned into an estate agent, next to – of course – a greeting card shop that used to be a fishmonger. Mum always hated that place, despite it being meticulously clean. I think it was more a case of her loathing the couple who ran it, who were constantly cheerful and got on wonderfully with Dad. It was just that they were 'common'. Mum thought most people were common or – worse – too pretentious for their own good.

This was pretty rich coming from somebody whose parents were a cook and a gardener respectively, but Mum had inherited a few airs and graces from rubbing shoulders with her parents' employers.

I allow myself a bit of nostalgia about the years when supermarkets first made their appearance and Dad struggled to keep going. He did, but only thanks to stocking a range of delicatessen-type goods that appealed to people. I honestly think that Dad was the pioneer of sun-dried tomatoes and good olive oil in Sheffield. Not that either ever made an appearance on our table. It was all 'that foreign muck' according to Mum – but it sold. As did the wonderfully mature parmesan, the Parma ham, and the spicy salami. Basically, Dad jumped on the bandwagon of Italian food, found a decent wholesaler, and made a name for himself.

The supermarket is open, and I hit the mother lode – the alcohol aisle – almost immediately. I've got Mum's shopping cart on wheels and fill it cheerfully. Sherry, brandy, and two bottles of wine to start with.

Then I find some chicken breasts and air-cured ham to wrap them in for dinner tonight. I'll make a sauce with a tin of tomatoes I've seen in the cupboard. The ham at the deli counter looks decent, so I ask for a few slices, plus some farmhouse cheddar. I spot some Wensleydale and grab it, because I can't get it in France and it's one of the few things I miss. That will make a decent lunch. The pre-packed ham in the fridge can go with some pasta for a carbonara at some point. I grab some fettuccini while I'm at it.

Moving onto the fruit and vegetables, I find them tired-looking but pick up some Little Gem lettuces, apples, bananas, and wilted parsley. Does Mum have olive oil for vinaigrette? I doubt it, but no way in hell will I stoop to buying salad cream. I pick up a small bottle of extra virgin, and suppress a chuckle, remembering Mum getting all huffy about vulgarity on oil bottles when Dad first stocked them.

I can't resist buying a little tub of olives, much as it makes me feel homesick, but Mum likes them.

There. I'm pleased with myself. I grab a couple of packets of biscuits as I know Mum loves those, too. I hover in front of the crisps and nuts and decide to be strong, and then see the cigarette rack on the way out and decide to be weak.

And off I trundle towards home, past the pub I worked in during university holidays. It's lost the air of a rather tatty local and is all spotlights and blackboards with chalked-up menus now. In my day, no food was served apart from crisps, pork scratchings and the free slices of black pudding to go with the brass band they brought in on Saturday nights.

There's also a sign that says *We serve morning coffee*. I suspect it will be thin brown stuff, probably worse than the cup of Nescafé I made myself earlier, but I'm tempted.

I'd better get back. I notice a small sign below the blackboard advertising happy hour saying *free wifi here*. That could also come in handy later.

Things are looking up.

***

By Monday night, when we're due to be picked up by Clive, I'm clinging onto my sanity by a thread.

Mum seems well. Since she came home, she's held court with several of her church friends and I've been sent off to provide tea and biscuits, this despite the fact I've got the wrong ones. Nobody eats custard creams any more.

I've been briefed on the need to avoid mentioning the boarding house project to her visitors because 'they wouldn't understand.' I let it pass, although aren't they supposed to have offered advice on plating meals?

I do as I'm asked.

Otherwise, life has been punctuated by television. I try not to be uncharitable about that – she lives alone after all. I'm seriously impressed by the fact that she's an expert at programming her video. Some of her favourites clash or there's the soap she'll miss when we go to Gillian's. She can even, she tells me, programme a whole two weeks of that for when she's staying with us. I could never even programme ours to record live, when we had one, but I'm not admitting it.

We talk a bit, but mostly it's a life history of her visitors and their ailments. Or Gillian. Again, I try to be patient although it does call for a quiet cigarette in the garage now and then. It's raining most of the time, or I'd escape to the garden, at the risk of being told for the second time that *nobody in Craghill Road smokes and what will they think.*

I learn that she needs her hair done, and we'll do that tomorrow. She's perfectly able to take the bus. She'd also rather like a little walk around town on Wednesday. She really needs a new handbag.

Lunch today was beans on toast, because that's what she fancied, not anything complicated. I made inroads into the Cheddar and got told off for getting the wrong sort of that, too. The supermarket's own shrink-wrapped brand apparently keeps forever so why I had to get the expensive farmhouse stuff she can't imagine.

Yesterday she'd finally arrived in the early afternoon because Gillian had just *insisted* that they went to their place for lunch once she'd been discharged and they'd had a *delightful* quiche. I don't say it would have been even more *delightful* if they'd warned me earlier rather than just as they sat down to eat. For dinner, she'd wanted one of her frozen chicken dinners, rather than my plans for ham-wrapped breasts, so we solemnly ate that in front of a quiz programme. It tasted uninteresting, but a couple of glasses of wine helped it down. Mum managed a couple too, while snorting at the incompetence of the contestants.

I've been pondering whether to actually *talk* to her – starting with the fact that every time I mention anything about my projects or my work or our garden, she cuts in and launches into how Clive grows wonderful kidney beans and Kevin just loves gardening, or how Gillian's doing voluntary work at a senior citizens' club since she retired, where she is universally adored.

It's not the right moment for that, though, because Mum's been unwell. That's my current excuse, because it hasn't been the right moment since I've been old enough to realise we don't get on. How do you broach that sort of thing with a parent anyway?

If you're me, you don't but you spend far too much of your life wishing you had.

So here we are. Mum has been upstairs to change into a pastel blue dress, complete with pearls and brooch. I'm encouraged to 'dress up a bit' because Gillian takes so much trouble for her guests, so I dig out some plain trousers and a burgundy top and put on a little lip gloss. Mum looks me up and down and tells me the top is badly made because the hem isn't level.

I calmly tell her it's asymmetrical on purpose. She sniffs, and I decide we need a pre-dinner sherry. I pour us each a generous one.

Clive arrives bang on time, before I've managed a refill, and drives us to their place in his usual silence, with classical music playing loudly. Mum whispers that he prefers not to talk when driving, but that suits me fine. Gillian talks for both of them, or at least in front of other people.

As predicted, we sit straight down at the table. Thank goodness for the sherry, I think. I'm almost getting a taste for it.

"You know," Mum says cheerfully, "the hospital food was excellent for what it was but there's nothing like a good Yorkshire spread."

"And good Yorkshire food's hard to beat," Clive nods knowingly. Is this a subtle insult or is it just part of Clive's fondness for his roots? A local council clerk for his entire life, he shares Mum's belief that Sheffield is great. I remind myself that there's nothing wrong with being proud of your roots, even if mine were pulled up decades ago and have been replanted in various places.

The spread starts with avocados filled with prawns. I resist the urge to ask if Clive has good Yorkshire avocado trees growing next to the kidney beans. The plate is trimmed with some curly parsley and a couple of leaves of lettuce, and the sauce is, if I'm not mistaken, salad cream mixed with a squirt of ketchup. There's a basketful of soft white bread rolls that could arguably feed twenty.

I dig in, making polite reassurances that it's delicious, and look around Gillian's new kitchen–dining room. The extension was a major topic of conversation during Mum's visit a year ago, and it looks splendid. They added an extra bedroom on top, too, which pleased Mum immensely and almost made up for the fact that she doesn't really like this part of town because it's 'rather working class'. The house had originally been a gift from Clive's mother, and it's a couple of streets from where he grew up. If I'm not mistaken, the extension is thanks to Clive's inheritance, which also pays for their cruise habit, according to Mum.

I wonder if they'll ask her to move in with them, in that brand-new room. Is that what they built it for?

I also wonder if she would accept, because she's very attached to Craghill Road.

I drag my thoughts back to dinner, and my surroundings, and have a pang of jealousy seeing the Aga in the corner. Much as I love my own kitchen, there isn't room for one without knocking down a wall or two and I think I've seen enough masonry work for a while.

I admire it all and push some of the salad-cream sauce under my avocado skin. Gillian glows at the praise, and I get a blow-by-blow account of the tribulations of the building work and sympathise a bit with that. Mum rapidly changes the subject to her neighbour's fancy sun lounge which is absolutely not in keeping with Craghill Road. It's far too modern and pretentious.

While we're waiting for the main course, I ask politely if I could use their wifi as I brought my tablet with me. I only need their code, I explain. I know from Mum's chatter that Kevin is 'always on his computer' when he's over, so that should be no problem.

Clive rolls his eyes slightly. Kevin set up their system, he says, and as they don't use the wifi, just their desktop upstairs, he has no idea what code I could be talking about. What's more, they never turn on the computer in the evening because they feel it's antisocial.

Quite right, my mother says authoritatively. All these young people getting addicted to their smart tablets and their play boxes. Kevin, Gillian adds, uses his computer for work so that's different. I feel like saying that my idea wasn't to nip up for a quick blast of Candy Crush or something, but simply point out that I do, in fact, rely on the internet for my translation work.

"At this time of night?" Mum says. "Who's working at this time of night?"

"It's to pick up my email," I say calmly. "Steve told me earlier that a big job came in, so I thought I'd download it. But it can wait until tomorrow morning. The pub has a connection. I can nip in while you're at the hairdressers."

We get back to the matter in hand, which is the main course.

Gillian hands out plates, chatting about Kevin and his job in sales in Northampton. I can never remember what the firm sells but it's something to do with pumps or compressors. Mum beams because he's done so well for himself, praises him for always helping her with the garden when he's up in Sheffield, and fortunately doesn't make any unkind comments about Emma being out of work. That's one crisis averted.

The Yorkshire spread continues with a ham roast in honey sauce, a huge tureen of broccoli in cheese sauce, one of buttered carrots, another of roast potatoes, plus a bowl of mashed ones with some gravy on the side. By the time we're all served, the plates are cold and so is the food, but everything's perfectly cooked. It just looks a bit like slurry with all the sauces and gravy and mash.

"Absolutely wonderful," Mum enthuses as she pauses for a sip of tepid Liebfraumilch. "I'm so fortunate to have such a superb cook in the family."

The urge to pick up my plate and throw it at her is strong.

"In fact," she adds, "both my daughters can cook. It makes me very proud."

I grab my glass and chug it down. This is probably the nearest thing to a compliment she has ever come up with.

Mum tucks in, and then has another thought.

"You should ask Gillian for her recipe for this, you know."

Gillian blushes faintly. If I'm right, this means the ham-in-sauce came from Marks and Spencer, but that's me being Mrs Überbitch.

"Definitely," I say enthusiastically, and she blushes a bit more, giving a furtive glance in the direction of the swing-top bin where she's probably hidden the evidence.

I decide to be kind and tell her we really can't get ham like this in Crest so it wouldn't be anywhere near as good. She shoots me a grateful glance.

In fact, the evening improves a bit from there on. Clive even breaks out a second bottle of wine and I genuinely enjoy the apple crumble. Fortunately, he's not in the mood for giving lectures on his pet topics related to local councils or the 'damned Tories'. Quiet as he is, we occasionally get treated to one of those. It gets rather uncomfortable all round, and particularly since, as shopkeepers, my parents were staunch Maggie Thatcher supporters. Clive's politics were always a major stumbling block for them both, but – as Dad would always say – as long as he was good to Gillian, they'd just ignore that bit.

All that was probably why I'd declared myself a Liberal when I was old enough to vote. It was more a case of not taking sides than actually caring much about policies or manifestos, but I've never admitted that. Just call me shallow. Or rebellious. Or both.

In a flash of genius, when the conversation about the glories of a good bit of pork dwindles, I manage to get the conversation onto some good memories, starting with Star Trek and toasted sandwiches, or digging barnacles off rocks in Whitby.

Mum, slightly pink from the wine, smiles at us all and declares that we've always been such a happy family. I'm not going to argue with her, because I'm about to announce the plans for the rest of the week, even without the added prop of a visit to their wifi.

I explain it all, trying to sound more regretful than I feel: I'll leave on Thursday because of this job that came in, which I'll need to finish for the Monday afterwards.

Mum starts frowning and insists she won't disturb me if I have to work. I explain that I'll need constant access to online glossaries and to discuss things with the client by email, so I really can't do it at Craghill Road. The good thing though – I pause for effect – is that Emma's coming over for a short visit to tie up some loose ends and will arrive on Friday for a couple of nights.

Mum smiles genuinely at that. She adores Emma, of course, and Emma seems fond of her too.

"Well, do what you have to do," she says graciously. "Will Emma come back to England, do you think?"

"I really don't know, Mum. First she wants to finish her dissertation but she's looking around."

"Poor girl," Mum says. "But she'll find something, I'm sure."

"Definitely," I say, glad this has gone relatively well. "And we'll be back at Christmas, of course. I'll not have to work then, at least."

Everybody nods, and Gillian starts clearing the plates. Feeling pretty contented, I ask about the cruise, which can be rescheduled at any time off-season. Gillian enthuses about it all: the fabulous cabins, the meals, the onboard activities, and I don't ask if that means bingo. There's even a complete spa on board, she says. Clive always insists she pamper herself.

"And quite rightly so," Mum agrees. "I've always fancied a cruise myself."

It would be evil to suggest they took her along, I suppose. Gillian doesn't comment on that, and I help her with the plates and start stacking the dishwasher. Scraping a bit of broccoli off one plate into the bin, I see the glossy cardboard and the M&S logo, and grin to myself. It's nice to be right. When I see Gillian watching and blushing some more, I even manage a wink.

"Wish they had Marks and Sparks in Crest," I mutter quietly, and she actually chuckles. By the time we've finished washing the glassware, we've actually managed a conversation of sorts, mainly about Mum. No way, Gillian admits, are they going to take Mum along on holiday. I sympathise, joking about the daily bowel movement reports, but we turn serious again wondering how much longer she'll be able to live on her own.

Gillian says they've thought of that, but Mum has insisted that she has no intention of going into a home until it's absolutely essential, or of 'being a burden' to either of her daughters. We decide to wait and see for a bit, but I promise to come over and help if it comes to a point where she needs persuading.

For a few short moments, we're actually behaving like sisters. We even sneak another glass of wine from a bag-in-box and she comes into their garage with me when I confess my need for a nicotine fix.

I apologise for losing my temper the night before, and she apologises for thinking I'd been making Mum work while she was over.

Mum has nodded off over the television, which is what she also does in France, I say. Clive has quietly switched channels and is watching football, and I tell Gillian that we do that too, but she often wakes up when we do. We have a couple of English channels on the satellite but they're pretty rubbish, I admit, and Mum complains. Gillian nods and says that Mum thinks all television's rubbish, but she's hooked on it anyway. A little more complicity.

By the time we've woken her up and Clive's driven us back in silence again, I'm feeling better than I could have imagined.

I text Steve to say I've survived, and it's been better than I thought. He texts back and says I'm a trooper, and he misses me, and then he gives me a quick call to tell me so in person once I'm in the garage where Mum won't hear the phone.

Steve's voice, a brandy, another cigarette, and I'm ready for the polyester sheets.

Chapter 10

Emma

So far, so good. Emma slid her key into the lock of her ex-flat, heart hammering, but it was as she'd asked: there were nearly a dozen packing boxes lined up in the hall, and no sign of Rainer.

Each box was neatly labelled, which was a plus. How very Swiss of Rainer, she thought, remembering her childhood in Switzerland and the way everything seemed so organised. Not that Rainer had ever been great at keeping the flat tidy until recently. His parents had hired help for that, so he'd never had to fend for himself as a child. All the same, she had the impression he'd be methodical and efficient at work.

She didn't want to think too much about Rainer and she'd tried not to for most of the journey. The right-hand-drive rental car from the station had been a bit of a challenge at first, but she'd got the GPS going and soon got the hang of it all and relaxed a little. Then she'd remembered the early days in London with Rainer, and him actually letting her loose on his Mini. That had brought a few pangs of nostalgia. They'd had a few trips out of town at first – even a couple of weekend breaks in the country and the one up to Sheffield. Over the last few months, it had hardly come out of the garage because it wasn't worth using it for work and he'd so often found other things to do at the weekend.

Those things, she told herself sternly, probably involved Alex. Seminars, extra work in the office – she probably even belonged to his gym, if he'd even been to the gym at all and that was just another excuse for not being at home.

That was enough. She pulled the tape off the first box, opened up the pack of bin bags and proceeded to whittle down her shoe collection.

A couple of hours later, there were two full suitcases to take home and just six cartons left, plus four large plastic sacks to be thrown away. She'd drop off those containing clothes at the charity shop nearby and the rest at the bins down the road before she headed north.

It was all going according to plan. Rainer had transferred the money she'd asked for – half the price of the television, plus a reasonable lump sum for some of the DVDs they'd bought together during those earlier, better times and that he wanted to keep, so that was it. The end.

She taped the last box closed, and let her mind roam, imagining herself in a new place that included her furniture that was stored in Lyon. It would be simple, airy. The days of accumulating clutter were the past. In principle. It was just that clutter seemed to happen by magic when she was around.

The flat looked good, even if it was still poky, she decided grudgingly. Clearly Alex expected no less of an illicit love nest.

Despite having decided she wouldn't, Emma went into the bedroom, noting the impeccably made bed – new sheets – and the absence of clothes over the chair back or on the floor. The wardrobe contained no women's clothes but there was a cream silk *peignoir* on the back of the door, underneath Rainer's own robe. The bathroom yielded an extra toothbrush, tucked away in the cupboard, and the linen basket included a few wisps of exclusive satin underwear.

The idea of Rainer chucking those into the washing machine along with his own stuff brought a wry smile. It was clear that Ms Big Banker hadn't ditched her husband and moved in yet, but she was still in the picture and he hadn't hidden the evidence very well.

A picture of Alex clutching a sheet to cover her breasts was imprinted on Emma's mind, including the wedding ring on slim fingers.

Thirsty, Emma headed into the kitchen and poured herself a glass of water. Nobody was going to accuse her of taking liberties with the fridge, although she did peer inside. Lots of organic juices, a bottle of champagne, and a small packet of smoked salmon. Very posh, she noted. Post-coital snacks, no doubt.

It was time to go. She rinsed her glass and then jumped. Rainer was opening the front door.

"I told you not to come," she snapped.

"Hello to you too," he answered calmly. "Don't be angry, Emma. I just thought we should talk."

"And I told you I didn't want to. We have nothing to talk about. And if we're honest, that was the case a long time before you got caught red-handed."

"Perhaps you're right. I wanted to apologise."

"It's a bit late. But accepted. Now go away. I just have to load the car and then I'm leaving."

"This –" Rainer waved his hand vaguely towards the bedroom "– I think I am a little crazy. It wasn't planned."

"What wasn't? Getting caught? Or having a fling with your boss in the first place?"

"Having… an affair. I am not proud of it, Emma."

"Well that makes it all just fine, then. I wasn't exactly proud of being the one you managed to fool for so long, either. Did you ever intend to tell me?"

Emma had promised herself not to ask that question.

"Emma, it was just a very few times."

"Now you're lying. And you're still seeing her – that's obvious, and yes, I was prying. So, what is it now? She's offering you comfort because your stupid girlfriend who was good for a shag but not for acting as your cleaning lady decided to walk out?"

Rainer didn't answer that immediately, and Emma's good intentions evaporated one after the other.

"I hate liars, Rainer. It was *not* just a few times. Also, next time you get caught in the act, don't leave your tablet running with your mail client open."

"You looked." His face went chalky white.

"I did." Emma could kick herself for blurting this out, but he deserved it. "I read German, remember? So yes, I know about your little arrangements dating back for weeks. At her place when her husband was off on a trip – that would be your 'extra project work', I suppose? Then here, while I was in France. She was here again at lunchtime that day because you were 'craving for her body' as I do believe you put it."

Emma's voice had risen, and she broke off suddenly, feeling sick at the memories of those mails.

"Now go. I'll put my key through the letter box."

"You hacked my mail."

"I didn't need to *hack* it, Rainer. You were sloppy."

At that, she picked up the first carton and shouldered past him to put it outside the door.

"Emma, I can't believe you did that. Did you… did you copy them?"

"And I can't believe you thought so little of me to have an affair with – with *her,*" Emma said, ignoring the question about copying them, and realising angrily that it came out as a half-sob.

Rainer picked up two of the cartons and silently placed them beside the hire car. Then he went back for the others.

"You don't need to do that," she snapped.

"I was wrong to cheat. But I still think we should talk."

"I may just be ready to speak to you without hating your guts by the time I retire. But don't count on it."

Tears were streaming down her cheeks, now.

"Emma –"

"Go to hell, Rainer," she said, wishing he'd stop loading the cartons and bags methodically into the boot.

"We will talk," he said quietly, actually pronouncing the *w* correctly. "I know you lost your job – I called your boss when you wouldn't answer my calls, and he told me. I could help you, Emma."

"I don't want your help," Emma muttered furiously. "I want you out of my life."

"You are so special," he said unexpectedly. "So independent, so stubborn. I even miss your mess. Emma… those emails –"

"Those emails of yours told me all I needed to know."

He didn't comment on that but just stood there looking at her.

Let him play the hurt little boy, she thought, fumbling blindly for her car keys and shoving the door key into his hand.

Hurt little boys, she reminded herself, did not screw their bosses when they were supposed to be in a relationship with somebody else.

By the time she reached the M25, the tears had stopped.

***

"You know, Gran, this could be a good night for some pizza and wine and maybe a really cheesy old film, if you've got one on video," Emma said.

"What an excellent idea. Do we need to get a pizza from the supermarket?"

"Most definitely *not*. Delivered to the door, and don't go giving me all those excuses about people talking if they see a Domino's van outside. If they do, tell them you have a granddaughter who needed a pizza fix."

That brought a smile.

"Your mum left some wine."

"Sensible woman. Give me a mo while I just send a quick email to her. I should let her know I didn't cause a multiple pile-up on the M1."

"I don't have the internet, Emma. That's why your mum had to go home early."

"I have 3G. That means I don't need you to have a connection," Emma said cheerfully. "I want Mum to get that as well but it's a bit technical for her, bless her."

Rapidly, Emma checked her inbox and smiled to see an email from Luc. It simply said, *Found any sushi in Sheffield yet?*

No. Pizza and girls talk with Gran coming up. Arrived fine, London done and dusted.

She hesitated for a second and then typed *Hugs.*

For somebody who wasn't into online communication, she'd been flattered he'd offered his email address over their beer the other day.

"So," she said, flipping onto pizza deliveries in Sheffield. "What's your pizza preference, Gran? Ham?"

"Oh yes, ham. Mushrooms as well. No peppers though – they give me wind."

"You're a closet pizza specialist?"

"The ones from the supermarket are smashing," her gran nodded. "One of them does me two days. They need a bit of extra mozzarella on them, sometimes. I like that, even though it's Italian."

Emma found what she wanted, typed in the order, and put *extra mozzarella* on the comments line.

"There we go, Gran. Half an hour. So, you seem to be doing fine."

"For an old 'un. I tell you, your mum and Gillian don't half fuss."

"Well, they're both mother hens I suppose," Emma acknowledged. "Remember when I was little, and Mum and Dad took you to France soon after Grandad died? And we ended up sharing a room and got into trouble for playing cards after lights out and making a noise in the room next door?"

"Oh, I do," her grandmother said. "But that was your fault for laughing so much when I taught you how to deal like a card shark."

"I should probably be shocked that you even knew how to deal like a card shark," Emma chuckled. "Right then, let's get that bottle open and you can tell me more about your misspent youth."

A large quantity of pizza and a full bottle of wine later, Emma squeezed her grandmother's shoulder and took the plates away, remembering about the card games and an admission about being a 'bit of a tearaway'.

"That was fun, Emma. Thank you."

"My pleasure. I love to hear about when you were younger."

"You do? It was very different." Her grandmother sounded wistful.

"You could have a snog in the cinema though? Go out dancing?"

"We most certainly could. But it was real dancing, not that jiggling about stuff."

"All terribly prim and proper?"

"Not so much. You obviously never had a waltz with somebody you fancied."

Emma decided the wine had definitely loosened her tongue a bit.

"I'm shocked. Next thing you're going to tell me is that you like books with sex in them after all."

"There's nothing wrong with sex. I just couldn't have your mother think I read that sort of thing."

Emma burst out laughing.

"You know, Gran, sometimes I think you and Mum need to have a long talk."

"About what?"

"About all the things you think each other thinks."

"Maybe."

She sounded thoughtful, and then grinned.

"You know your mum brought me some more sherry as well, and brandy. I'd rather have brandy, I think."

Amazed, Emma opened the sideboard and found two brandy glasses.

"Ah," her grandmother smacked her lips. "Jim was so funny about alcohol. All that Methodist upbringing, you know. Mind you, I didn't want your mother turning into an alcoholic, so it was probably wise to warn her about drink."

"I don't think she's likely to go off the rails now."

"Probably not, but you never knew with Shirley. She was wilful even as a child, your mother. Stubborn as a mule."

"And who did she get that from?" Emma asked, watching Gran swirl the amber liquid around the glass.

"Jim, of course." The blue eyes twinkled. "But no, your granddad was just a bit set in his ways. He was never ambitious like her apart from with his fancy groceries. He was a bit boring in bed as well."

Emma nearly choked and wondered whether to remove the glass from her grandmother's hands.

"Am I shocking you?"

"You might say that, Gran. But being good in bed isn't everything you know. You must have loved him."

"I did, in a way. But…"

"But?" Emma asked gently.

"My parents virtually forced me into marrying him. A nice, solid young man. You know, Emma, nobody should have to marry nice and solid if they can have sparks."

There was silence for a second or two. Emma didn't want to force her gran to speak, either.

"It's important to enjoy life. And to find somebody to enjoy it with. In every way."

"Definitely," Emma half-whispered.

"I was probably hard on your mum," her grandmother said unexpectedly, after a few moments of silence and cognac-sipping.

"She thinks you were."

"I wanted her to be carefree and sweet-natured, you see. Like Gillian. Like I wanted to be, but I ended up living behind a grocer's shop. Your mum was such a serious little thing, always with her nose in a book. I wondered if she would ever be interested in boys."

Emma decided that honesty was the only way.

"She always feels you compare her with Gillian, and that you criticise her all the time, Gran. That's the impression she gets, anyway."

For a moment, there was silence again. Had she gone too far?

"Maybe I do, Emma. Maybe I've alienated her. I probably just never told her some things I should have done. She's turned out so well, but I probably made it hard for her."

Horrified, Emma saw a tear slide down her gran's face.

"Oh Gran don't – Mum really isn't doing so badly you know? She really loves Dad, and what they're doing now."

"I know, and I'm glad about that. I just wish sometimes we'd been closer, but I kept wishing she'd be a little less rebellious, a bit more *normal.* But I also thought sometimes that it would be better if Gillian was a bit less placid – have a bit more oomph. Heaven knows her father did."

"I thought you said he was a solid, sensible Methodist," Emma teased gently.

"No, her real father." She was weeping openly now. "I was seeing an American serviceman you see. Even when I was engaged to Jim. We were supposed to elope just before I married Jim."

Emma felt her heart start to race.

"I had to tell somebody, Emma. And I never found the courage to tell either of the girls. Or even Jim."

Emma got up and knelt by her grandmother's chair, hugging her tight. What on earth could she possibly say to that?

"Gran, don't cry. Please don't cry. Both Mum and Gillian are great, and Grandad adored you – that's also important, and you were a good wife to him, no?"

"He did adore me. He always did. So, I tried to be the sort of wife he expected. I just never loved him like I should. I fell in love hook, line and sinker with Brad."

"Tell me about him, Gran?"

"He was tall and blond and so damned handsome, Emma. I met him at the tennis club, and he used to come into the servicemen's canteen. I used to volunteer there."

Emma listened to her gran speak, falteringly at first, about the dashing young American soldier. The silk stockings he gave her when they were impossible to get, even though the war was over. The cigarettes too. How he'd kissed her until her legs nearly gave way. How he'd made her laugh, spun her around a dance floor. He'd been there for a couple of months, she said, waiting for his final transfer back home and to be demobilised, and feeling stuck in a boring administration job in Sheffield. He was so different from all the others at the club. So special.

She'd trusted him, she said. Including with her virginity. She'd been all set to call everything off with dear, sensible, portly Jim who'd spent the war in a tank and had just wanted to come home and be a grocer, but no, Brad had told her just to act normally. He'd get a few things sorted out at home and then he'd whisk her off her feet and take her to Texas, where he'd treat her like a queen.

"And then?" Emma prompted gently.

"And then I got pregnant. A couple of weeks before the wedding, but I knew straight away. We got careless about condoms one night and then I missed my period and started feeling sick every morning."

"You told him?"

"I did. He said he'd go down to London to try and hurry up his transfer back home, and then he'd come back for me and we'd go up to Gretna Green – that's where you had to go to get married without all the formalities."

Emma felt tears in her own eyes, half knowing what was coming next. Her grandmother took a deep, shuddery breath.

"But he never came back. I never saw him again."

"Oh Gran. Did you ever find out why?"

"I did. I talked to some of his friends at the canteen when he'd not been in touch for days. I was sick with worry as well as with being pregnant. It was really hard to hide that from my parents and from Jim, but I had to. They – Brad's friends – said he'd gone back to his wife and kids in Texas, and that he'd been missing them terribly. He was always passing photos of them around."

"The bastard," Emma swore softly.

"A real bastard. No wonder he always met me in secret. So, I got married to your granddad as planned, less than a fortnight later."

"He never knew anything?"

"No. Or at least I don't think so. I was only about a month pregnant when we got married, so it was easy enough for people to believe I'd conceived straight away. Gillian was born a bit later than I'd calculated so it just seemed as though she was only slightly early. I suppose I was lucky," her gran said wryly. "Jim didn't even realise it wasn't my first time – I should have got an Oscar."

Her grandmother took another sip of her drink.

"Gillian was such a pretty, sweet-natured child and it was love at first sight. I wondered if I'd hate her because she looked like Brad, but I couldn't. She was the sort of child everybody admired. Your granddad loved her so much. He was always such a kind man."

"I can believe it," Emma told her. Although he'd died when she was tiny, she had some rather blurred memories of him, always smiling at her, always gentle. "And he loved Mum too, right?"

"Oh, he did. You know, your mum was the image of him, even when she was born."

"Was she – did she come as a surprise?"

"She did. Not really an unwanted one, but yes, we didn't expect it. It was hard to start all over again with the nappies, you know, after so long. She was a difficult baby as well: she hardly ever slept through the night."

"I get the impression Mum thinks she was an accident."

"She's not entirely wrong, Emma, but I tried really hard to love her. I just found her so different to Gillian, right from the start."

"I suppose everyone wants placid, easy babies."

"Yes, I think so. I told myself I'd never, ever, let myself have favourites but your mum seemed so… I don't know, so driven by something. So complicated. Always having to prove herself. She was brilliant at school – she seemed to find it all so easy, and I didn't want it to go to her head. Particularly because Gillian just wasn't very academic."

"I don't think it did go to her head," Emma said thoughtfully. "Quite the opposite, in fact. She never thinks she's good enough. She's never felt good about her looks or been proud of what she's done."

"That's stupid," her grandmother said with a flash of spirit. "She's done what I'd like to have done, in the end. Got away, did something interesting with her life. Poor Gillian never did."

"Gillian chose her own way, though, didn't she?"

"Well yes, she did, and she's happy with it. And I'm glad she lives close by. She's been wonderful to me. Your mum's so far away now. And she did get to do something different, and exciting."

That, Emma realised, sounded a little wistful but they'd been through enough in one evening to delve any deeper into it all now, including why she suspected her mother had moved away from Sheffield. In Emma's opinion, it had been as much about escaping than a taste for adventure.

"You know, Gran, I think they're both happy, both have great marriages, and that really means something these days."

"I suppose so." Her grandmother took a hefty swig of the brandy. "Although I'm probably a burden to both of them now."

"Oh come on, Gran. You're a tough old pizza-eating, brandy-swigging broad and I love you to bits. But look – neither Mum or

Gillian know about… you know? Even without mentioning the fact that Gillian was his?"

"Brad? No. I told myself I'd never tell anybody a thing. And I never have. But it's been upsetting me lately. I don't like dishonesty, Emma. Not even in myself."

"I don't think you've been dishonest with anybody exactly, Gran. You were just a bit sparing with the truth. And the person who's suffered most over it all has probably been you, not Mum and Gillian."

"Maybe you're right."

"I think I am. You know, Mum's a tough old bird herself in a lot of ways, so it's up to you whether you ever do tell them or even just talk to Mum about why you two never seem to get on very well. I won't say anything. But it might help Mum, at least, to understand where you're coming from and for her to know you admire her."

"I do. She's achieved a lot. She can be funny, and she's always been determined."

"Then tell her so – even if you don't mention Brad."

Her grandmother considered that for a moment.

"I should tell her about him. You know, I heard from him a couple of years ago. Out of the blue."

"Wow. And?"

"I didn't reply. It was too long ago. But yes, I'll talk to your mum about it at Christmas, face to face. I'll have time to think about how to say it by then. I should talk to Gillian, too."

"That sounds like a plan."

"Thank you, Emma. You're a remarkable young woman. You deserved way better than that bastard you were with. I never did like him much – he looked like somebody stuffed a broom handle up his backside. I hope it didn't show that I didn't really take to him?"

Emma loved the description, and there was definitely some truth in it.

"Not a bit, Gran. You were an absolute lady with Rainer – like you are with everybody."

"Flattery will get you everywhere, miss. But, Emma –" she paused, "I have no idea why I told you all this."

"Because we've both suffered from cheating, lying bastards," Emma said calmly. "They didn't deserve us."

"They most certainly did not. Now, young lady. Pass me just another tiny drop of that stuff. I actually feel much better."

Emma gave her a trickle and was pleased to see her grandmother smiling again.

"You know what, Gran? I always thought you were dead against, you know, sex and things. I mean, like I said before, you never wanted to read a book with sex in it, and got all uptight about it?"

"That wasn't it at all. When your mum was little, she'd read anything. I know for a fact she managed to read the James Bond books I hid under the stairs, and she was a bit young for that. Didn't want her to get into trouble too early, like me."

"Ah. That explains a lot. And me who always looks through books to see if they're too daring for you."

Her grandmother sniffed. "I did notice. They're all very proper, more's the pity."

"Well, duly noted. As long as you don't start getting into things like Fifty Shades of Grey?"

"Oh, is that good? We have a reading group at the church seniors club and –"

"No, Gran. That would not be a good idea. Most definitely not. Nor do you want to go and ask the library for it."

"You're a spoilsport."

"And you're terrible," Emma chortled, hoping her grandmother hadn't made a mental note of the name – she wouldn't put it past her. "You do know that?"

"I suppose I am. So, tell me, Emma – was he at least good in bed, that Swiss of yours?"

"*Gran!*"

Chapter 11

Shirley

The boarding house gods are being kind to us. The whole plan is still on track. I'm cautiously excited now because it's all gone so well, with the exception of the odd few glitches like things arriving late. Even the translation and editing jobs have – mostly – come with reasonable deadlines, so I've managed to combine that side and all the planning quite nicely.

It's uncharacteristically dry for the season so Steve has done everything he wanted to do in the garden, and we're almost ready to do the painting in the new rooms. The plumbing's finished, the heating works, and Steve has just finished wiring up the lights. All we need now, he grumbles cheerfully, is for me to decide on the light fittings and the 'bits and bobs.'

We've already freshened up one of the two upstairs guestrooms in the main house, but I've left the one Emma uses as it is until she's decided what to do. In any case, the three new rooms are really the basis of the whole venture, but if we ever do get popular, we can use the other two rooms as well.

Emma got her head down and worked on her dissertation as soon as she came back from Sheffield and now says it'll be finished soon. In parallel to all that, she's coaching me patiently on things like Facebook and websites, and I'm slowly getting to grips with it. In return, she says, I can edit what she's written, and she can submit it well before Christmas.

I cut up a chicken and browned it ready for a *coq au vin.* Another glorified stew.

I'm generous with the brandy and then set it alight, remembering the time Emma was about five or six and had told our dinner guests I'd burned dinner just for them.

I wonder if Mum's touched the brandy I bought?

According to Emma, she was in great shape when she'd left, and they'd had fun. I wish I knew how my daughter can get on so well with her, because fun with my mother is hard to imagine.

Families are strange, complex things. I always felt jealous of people who seemed to be part of one happy whole, but even then, there's often one misfit. In our little unit of four that was me.

I'm not going to wallow in self-pity. Not when everything is going so well.

Emma drifts in and sniffs rapturously.

"Can we have *gratin* with that?"

"We can if you make it."

"Oh *Mum.* You know that when I make it, it ends up too dry and burnt, or there's too much cream and the potatoes aren't cooked."

"Practice," I say calmly.

"It really doesn't help when I ask how long you cook it for or how much cream to put in and you say, 'as long as it takes' or 'as much as it needs'."

"And that is why I shall never be a cookbook writer. So, get peeling, I'll supervise while I have another look at the bedding catalogues."

"Bedding sales are in January, Mum. Why don't you wait until then?"

"Because *somebody* said we should have the photographs of the rooms up on the web when we go alive around Christmas."

"Go *live*, Mum. And for the photos, you could just use the bedding you already have. Use it in different combinations. Same with the décor bits. We can easily update the photos when you've finished faffing.

"Faffing?"

"Doing your interior designing. How many photos of meals have you taken? We don't need that many on the website."

"A couple," I say. "Well, one. And it's a bit out of focus."

"We'll work on that next week," she says firmly. "Or even tonight, with the chicken."

"Coq au vin isn't very photogenic."

"Chocolate mousse with candied orange strips is," she says sweetly. "Or that strawberry soup you do with balsamic vinegar."

"I can take a hint."

"Good," she nods. "Otherwise I'd have had to resort to blackmail. No chocolate mousse means you really need to learn more about updating the website. Today."

"Anything but that," I grimace.

"Oh, and Mum?"

When Emma is acting this casual, something's afoot. "Now what? I've finished the blurb for the title page."

"No, no. I just wondered whether to invite Luc around tonight, as it looks like there's enough for four."

I haven't asked about how their dinner went a few days ago and she hasn't been forthcoming, but they did go and see a film the night before last.

"Why not?" I aim for casual too.

"And before you start, don't read anything into this. We're just friends. You did promise to decide on a name for the place and to talk to him about the logo. We can all brainstorm tonight."

"Oh. Well… we've narrowed it down a bit."

"That doesn't help, Mum."

"I know, I know. Your dad isn't helping either."

"Not helping with what?" Steve comes into the kitchen and sniffs in a way that's so exactly like his daughter I have to laugh.

"Names. Logos. Believe me, I'm not complaining about your DIY skills, love, but when it comes to choosing colours or finding a catchy name…"

Steve shrugs cheerfully and leans on the kitchen counter.

"I could name names about people who can't read a balance sheet."

I shake my head in mock exasperation and fire up the coffee machine. This is sheer contentment, seeing my husband and my daughter exchanging knowing looks, and having them around me.

"Oh, some news," Emma says, doing that casual thing again. "I caught up with a few people and I might be up for an interview in Lyon."

"Well done," Steve says. "Doing what?"

"Marketing strategy, mainly telecom and media. It's the French branch of a US company that seems pretty solid. But don't get your hopes up yet – I only just sent my CV in but a friend from London knows somebody there."

"That's great. I'll be keeping my fingers crossed. "

"Sophie – she's the girl who told me about it – says there might be a lot of applicants, so I'll wait and see. Just don't mention it to anybody else yet."

I nod, but I'm secretly delighted. To have Emma close enough for weekends again would be wonderful. Me being me, I'm scared to hope because it will make the disappointment worse if it doesn't work out. That's the story of my life, really – I feel a bit the same about the B&B – I'm still trying to imagine worst-case scenarios so that if they happen, I'll be ready for them.

"Funny," Emma says thoughtfully. "Sophie used to go out with one of Rainer's big buddies. She walked out on him. It's sort of a female solidarity thing, I suppose, her helping me now."

"Rubbish," Steve says uncharacteristically categorical. "You'll make it on your own talents, Em, but a bit of support never goes amiss."

"Thanks, Dad," Emma gives him a hug. "You really know how to talk to the girls."

"Put him down," I say mock-sternly. "I saw him first. He's a keeper."

Steve snorts. I tell him Luc's probably coming over tonight and he raises a quizzical eyebrow.

"He. Is. Just. A. Friend." Emma says and stalks off – I hope in the direction of the cellar to get the potatoes.

"That's about as convincing as us calling the place Bellavista, or…"

"Le Boarding 'Ouse" I nod. "The trouble is, it's starting to have a bit of a ring to it. Now, Mr Sandford, please get out of my way. I have a chocolate mousse to make and I'm *quite* sure you have a balance sheet to drool over."

***

Steve breaks out a couple of bottles of good red wine as I'm setting the table – the good mood seems to be infectious.

"I think we may need a little wine-buying break soon," he says cheerfully.

I'm never against that idea. Steve adores his wine and so do I, and to be able to buy it from the producers is always fun. We've been all over the area, stopping off to taste and buy a couple of bottles and then deciding on what we like best before investing in a case or two. Steve has made himself a wine cellar in the crawl space beside the cellar – it's roomy, high enough to stand up in, and cool thanks to the beaten earth floor. It is, as I tease him occasionally, his man-cave. Much as he can't find the butter in the fridge unless it leaps out at him, he could probably home in on any given bottle without thinking twice.

"Sounds perfect," I nod enthusiastically. "Any time after they've delivered the mattresses and the bed frames. They're due next week."

I'm looking forward to that. We've gone with the sober theme again, with plain frames and excellent mattresses. The bed heads will be plain wooden boards, covered with superb Moroccan fabrics that are both vibrant and washable – I'll make them so they tie on. I'm planning to make the curtains to match.

"Better get on with the painting as well, then", I add.

"We can once you stop dithering about colours."

"I'm not *dithering*. I'm engaging in careful reflection. And I'm definitely leaning towards off-white everywhere, and bits of blue."

"The trouble with you," Steve says, uncorking a bottle to air and sniffing the cork appreciatively, "is that you're going to tell me there are all sorts of different shades of off-white and blue."

"Well there are. So don't go buying the paint without me. I think we need one wall in navy blue in the bathrooms as well, remember?"

"And there are even a dozen different navy blues, don't tell me."

I frown at him, although he's laughing. His patience will probably wear a bit thin once we go and order the paint, but he'll survive.

"You two are so romantic," Emma says, coming into the kitchen. "Canoodling over paint colours, or mattresses…"

"It's an improvement on the saga of the taps and shower fittings," Steve says. "I think."

"And way, way better than the tiles and the flooring," I admit. "You look nice."

Emma shrugs casually and peers into the oven.

"When I say that," Steve tells her, your mum says 'oh, this old thing'."

"Oh, this old thing," Emma nods. She's wearing a stretchy black top that shows off her figure, with tiny red bows down one sleeve, paired with a black pencil skirt and heels. It looks vaguely 1950s. "It's one of the outfits Rainer thought looked cheap."

"Then Rainer's stupid," I say firmly. She's even done her hair in a vaguely pinup style, but the effect is anything but cheap.

"Anybody'd think you were trying to impress somebody," Steve tells her. "But as we know you're not, let me just say it's nice that you dress up for your parents."

Emma rolls her eyes and helps herself from the open bottle of white wine on the counter. Then the doorbell rings and she sets off like an athlete on a starting block, until she slows up and seems to remember how casual this all is. Or isn't.

Luc walks in with flowers for me and a bottle for Steve. I find myself not staring at the flowers though, but at Luc. He's cut his hair.

He runs a hand through it, obviously self-conscious.

"Don't say anything. I'm going up to Lyon to see my parents tomorrow for a couple of days. It's – well…"

"A parent thing," Emma finishes the phrase for him. She's admiring the effect and so am I. It's not short, exactly, but it's a tidy, curly mop that makes him look frankly angelic. He's made an effort too, with a plain shirt under a smart jacket and dark jeans.

"A mum thing, to be absolutely correct," he grins, and then peers into the bag he's used for the wine and brings out a single rose. "And this is for the *gratin* cook – Emma told me she was slaving over a hot stove today."

Emma takes it graciously and rushes off for vases. Steve offers Luc a glass of wine and they wander down to the wine cellar when he praises it. Luc, it seems, also likes good wine and so do his parents, so Steve wants his opinion on wine storage racks. Or Steve just wants to give him the third degree, but I doubt that somehow. Not yet, at least.

"How thoughtful," I say, as Emma puts the rose on the table.

"Mum," she glowers.

"Don't scowl. Gives you wrinkles."

***

The meal, and the evening, are a great success. Luc always enjoys food but tonight he is more open – almost chatty. He groans with pleasure over an appetiser I've made with roasted bell peppers and goat cheese, which I'm pleased about as it's a family favourite. Emma adds that Luc knows his way around the kitchen as well, judging from the other night, and he grins and says his repertoire is a bit limited.

His parents have the usual *Lyonnais* passion for food, he adds, and he and Emma are swapping memories of Lyon when I remember the camera.

I put the big dish of *coq au vin* on the table, and then the one with the *gratin,* and hover for a bit with the camera, which I forgot to get out for the starter.

"Can I help?" Luc asks.

"I don't know where to start," I admit, handing him my camera. "Too many buttons."

Emma rolls her eyes. Websites have too many buttons as well, and I seem to be a rather slow pupil, but I'm getting there.

Luc has a quick look, adjusts a couple of things and then snaps away, moving a couple of wineglasses, putting the bouquet he's brought closer and then leaning the serving spoons on the edge of the dish. For once I've not plated it, preferring to let people dig in, so he suggests showing a plate ready to eat: we do that too. By that time, Steve looks as though starvation is about to set in, so Luc gets the message and stops. The murmurs of appreciation make me very happy.

I give the camera back at dessert time, and he repeats the exercise with the chocolate mousse and a little thimble of strawberry soup, this time using the single rose in the background.

"All these arty-farty people," Steve says, not unkindly. "Does this mean you know the difference between the various shades of off-white when it comes to painting walls, Luc?"

"Hardly", Luc shakes his head. It turns out his mother is a professional photographer, so he knows his way around cameras.

We linger over coffee, and the conversation flows freely. I notice Emma watching Luc as he waves his hands around, talking about his work, and she looks positively glowing.

She catches me looking at her and gives me a scowl.

"Names, Mum. Logo."

Ah yes. I sigh and reach for a sheet of paper with half a dozen names scribbled on it and crossed out. They all seem too trite, somehow, or too contrived. We have cypresses by the front gate, and three of them are a sign of welcome in Provence, so incorporating those in the name was one idea. Another was "*Les volets bleus*" because of the traditional blue wooden shutters. Emma grimaces, whips out her tablet, and tells me there are dozens of those already.

My favourite at the moment is '*L'olivier*' because of our remarkable olive tree but I expect there are literally hundreds of B&Bs called that. I'm right.

"Thing is," Emma says, "you need quirky."

Quirky, I say gloomily, is going to be hard.

Marketing strategy, however, is Emma's *raison d'être* and she insists that we need something memorable but evocative. Twisting the known with the unknown. Somehow showing the English–French mix.

"The money pit," Steve jokes. "The crazy house. Off-white blues."

"Wait," Emma says thoughtfully. "Blue. You use blue everywhere, Mum. But calling it "*La maison bleue*" wouldn't work. Too ordinary.

"Blue olives?" I say doubtfully

Emma virtually jumps off her seat. Then she taps frantically on her tablet and looks up.

"Olive blue. Blue in English, not *bleu*. Olive works in both languages, which is a plus. And there are lots of *olive bleue* references, and a couple with blue, but not in France."

We all digest this for a minute. I say it over and over in my head and decide I quite like it.

"Also," Emma is positively bubbling over, "the logo could be in a deep blue."

"Don't," Steve groans. "There are probably several hundred shades of deep blue – we've been through that over the bathroom walls. But I think I like it."

"I love it," I say firmly. "Luc?"

"I do too," he nods.

"Good. So, Mr Theyroux, you have a commission," I say cheerfully. "Can you come up with something? Something we can use on stationery, on the doors beside the numbers, on the web…"

Fortunately, I've already talked about this with Steve, and with Emma, or there would be raised eyebrows. They were both suitably enthusiastic.

"Me?" Luc looks stunned. "Well… yes I could. In fact, I'd be delighted to. I could start once I get back from the exhibition and fair that I'm taking part in. Say a couple of weeks or so, then about a week to do it?"

"Perfect," I nod.

"What about a sign for the gate?" Emma asks. "That could be complicated."

"It could be done on enamel," Luc says. "I know somebody who could do that, if I gave him a good print."

Steve gets up and comes back with a bottle of his prize Armagnac. Emma's babbling about size ratios and Luc's talking about inks and pigments, and I'm just sitting there feeling almost dizzy with the realisation that we've actually named the place. It feels symbolic.

"I'll need a price estimate," Steve says, pouring four glasses. "Mainly for the accountants. Don't under-price for the work it entails, either."

"I wasn't going to charge. I've enjoyed working here so much."

"Don't be daft." Sometimes the Yorkshire comes creeping back when I'm feeling mellow. "That's not an option, Luc. We could even sell your prints of the logo, maybe?"

"You could sell his prints in general," Emma says. "Couldn't hurt. Or at least advertise them, with a flyer showing his website. Which he doesn't have yet."

Luc glances over at her, thoughtful, but doesn't comment.

I raise my glass.

"To Olive Blue," I say. "And to us."

"The A team," Steve says.

"I'd like the logo on an apron," I muse contentedly. "I've always fancied that."

"Or t-shirts," Emma nods. "Merchandising. Crockery, serviettes, towels…"

"Whoa," Steve says. "This is a small B&B, Em, not a five-star palace." He's chuckling, though.

"Maybe not yet, for the rest," I tell Emma. "But it's tempting."

"I'll get started on some sketches tomorrow, while I'm in Lyon," Luc says. "Keep me from getting under my parents' feet. I'll mail Emma when I've got a few? And I won't forget to fiddle with the food photographs. I expect my mum will give me a few pointers, as well."

"Sounds like a plan," Emma says, still tapping away at her tablet. "There are no cookbooks called Olive Blue either, by the way."

"I wasn't thinking of writing one."

"You are now," Emma says. "You gave me the idea while we were cooking today. People would buy them as souvenirs. That *gratin* was fabulous if I say so myself. So was the mousse."

They toast me as the chef and my new career as a cookbook writer. I don't think she's joking about that, but we can argue about it later. By that time, Luc decides that if he's going to make it back home without losing points on his licence, he'd better go.

Emma decides to see him out, and I glance at Steve.

"We should toast our daughter for coming up with a name, and maybe also for most definitely having an admirer," I say. "And our future artist for having excellent taste."

"We should," Steve holds up his glass up again. "And I did notice those two. Maybe I can't tell sludgy beige from mushroom, but if they're going to be 'just friends' for much longer, I'm a bloody Dutchman."

Chapter 12

Emma

Her legs dangling off the end of Luc's sofa, she leafed through the sketches again.

"They're fabulous. I think I like the one with just the two olives and the really plain lettering best."

"I think I do too," Luc glanced over his shoulder from the kitchen area. "Your mum's tastes are fairly unfussy."

"Mmm," she agreed, glancing round the apartment again. So were Luc's, she decided. His place was tucked under the eaves of an old stone house in town, up a flight of worn stone stairs. He'd taken it, he'd told her the first night he'd cooked her a meal, because of the cellar and garage that went with it, and where he'd put his printing press. He'd showed that to her, and how his wood blocks pressed the design onto the paper, how the inking worked – it was low-tech but fascinating.

Upstairs, nothing was square. The kitchen was tucked under a sloping roof and the bedroom was up a steep flight of ladder-like wooden stairs. The main room, with a view out onto the old roofs, was airy and painted simply in white, which contrasted with the rough, unvarnished wooden beams. A few cushions gave it colour, as did a couple of very modern paintings that she wasn't sure she liked. A couple of photographs of his family were on a shelf. One of them showed a much younger Luc and, she presumed, his sister, laughing.

She wasn't going to pry, so she'd admired some more photos of cityscapes. His mother's, Luc had confirmed.

The fireplace was a nice touch and judging by the basket of logs, it worked. The room would look lovely in firelight.

His work desk was under the bigger window, and there was a battered couch and low table in the corner, next to a bookshelf and, surprisingly, a PlayStation. Being nosy, she'd looked at the books as he cooked and found anything from travel books to some old classics, and video games that had nothing old about them at all. She hadn't seen him as a video games fan, and felt a pang of regret that Rainer had enjoyed them too, once – until he'd discovered the joys of sleeping with his boss.

Luc had promised her a games evening that first night, and she'd tried not to seem too enthusiastic even if the idea had delighted her and she'd been looking forward to it.

The first time she'd been to his place, they'd talked about his work and all it entailed and continued over the meal, and then she'd made a few more suggestions about promoting it. He'd been interested but still non-committal and she hadn't pushed it. She'd enjoyed the evening, just as she'd been pleased to go and see a film a few days later.

Less pleasing was the fact that she was trying hard to stay detached and casual and finding it increasingly hard, but Luc had never made the slightest move beyond a casual kiss on greeting and another at the end of the evening, on both occasions.

That was logical enough and how she'd wanted it, and she had said so that day on the tower. But the flutter of pleasure when she saw him was turning into something more. And yet, when he'd left her parents' house the other night, there'd been just another chaste and proper kiss on both cheeks.

He did bring a rose, though. Surely that meant something?

Did she *want* it to mean something?

What the hell did she want? To kiss him properly seemed like a good place to start. Watching him at the stove, she started to imagine how it would be, held close against the slim body, lifting her head and feeling his lips find hers.

What if she went over there, right now, and just happened to brush his arm?

No. Better not. In the cinema, sitting beside her, he'd gone to great trouble not to make any physical contact.

Damn.

"Come and get it," Luc said, waving a spatula. It smelled good.

Emma sat down at the battered old table, smooth with wear but obviously stripped and waxed – probably by Luc.

She tossed the salad, as instructed, and pulled off pieces of the baguette as he put a large dish in the centre.

"My mum always says that nobody can ruin spaghetti Bolognese," Luc said. "And after that chicken with olives I did last time, that's about my limit when it comes to cooking for guests."

"This is so good," she said, honestly, cheerfully sucking up a few strands of pasta. "Even if I've never found a way to eat it elegantly."

"It's not meant to be eaten elegantly. But it's better not to eat it wearing a white shirt. They attract the sauce."

Emma glanced down at her dark red top. "I came prepared. I must have read your mind about what you were cooking."

"I'm glad you came," he said simply, pouring her a glass of wine.

"For video games, you can't keep me away," she said lightly. Did that sound like a brush-off?

"Not just the video games. I like your company. Very much, Emma."

She looked up at him, seeing sincerity in the grey eyes and immediately regretted being so offhand.

"I'm sorry," she said. "Never forget I'm the hard-nosed bitch from marketing. I like your company as well, Luc. It's just –"

"It's just that it's not a date. It's okay, Emma, I won't ever push you. Stop agonising, will you? Oh, and stop saying you're sorry."

"I'm –" she started, and then stopped herself. "Thanks. It's just better if it's –"

"Clear. You have sauce on your chin."

Emma grabbed the napkin and scrubbed furiously. Of course things had to be clear. She had no idea where she'd be a few weeks from now. She was never going to settle in Crest, not given her line of work where big cities were the best option. And Luc – well, he didn't want to push her. Meaning he wasn't interested in anything more either.

Damn it. Her mind couldn't stop imagining not only kissing him now but climbing up those steps into his bedroom.

What if he'd been thinking of that as well?

He wouldn't be, she reasoned. He was just sorry for her, and pity sex was never a solution. What she did need was a friend.

With Rainer, she remembered, they'd moved from their first encounter to the bedroom within two days, when he'd been in Lyon on business and she'd met him through a mutual friend. And a couple of months and a few rapid weekends in London later, she'd found a job there and joined him. On reflection, it had been ridiculously fast but then there had been absolutely no reason not to simply follow her instincts.

Except, she reflected, her instincts had been wrong. The sex had been good, London had been glamorous, and the rest had just followed.

She missed the sex, but she wasn't going to think about that. Except that she was suddenly, terribly aroused and sitting opposite somebody kind, intelligent and extremely desirable.

"Are you all right, Emma?" Luc was staring at her.

"I'm fine," she said faintly, stirring the spaghetti around and trying not to think about him naked. "Just daydreaming."

"Time to stop that. I am going to thrash you at every video game you choose. You do know that?"

She burst out laughing despite herself. Yes, definitely an excellent person to have as a friend.

"Luc Theyroux, you are extremely sure of yourself for a guy who says he hates technology. And maybe a bit of a macho on the side, no?"

"Guilty as charged for the first. Maybe the second but I try not to be."

"Right. Don't you dare say something as corny as being in touch with your feminine side or I'll…"

"You'll what?"

"I'll…" Emma was lost for words, and then made a conscious effort to come to her senses. "I'll have to write you off as a wimp."

"Maybe I am," he said. "But my mum said that with shorter hair I at least looked the part less."

"She liked it?"

"She said it was a start. I told her that if she wanted me to be more of a he-man I could always go out and get some tattoos and piercing."

"And how did that go? My parents seem to think that any man with a tattoo or piercing is automatically a drug addict or at best a hooligan."

"Your parents would probably get on very well with mine. They left me alone after that – or at least as far as my appearance was concerned. I got the usual pep talk about…" Luc broke off.

"About?"

"Nothing. Forget it."

"Settling down with a nice girlfriend?"

"Something on those lines, but not exactly." Luc sighed deeply. "It's complicated."

"Want to enlighten me? Friends can say stuff that lovers can't," Emma said more boldly than she felt.

"I think we should change the subject," Luc said firmly. "Or I may forget I'm a gentleman."

What on earth did that mean, Emma wondered? She started to let her mind wander to Luc being anything but a gentleman and forced herself to stop before it got out of hand.

"Agreed," she said. "Let's do the washing up, and then be prepared to be shamed by a poor weak girl."

"The washing up can wait until tomorrow. Select your downfall, woman."

Emma went back to the shelf of video games, trying hard to refocus.

Two hours later, they were neck and neck in front of the screen, and they'd laughed a lot. She'd had a couple more glasses of wine and then moved onto water. Her mum had lent her Tweetie, the famous yellow peril of a Renault, and at this moment was probably imagining her in a ditch, or with her licence taken away. There was a lot to say for being well out of the way of parents when you wanted to stay out late, or drink too much.

"Last attempt," Luc said. "My honour is at stake."

"Prepare to lose," Emma said.

She let him win. Why, she had no idea. Normally she would have gone all out to prove she could, but not this time.

Luc got up and turned it off, and then pulled her to her feet.

"Emma, listen –"

"Nicely played," she murmured.

"Except you lost on purpose. I want to ask you something."

At that moment, if he asked her to go upstairs, Emma thought she would be on the first step without thinking twice, whether it would be pity sex or not. Just the touch of his hands – he'd held onto hers just a moment longer than strictly necessary – had made her mouth go dry immediately.

"Ask," she said quietly, suddenly realising she wasn't the only one who was aroused. Luc was breathing hard, looking at her with such intensity that the temptation to touch him again was almost unbearable.

"I want to ask you out. On a date. Somewhere on neutral ground."

"A date?" Emma stared at him. "As in a proper date?"

"As in an evening where I take you out to dinner and we discuss the sort of things that people do on dates. Not me explaining about engraving and you plugging the social media. And no video games, much as it's been fun. Nor sitting in a cinema and trying to keep my hands to myself."

Emma kept staring at him.

"It's okay if you say no. We can just keep on doing the not-dates but quite frankly I'm starting to wonder just how long I can keep it up. So maybe we should have a date and *then* decide if it all stops at friendship?"

"Oh."

Very eloquent, Emma.

"And although I know full well that we could take this further now – right now, and God knows I want to – I still want you to think about it first. So please, Emma, get into that yellow monster of your mother's and do just that. You can email me to say yes or no anytime between now and Saturday night. That gives you nearly 48 hours."

She didn't need 48 seconds, Emma thought, but she nodded, still watching him.

"Luc, I don't need –"

"Shhh," he put a finger on her lips. "You do need time. Please, Emma. There are things you need to know about me. I have an unfair advantage here – I know your parents, and I know what you've been through."

"You're married?" she blurted out.

"Nothing like that. And no, my parents don't live in a museum, far from it."

Emma half-chuckled – she'd mentioned Rainer's home territory at some point.

"Well that's good news then. All I know about them is that your mother's a photographer – oh, and she prefers you with short hair."

"There's a story to that too, and I may tell you before long. But right now, if you aren't out of here in twenty seconds, I shall have to haul you downstairs by force, because if I don't take a cold shower soon..."

"Consider me gone," Emma said, trying to sound calmer than she felt. "But first –"

She reached for him and gave him a fleeting kiss on the lips. He moaned slightly, and pulled her closer, returning it.

It was good – so good. She could feel his hardness against her and could so easily lose herself in his lips, his body – but then he took her face in his hands and gently moved away.

"Go, love," he said softly. "Email me."

Go *love?* Well, it was a term of endearment much loved in Yorkshire, where everybody seemed to be loves or ducks or flowers, but if she remembered correctly, his mother was from down south somewhere.

It sounded good, though.

"Shower." She pointed towards the bathroom. "I'd say think of me in mine within ten minutes or so, but –"

"You are impossible. Anybody ever tell you that?"

"Often. And yes, I'll email you."

"Not before tomorrow. And now, woman, and for the last time..."

"Gone," she said, virtually skipping down the stone stairs.

Chapter 13

Shirley

Emma looks like the cat that swallowed the cream, and she helps herself to a glass of Steve's whisky. Yes, she's had a wonderful evening. And no, it wasn't a date. You didn't play video games on proper dates, she says, as though explaining things to a couple of kindergarten kids.

She brandishes Luc's sketches. We admire them and agree with the one Emma prefers. She raves about his talents, and his cooking, and then obviously realises she's giving too much away and decides that making a cup of tea is suddenly urgent.

I follow her down to the kitchen and she passes me a steaming mug of something herbal. I raise one eyebrow.

"Yes, Mum, something's happening. But slowly," she says. "We're going out the day after tomorrow just to talk. Well, on a proper date, in fact. But we haven't – you know…"

"I wasn't going to ask, believe me." The phrase 'you know' covers a multitude of sins when it comes to the English talking about sex.

"But you were dying to know," she gives one of her typical, growly chuckles. "And I'm sure as hell not going to give you a report when – if – it happens."

"I wouldn't expect you to," I answer sweetly. I'll know, though. And I think 'when' is far more likely than 'if'.

Emma glances at the clock – two minutes to midnight.

"I'm off to bed, Mum. It's nearly tomorrow." She gives me a hug.

***

Mick Jagger ain't getting no satisfaction this morning, and the Stones are still among my favourite kind of music to iron to. That, or Rod Stewart. All ancient, but who cares?

I've brought the ironing board into the living room, where I can look out over the pool, and I've turned the sound right up. Steve's in the garden and Emma's upstairs working on her dissertation, so I can wriggle and grind away to my heart's content.

Being virtually geriatric, I've informed Emma, does not mean I can't strut around using the sticky roller I use to remove cat hair as a microphone between ironing two shirts.

Ironing is almost as cathartic as pruning or making bread and it produces results while being a whole lot more zen than snipping stems or thumping dough. I'm an expert at shirts – I've only told Steve a million times how fortunate he is to have a wife who *likes* ironing – and there's something about a pile of sun-dried washing, all ironed and folded neatly into a basket that makes me smile.

I'm odd, of course. Emma has said so more than once and I've had a lifetime of being told so by my mother. Emma can't understand how anybody could possibly enjoy the very symbol of household drudgery and doesn't even possess an iron. Rainer apparently sent his shirts to the laundry.

There's little point trying to explain that it's one of those jobs that doesn't require my mind to focus on much, so I can just let my thoughts go where they fancy.

Today, I start by chewing over the last couple of phone calls with Mum. She's feeling fine. And she was different. No comparisons with Gillian, no criticisms of the B&B – she even thinks the name we've chosen sounds fun, because she loves our olive tree and how it reflects in the pool.

There were no lessons on how to present meals or to dress for Craghill Road at Christmas.

I wondered, probably unfairly, if she's been hitting the booze I left at her house. Whatever brought this change on, it's extraordinary.

I've grilled Emma a bit on her visit to Sheffield and she just shrugged, saying that they had a blast, which included eating pizza in, sushi out, and a bit of online shopping. I dread to think what that entailed, and Emma's not saying, although knowing my daughter it involved shoes or handbags.

That's all the bedding done. Now for the shirts. One of Emma's tops could use a bit of steam, too.

I'm fighting with one of Steve's shirts that is a pig to iron when Helen calls.

Yes, I agree happily. Doing the market tomorrow and having a good long girls' gossip sounds like an excellent plan. It could, I warn her, involve lunch so she may have to leave Joe something to eat.

I make a mental note to leave something for Steve and Emma and then decide that they can fend for themselves. I might enjoy ironing, but it doesn't mean I have to be tied to the kitchen when there are two capable adults there.

The Stones have finished, but I haven't. What next? Something French? Johnny Halliday? Eddie Mitchell, maybe.

My parents hated my music – the Eagles and Fleetwood Mac drove them insane. When Emma was small, I thought I'd strangle her for her own choices, and particularly during the heavy metal period.

I'm singing along happily to Eddie and *Couleur menthe à l'eau* when Emma bellows downstairs.

"Yuck, Mum. Turn it down."

Some things never really change, I smile to myself.

"It's either that or I'll dig out something by those boy bands you used to love," I bellow back. "Oh, and I could mention your crush on them to Luc in passing."

That meets with silence.

We go with Eddie. I turn it up a bit.

***

Armed with large wicker shopping baskets, Helen and I meet in the car park and walk across the main *Pont Mistral* into town. I'm looking forward to this, because since Mum's visit I've hardly had time for a good wander around.

France's last wild river – it's never been dammed or otherwise messed with – is blue and clear this morning. If it rains up in the *Vercors*, it turns muddy and brown, and swells impressively. In summer, tourists swarm to it for picnics, kayaking, or to fool around in the water.

It's still warm for November, and people dodge and pass on the footpath, heading for the market or on their way back with several baguettes peeping out of their bags. I have a theory, I tell Helen, that nobody ever arrives home with all their baguettes intact – the temptation to bite the end off at least one of them is impossible to resist.

I remember my mother's last visit, and sipping wine in the square, and I smile.

We go into my favourite bakery and munch flaky, buttery croissants as we head up into the old town.

Stalls still line the streets, even though there are fewer of them than in summer, and particularly those selling the touristy items like Provençal fabric or olive wood bowls and boards. The Locals frequent markets assiduously; everybody has 'their' stalls for vegetables, cheese, meat or fish. Tiny counters boast modest displays of honey, huge bowls of olives, lavender. A fishmonger sells oysters brought down from the coast that morning. A Vietnamese trader sells rotisserie chickens that smell so good it makes your mouth water a dozen metres away. Bread is piled up in all shapes and sizes, with olives, nuts, and then there's the traditional *fougasse,* a bread cut and twisted and heavily spiked with cheese, bacon or ham.

I approach my supplier of goat cheese, the famous *picodon* of the Drôme. You can get them from creamy-textured, freshly made ones to those that are almost rock-hard.

We grab tin basins and pop in whatever vegetables take our fancy, in whatever quantity. No shrink-wrapping and polystyrene trays here, thank goodness. And where else would you find a line of people waiting to choose misshapen but exquisitely fresh organic produce, often with a good coating of dirt still attached?

The roast chicken smell reels me in as it always does. A creature of habit, I buy one for tomorrow's lunch and add a couple of home-made spring rolls for good measure. The stallholder throws in a couple of *samosas.*

My last call is at a stall selling fresh mushrooms. Not the round, white, tasteless things, but *cèpes, girolles* and *chanterelles* and some I don't recognise. I don't even know the English names for these, as they weren't something that got served up in Sheffield.

I go for some *pieds de mouton* – 'sheep's feet' – but still mushrooms, despite their name – to go with some veal I plan to cook tonight. I've decided Steve and I should have a date of our own. I have a tiny roll of *foie gras* I can serve with some fig jam and bread with walnuts, and for dessert I'll do a *panna cotta* with some blackcurrants from the freezer.

Helen and I haven't chatted much yet apart from a few bits of news about her garden and our progress with the building, mainly because another feature of the market is that you always come across people you know. It's a social occasion bar none, and you have to get used to knots of people standing in the middle of the road, while everybody else has to dodge them.

Some people say that this is French arrogance, but it no longer bothers me, this habit of stopping to chat wherever you feel like it. I'm guilty of it myself these days. So far, we've run into our neighbours, her neighbours, and half a dozen other acquaintances and friends.

During the tourist season, the Drôme comes under siege by half of Holland and a good chunk of Belgium, all in campers or towing caravans. They adore the area – it's pretty, it has mountains, it has dozens of campsites, and prices are low compared with much of France. Now, most of them have gone home. They also love the markets even if they only buy a carrot or two or a couple of lavender bags to take home. That makes it even more of an obstacle race, but I love it anyway.

Over the last couple of years, we've had more British and Swiss visitors, and they are among my target markets for the B&B. The French, too, are tending to explore places a little off the beaten track rather than beaches. Crest, I was delighted to discover when we moved here, always gets itself in the official handbook of the 'best detours in the country'.

I'm proud of my little town.

"Right, all done," Helen says, looking wistfully at the handmade chocolate shop. "We shouldn't go in there, should we?"

"We shouldn't. But those little dark chocolate twigs with orange, or the bilberry cream ones…"

Quite by accident, we go inside, and I indulge. It's mostly for Steve, I say airily. Helen gives me one of her looks, and says Joe is not getting his hands on her bar of almond-studded pleasure and that is that.

Then it's time to search for a table outside one of the cafés, and our luck holds. We slide into two seats as people leave, and sigh happily. It's a little chilly but sunny, and there's my nicotine habit to indulge.

It's only just past eleven, so we start with coffee, and a little chocolate, just to test it.

Helen gives me a run-down of her kids and grandchildren, all in England. She must be an adored grandmother, I often think. Slightly plump but constantly on the move and completely unflappable, she's always doing ten things at once and still finds time to rush over to Kent now and then to babysit or to visit friends.

"Sometimes you make me want to be a grandmother," I tell her.

"That rather requires Emma to co-operate and last I heard she was single."

"Aha!" I say. "That is a subtle introduction to the latest developments."

I give her a potted version of the Luc and Emma saga, and she looks pleased.

"She's got her head on her shoulders, that one. Have they... you know?"

Those two words that mean so much. I chuckle.

"Not yet, I think, but they're having a proper date tonight. She's probably trying on her entire wardrobe as I speak."

Emma would be horrified at this conversation, I think. Mothers do not discuss people's sex lives, even using the appropriate euphemisms. Not anybody's sex lives and especially hers. That was very clear with Emma the other night. One of these days, however, I'm going to have to tell her that being over fifty doesn't mean you lose interest.

"I remember him from when we came over. Nice-looking lad with long hair?"

"That's the one, but the hair's short now. To please his mother."

"Now that is a *very* good sign," Helen nods. "And rebound or not, it would do her good. Even if it's just, well…"

"I know," I agree. "But somehow I think they're working up to a bit more than just a bit of casual sex."

I've moved on to calling it by its name.

"Even better. You know, if my kids heard us, they'd have a heart attack. The words 'casual' and 'sex' spoken by my generation are just too shocking for words." Helen casually nibbles another chocolate, and grins.

"That is *exactly* what was going through my mind. Do they think we talk about knitting and gardening all the time?" I ask.

"Probably. Although I suspect that men *do* actually talk to each other about cars and lawnmowers and DIY and wine. Or at least once they've stopped sowing their wild oats."

"You could be right about that."

Helen sighs. "Getting old's a bitch. Maybe we should consider toy boys."

"Nah," I say. "Too high maintenance. Although Emma's ex took up with his boss, who is apparently forty if she's a day."

"Hmph," Helen snorts. "And he's what, thirty? No, if we need toy boys at our grand old age, they need to be very young and very disposable. Let's go and have a month in the Caribbean and test the concept."

This is about as likely as hell freezing over but we go with it a bit, deciding we'll need somewhere hot but not too hot. Lots of tropical fruits and softly waving palms. An unlimited supply of silly, girly novels and films. Definitely no mosquitos. And, of course, the pool boys.

That takes us neatly to aperitif time.

"I'm glad not many people are likely to understand English on this terrace," I say. "In Switzerland, you can never count on that, with all the languages they speak."

"Do the Swiss even *have* fantasies?" Helen asks, ordering some rosé. "And no, I'm not going to do the cunning linguist joke."

"Good – it gets old," I chuckle. "And about fantasies, ask Rainer. Or rather don't. But the Swiss are probably very... precise in bed."

Helen guffaws. "Let's include one in our pool boy selection then. Research."

Suddenly, I catch the young waiter looking at us. I bet that one speaks English, but tough. Right now, I don't even care. Helen catches my quick wink as I nod vaguely in his direction and raise my voice just a fraction.

"The French now... best lovers anywhere, I've heard. Not that I have first-hand experience, you understand."

"Me neither," Helen says, eyeing the waiter up. "I've heard waiters are particularly good."

When the wine comes, it's on the house. Helen, all grey hair and twinkling eyes, thanks him sweetly in English and he blushes.

"Always nice to make somebody's day," she gurgles as he rushes off. "Are we really terrible?"

"Terrible is great," I say contentedly. "Here's to terrible."

Chapter 14

Emma

Hair up or down?

Emma tried both, twice. In the end, she settled for down, and reached for the tongs.

Her tablet pinged. Another email from Luc, this time asking her if she'd tried on her entire wardrobe yet.

Cheek, she typed. *Not quite. Scruffy jeans and trainers OK?*

The reply came only a few minutes later. It said, *as long as you wear heels, no problem. Those are official date wear.*

He was as bad as her mother about the gentle art of texting, as in he couldn't get his head around it and stuck to emails, but he'd definitely got into that over the last 48 hours.

It was still weird, though. Who didn't know how to text in 2014?

Luc. That was who. But it added to his charm.

She'd sent her first email accepting his offer of a date at 12.01 a.m. *It's tomorrow. Consider this a yes.*

He'd replied immediately. *Great news but cancellations still possible.*

I am not a woman who changes her mind, she'd typed. *Had your shower yet?*

Yes, but round two with colder water may be required if you don't stop all this. GO TO BED.

She had, but she hadn't slept that much.

There had been a couple of emails since – one to say he'd pick her up at 7.30. She'd just replied *OK* to that at first, and then she'd mailed again to say *I'm nervous. And excited.*

She'd waited, worried that she'd said too much, until the reply came: *That makes two of us.*

If only, Emma wished, he used messenger to have a conversation, if he really was that bad at texting. On the other hand, the short emails seemed just right. It was like writing each other letters the old-fashioned way.

Her mother was adopting a matter-of-fact approach, which was always how it went, even with her daughter's first boyfriends. It was better than not being interested at all, or prying for too many details.

"Emma?" Her mother called through the door.

"Yes, Mum. I do know it's after seven. I'll be down in a minute. I'm not going to do the 'arrive late in a waft of perfume' thing. I probably need a drink first, anyway."

"And me thinking you were going to shimmy down the stairs like Rita Hayworth."

"I'd need a ball gown for that, and I don't think Crest can really cater for it."

"They still have tea dances here," her mother said. "Did you know? And no, Dad and I have no intention of going to them."

"According to Gran, ballroom dancing is sexy," Emma said airily.

"She said *what?*"

"Look, Mum. Stop hovering outside the door and either come in or go away. And yes, she was talking about dancing after the war. Men in uniforms and stuff."

"Well now I've heard everything."

No, you haven't, Emma thought. But come Christmas, you might.

Her mother came inside the room, a bit flushed from doing something fancy in the kitchen.

"How's your own romantic dinner coming along?"

"Very nicely, thank you. You look great, but just a bra and pants might be a bit chilly?"

"Very funny." Emma swept her dress off the hanger. "What do you think? Too glam for Crest?"

"It's unusual," her mother said, studying it once Emma slipped it over her head. "Difficult to categorise. But don't tell me Rainer thought *that* looked cheap?"

"He did. You like it?"

Emma stared at herself in the mirror. The dress was deep blue, softly clinging and with an asymmetric hem. Was she getting a taste for those from her mother? The fabric was a screen print, with a photographic image of a galaxy spread from one shoulder to the other hip.

"It's fabulous. Not for oldies with a waistline problem, but it suits you perfectly. Shoes?"

"Those," Emma pointed. "And before you start, yes I *can* walk on them. Slowly and carefully."

"It's your ankles that are going to suffer. And if you're going somewhere in the old town, mind the cobblestones."

"I thought of that. I actually don't know where we're going."

Emma found herself hoping, it wasn't too far from his apartment. The last 48 hours had been long enough, although the idea of a leisurely meal to start the evening was all part of the anticipation.

But what if it didn't go well after all? What if, when it came down to it, the 'proper date' ended up a dismal failure? What if he found her too easy and regretted the fact that he'd been so turned on the other night?

"Cold feet?" her mother asked, so she must be scowling.

"No. You know, Mum," Emma took a deep breath, "I just don't want to come on too strong. Not that I don't want to but – oh *hell* I can't believe I'm telling you this."

"Don't go with any preconceptions, Em. Just go with the flow. Although I suppose nobody says that anymore."

"No, they don't, but I know what you mean. That's what I keep telling myself, but I wonder if I'm too much on the rebound and I'd be using him, because I'm missing… you know." Emma saw her mother smiling and raised her eyebrows. "What's funny?"

"It's normal to miss sex, Emma, and stop looking shocked at me calling a spade a spade. I decided it was old-fashioned of me to keep tiptoeing around the actual words."

"Wow, Mum. But okay."

"But more seriously, you don't really think any of that or you wouldn't be going. I don't think you'd do that to Luc, for a start. I get the impression he's very serious in a lot of ways."

"There's a lot I don't know about him. I do know his sister died six years ago, but that's all. He didn't mention anything about past girlfriends."

"I didn't know that. And as for the girlfriends, some men don't like to talk about them. Your Dad never did. Or maybe it's different now."

"I think these days, couples talk more about their relationships –
analyse them more," Emma said thoughtfully. "Let alone calling
a spade a spade. Rainer and I did, but it didn't get us far, did it?"

"Forget Rainer," her mother said.

"I intend to, but I've learned from it. And is that a certain pickup
coming into the drive? Can I borrow your cape?"

"I do believe it is, and yes you can. Now, go and make your
entrance. We shall *not* wait up for you, miss. Nor will we ask any
embarrassing questions. That's a promise."

"Thanks, Mum." Emma picked up her bag, slotted her phone into
it, and wondered whether to take a toothbrush. No, definitely not.
Or maybe…

No.

***

Luc seemed as tense as she did, Emma noticed as they drove into
town. He'd exchanged pleasantries with her parents, who were
still being casual, given her the usual pecks on the cheek, and
then didn't say much until they parked near a new, tiny restaurant
up one of the cobbled streets.

What he did do, however, was to reach for her hand as she
climbed out of his pickup and didn't let it go. That, she decided,
was a very good move.

He lifted her hand to his lips and kissed it gently.

"Hello," he said softly.

Emma let herself be guided to the door. He helped her off with
her cape and looked approvingly at her dress.

"I really like that," he said simply. "Definitely you."

"Thanks."

"The first time I saw you, you had jam on your chin and your pyjamas. Not that I made much of an impression on you."

Emma was amazed he'd remembered the first time he'd seen her, let alone the pyjamas or the jam.

"I was a bit distracted at the time. This place is lovely," she said lightly.

"It looked nice – I've never been before." He took the menus and they both laughed when the waiter attempted to speak in English before they explained that French would be just fine.

They chose from the menu, and then there they were, Emma realised. On a date.

"So," they both said in unison as they were left alone, in a quiet corner, and then laughed again.

"This date idea," she said, lightly, "has something going for it so far."

"It's a far cry from London."

"It is. I miss the place sometimes. I still feel in limbo."

"Hardly surprising," Luc nodded. "But better?"

"Better than when you picked me up in Valence. Did I say I was sorry about that night?"

"Several times. So how about we forget all that?"

"It wasn't one of my great moments, no. But the hug was… memorable."

"It was?"

"It was. You're good at helping damsels in distress."

Luc's face clouded at that, and he took a sip of water and stared at the menu again. Had she said something wrong? Well, there was only one way to find out. She asked.

It wasn't important, Luc said, but once they'd ordered their meal, she looked at the serious grey eyes again and knew something was on his mind.

"I've put my great big size forty shoes right in it," she said frankly. "I'd promised myself not to pry and just let you talk – I can be too nosy."

"I suppose you should know, then," he said quietly. "My sister. She was a damsel in distress as well, and I didn't manage to save her. If you want the short version, she had something of a drug problem thanks to a very bad choice of partner who got her into it. They got high one night, he took videos of her naked and of them having sex and put them all over the internet."

"Oh God," Emma said quietly, taking his hand. That explained his aversion to all things online.

"It gets worse. She was so upset, she took an overdose. A massive one."

The pain on his face made Emma want to reach over and hug him.

"We were close. Very close – she was two years younger than me. She was a brilliant classical dancer, with every chance of a great career. She met the wrong guy. Anyway," Luc attempted a grin, "now you know the worst, or most of it. The final bit of the story is that I went to find the guy and beat the crap out of him. I'd probably have gone to prison for it if he'd made a complaint but he didn't. Maybe it would have meant details coming out about his suppliers – I don't know. I managed to stop before I did him some permanent damage, but I still wonder how."

"Jesus," Emma breathed, still gripping his hand. "I don't know what to say except it must have been hell for you. Your parents as well."

"It took them years to move on, and I'm not sure my mum ever has, really. I was a mess for a year – spent most of it down here, working, just because I couldn't stand the atmosphere at home. Then my other uncle – not the one at the masonry firm here, the one who lives in New Zealand and has a building company – told me there was work for me there if I wanted it, so I went. You can't get much further away from Europe than that."

"Complete break," Emma said quietly. "I can understand that but oh Luc –"

"Shhh," he put a finger to her lips. "I was going to tell you all this at some point. It just came out earlier than I expected. But it's only fair you know about Marie. And the fact that I have a filthy temper with people who deserve it. The little shit spread that all over the internet as well, by the way. I found him through some of her friends and sometimes I wish I hadn't. When I went to see him, he said I was a thug seeking vengeance and that he'd done nothing wrong."

"That's just horrible. But I'm glad you told me," Emma said, unaware of the plate that had appeared in front of her.

"Don't let it spoil the evening," Luc said, firmly. "You want to hear something more cheerful?"

"Try me." Emma kept looking at him, seeing his face soften.

"My hair. I went off relationships for years. Even when I got back to France. It's a trust issue. Marie always defended that bastard, saying he was harmless, and she loved him and trusted him, and then he killed her, basically. I ended up with long hair and avoiding relationships. I always told my mum that the day I cut it would be when I found somebody I trusted again."

Emma felt tears come to her eyes and stared into his.

"I also told her that I was probably just deluding myself that you felt anything for me. That got me the pep talk I mentioned, so let's say I acted on it."

"Glad you did," Emma said, reaching over and squeezing his hand.

"And now, young lady, please eat that excellent-looking starter or I'll think I've completely screwed up the evening."

"You haven't," Emma said immediately. "Believe me, Luc, you haven't. I'm stunned you told me. And that you trust me. I wouldn't betray that, ever."

"I think I realised that very early on. Just like I realised you can never eat without getting things on your chin, and that just makes me want to kiss you and lick it off."

Emma felt her eyes widen.

"It does? You do?"

"I do. Jam or Bolognese, at least. You should also know, by the way, that I am never, *ever* going to eat second-hand fondue. I hate the stuff."

"Fondue is part of my cultural heritage."

"Fine. When you cook it, I'll make myself a steak, then," Luc said firmly. "Can I have a bite of your pâté, though?"

"Maybe," she smiled at him. "As long as I get a bit of your goat cheese whatsits."

"Could happen," he said mildly. "Although I think it was called something a bit more sophisticated than that. And Emma? I'm just so glad to have got over that particular hump. Can we relax a bit now?"

"We can," she agreed, spreading a little pâté on a corner of toast and handing it over. "And if you think I was going to be scared off, you're wrong. I just feel so sorry for putting my foot in it."

"Stop saying you're sorry. Please." Luc sighed dramatically and held out a forkful of his starter for her to try.

It felt as though she'd known him for years. They talked about films, about everything that came into their heads, including Luc's guarded excitement about the craft fair he was taking part in the following week, further south in the Drôme, and Emma's guarded optimism about a job in Lyon.

"Lyon's not so far," Luc said thoughtfully. "I was starting to think we might be spending a fortune on air or rail tickets."

"Did you indeed, Mr Theyroux. How –"

"Presumptuous of me? Yeah, maybe. Hopeful, definitely. But I want us to take the time we need, Emma. Well, at least with some things."

"Hopeful sounds like I feel as well," she admitted. "And yes, taking it slowly for – some things – sounds good to me too."

'Some things' was a bit like saying *'you know'*, she thought, remembering the conversation with her mother. Although there were times when saying *sex* was a bit too much like calling a spade a dirty great shovel. There was no doubt what he meant. His hand reached across for hers.

By that time, Emma had shared her guinea fowl, Luc had shared his steak, and he'd decided on a lemon meringue tart for dessert. She felt more like wrenching the dessert menu from his hands and dragging him outside for a taste of *some things*.

"Emma," Luc said, mock-offended, a few minutes later. "You do realise you were going to have just one bite and you've eaten most of it?"

"I like lemon tart," she said cheekily. "And food in general. I'm too weight-conscious to indulge myself in a whole dessert. Maybe I should get a bit of it on my chin?"

"Maybe you should," he chuckled. "I feel like finding some runny jam to spread on a baguette early one morning."

"Oh yes?" Her mouth went dry.

"Like... tomorrow morning? Or am I rushing you? I'd told myself I was not going to let you think that a date came with... obligations."

"You're not rushing me," she said quietly, firmly, appreciating his diffidence. "I hope you have spare toothbrushes. I didn't want to seem presumptuous and bring one."

Luc laughed – a rich, deep laugh that spelled relief but also anticipation.

"Let me go and pay and then we can check that out?"

Desire swept through her, and she saw it in his eyes too. She wanted this man and wanted him badly. And it was mutual. Some things couldn't wait.

"Be right back. Don't eat the tablecloth while I'm gone."

"I can wait for breakfast, thank you. You can go out and get me a croissant. And a *pain au chocolat*."

"You'll get chocolate on the sheets as well as your chin, right?"

"Probably," she said cheerfully, feeling her heart rate speed up, and fire flicker in the pit of her stomach.

Her phone rang as she was reaching for her cape, and she pulled it out of her bag, hoping it was a wrong number. Who on earth would call her at ten at night? At possibly the worst moment ever to be disturbed?

When Luc got back to the table, she was standing by the door, tears running down her face.

"Luc…"

"Emma, what? What is it?"

"That was Dad. My gran just died."

He reached for her, pulling her into his arms.

"I'm here, Emma. I'm here."

"Oh Luc. She was fine while I was there."

He steered her outside.

"I – Luc I don't know what to say."

"Shh", he said. "I'm here."

***

When she finally sank onto the bed and pulled out her tablet, Emma felt drained. Her mother seemed angrier with her dad for calling her than anything else.

No, she'd said – it was fine. Then she'd worked with her father to book flights, all the time remembering her last few days with her grandmother.

Her mother wasn't saying much at all as they made the arrangements, which was probably her way of coping with it. It wasn't the time for revealing family secrets, Emma had decided.

Poor Gran. She'd died quietly in her chair in front of the television, with a sherry glass beside her, Gillian had said. They'd tried to call in the early evening and she hadn't answered, and then they'd called the neighbours who said there were no lights on. Worried, Gillian and Clive had driven over and found her.

At least she hadn't suffered, Emma's mother said at one point. Emma felt like saying she'd suffered ever since she'd been abandoned by an American soldier.

Wearily, she opened her email and smiled despite everything.

Hello my sweet Emma. Thinking of you and waiting for news. Also, have installed some gizmo called gtalk and got a gmail address in case you want to type rather than talk. Or you can call me. Doesn't matter what time.

It didn't take her long to add the address, and she smiled again. Who but Luc could think of a name like *artistcarpenterbloke*?

So, she typed, once she saw his 'available' icon. *Has the artist bloke suddenly discovered technology?*

Yes, he typed back. *But more of a case of discovered a lot more about somebody wonderful tonight.*

So did I. You're making me cry, Luc.

Can I call you?

I'd like that. Not the world's fastest typist here.

He did. She told him about the flight plans and heard him scribbling them down, and didn't suggest he get an online calendar. The messenger was already a huge step forward, she realised.

"Can I see you Friday night, when you get back?"

"I'll be there as soon as we get in – around eight or nine by the time we get to Crest?" she smiled. "I'll send you a text when we land?"

"Texting? You want miracles, woman?"

"You don't have to reply." Emma found herself holding back a chuckle. "Just find a bottle of wine."

"I have to leave very early on the Saturday for the exhibition," he said. "But at least I'll see you before I go."

"Weren't you supposed to go on Friday?"

"And miss you? No way. I'll leave at the crack of dawn to set up. And maybe you can come down and see it on the Sunday?"

"I'd like that."

"If I wasn't sharing a crummy room with two other blokes, I'd suggest you stayed over, but…"

"I understand," she told him. "When you're famous and staying in five-star palaces, then yes."

"Still thinking big. Give you an inch and you'll be pre-ordering a private jet as well. But Emma, enough joking around. Are you really alright?"

"I'm all right because I'm talking to you. There's stuff with Gran and Mum that's complicated and I'll tell you about it. Just not now."

"We'll have time," Luc told her gently. "Right?"

"We will," she said softly. "Tonight was fantastic, Luc; and Friday seems a long way away."

"Can I come by tomorrow, before you leave? Just to offer your mum my condolences?"

"I'd like that."

They broke the connection and Emma lay there, her emotions going wild.

Gran, she thought to yourself, you'd have liked this one. And he won't walk out on me like your bastard of an American had, either, or cheat on me like Rainer.

Chapter 15

Shirley

How are you supposed to act when your mother dies and you never really knew her?

I don't know. I don't feel like crying and I suppose I should. Steve is treating me like fine china and Emma's gone into efficient mode, which included making breakfast and leaving the kitchen like World War III. She clears up afterwards. She's on a rollercoaster of tears and what looks suspiciously like contentment. I feel terrible that Steve ruined their evening and say so.

"Mum, it wasn't ruined. I promise you that."

"I'm glad. I told Dad not to call."

"But I'm glad he did. Just – don't go into a corner and refuse to talk."

"I'm not refusing to talk. I don't know what to say."

"Whatever comes to mind. Even if it's about you thinking Gran didn't love you."

I stare at her.

"Look, Mum, I know you often thought that, but you were wrong. I talked to her about all sorts of things in Sheffield, and she really admired you."

"She had a funny bloody way of showing it."

"Stop it, Mum. Whatever you thought of her, you've got to admit she could be really fun at times."

"At times," I say bitterly, and march off to the laundry. I'm not in the mood for the third degree.

"Mum?" Emma calls as I go, "Luc's going to drop by before we leave for the airport. Just –"

"To offer me his condolences," I sigh. "That's kind of him."

I realise that didn't sound very enthusiastic, so I pick up the basket of clothes and go back into the kitchen.

"I'm sorry, Em. I'm not trying to be difficult."

"You? Difficult?" Emma asks airily. "How could that ever be?"

Despite everything, I find myself smiling back. "Apart from your evening ending a bit prematurely, it was good?"

"It was fantastic, Mum."

"Good." This time it comes out with feeling, and Emma hugs me.

"But I'm not going to go mooning around acting soppy."

"Why ever not? You deserve somebody who cares, love."

"Thanks Mum."

Emma's eyes have tears in them again. Yet once Luc turns up, she looks like a young woman who's fallen hook, line and sinker in love.

It's a good thing, and it cheers me up. At least her relationship with me – and vice-versa – is light years from mine with my own mother, who never really approved of my admittedly limited number of boyfriends. Steve was the exception. Good job, good prospects. Meeting him when we were both working in Switzerland had also meant I'd never gone back to England despite my original idea of only staying abroad for a few years.

Mum liked Switzerland for its orderliness, the scenery, and the opportunity to show off about her daughter marrying somebody with an up-and-coming career. My career, she didn't care about much. Working for an international organisation was something like being a glorified typist in her eyes, but it probably got her Brownie points when she name-dropped about who I worked for. Once I gave up that job and started freelancing, she didn't consider that to be working at all – more like some sort of paid hobby.

The past is the past. She probably spent the last year or so carefully skipping over the fact that we were moving into the boarding house business when talking to her friends. She'd also had dozens of free holidays in Switzerland and then in France over the years, so no doubt she'd managed to find something to show off about even if it was only that we had a pool – something neither common nor practical in South Yorkshire.

I'm a bitch. I shake my head at such spiteful thoughts and carry on folding underwear.

Luc comes, and is polite. He doesn't stay long.

"You doing all right?" Steve comes into the kitchen as I'm putting together lunch before we leave.

"Sure I am. Luc gone?"

"Yep. Not that they didn't grab a quick snog in one of the guest rooms."

I sigh contentedly despite everything. "Well good for them. Nothing wrong with a quick snog, Mr Sandford. You weren't spying on them, were you?"

"Oh please. I might be a man, but I'm not blind. Our daughter has it bad. And I suspect he's in the same boat. I don't need to peer through keyholes to confirm it."

"How very perceptive," I say, moving closer to him. "Love you, Steve."

"Well that's useful," he says. "Love you too. And Shirley, if you want to talk –"

"You and Emma need to stop this fussing around me," I say a bit testily. "I'm fine."

"Well, if you say so. I'm just trying to be helpful."

"You are," I tell him. "And a snog isn't reserved for the under-forties, is it?"

***

The hotel in Sheffield is everything I don't want our B&B to be. It's a big chain, built of plastic and cardboard, and there are health and safety notices everywhere.

Who would have thought that you couldn't have a toilet brush in the bathrooms because of rules on sterilising them? Or that you couldn't walk more than a few steps outside the bar with your drink before risking fines?

As for smokers, I'm a leper, and I've been taking in nicotine like there's no tomorrow since we arrived, much to the disgust of my husband and daughter. Their disapproval has been carefully disguised. Mustn't upset wife or mother, who is still in that weird state of not really feeling very much. At least there's a special ashtray bolted to the wall outside, with the usual little notice about using it or being shot on sight for littering.

I wake up after tossing and turning in an overheated room with ridiculously soggy pillows that have probably been approved by the health and safety authorities, but that are frankly horrible. It makes me wonder whether our future guests want these non-pillows or whether they want nice hard ones that actually support your head. I'll have to give that some more thought, and probably have a few of each.

We arrived as planned. The air traffic gods were kind to us. I'd have preferred the train, because airport queues, security and frequent delays bring out the worst in me, but I managed not to reach out and grab people trying to skip the check-in queue.

Emma reminded me that the Eurostar isn't a paragon of timeliness, or even free from strikes either, but in my mind it's still infinitely preferable to the frustrations of air travel. Steve had decided that a flight would save time in this case and he was right. We arrived late in the evening and went to the hotel's so-called coffee shop because it was still open. We ate something that sounded wonderful and tasted like nothing. Although that could be just me. Twenty-four hours ago, life seemed fine. Now, it doesn't.

This morning, we embark on the 'who-does-what' marathon, starting with meeting Clive and Gillian at their house. Clive, logically, is the executor and is taking it all very seriously, which is a good thing. He is going to put Mum's house on the market and organise the house clearance. The will, to my surprise, divides everything fifty-fifty. I told Steve I had expected Gillian to get the lion's share, and he told me I was being silly.

Clive also adds that the funeral booking for Thursday is confirmed, and that we just need to sort out the details. First, he suggests, we should go out for a pub lunch to save Gillian cooking. We agree. It's mediocre but at least it's a welcome change from their overheated lounge with its overstuffed furniture and its bizarre collection of Murano glass on the shelves. Nobody talks as we plough our way through bland lasagne. Gillian is sniffly and pushes her food around her plate.

Then we go back to their place to sort out the funeral service itself, which is to be held at our local church.

I find myself thinking about Sunday School classes there, or the odd times my parents went to the family service. Dad wasn't much of a churchgoer and I always suspected Mum only went for an opportunity to dress up and make an appearance at the coffee morning afterwards prior to going out for Sunday lunch, which she liked a lot as it freed her from the mammoth task of the Sunday roast. I enjoyed Sunday lunches out too – the thrill of choosing what you got to eat, even though I always had roast chicken and Dad always had beef. And there was no washing up.

The Sunday post-lunch washing-up exercise was a major one because I swear Mum used every pan and utensil in the place to produce 'all the trimmings.' Dad washed and I dried, as we did most evenings. Gillian, if she wasn't off with the boyfriend of the moment, would be pressed into service to put things away. Mum? I can't remember what she did, but she'd often say that it was her one moment's peace from all the cooking and looking after the house. I used to think she was exaggerating a bit as the dusting and vacuuming were my domain. The ironing too, as I got older and Mum discovered I liked it.

Those thoughts lead me to other ones, slightly more pleasant. The superb Yorkshire puddings that I've never been able to equal, the trifle scattered with hundreds and thousands and made exotic with a thimbleful of sherry, and as time went on, a sip from Dad's glass of tepid Blue Nun.

My moment of nostalgia comes to an abrupt halt when Emma reminds me that we're supposed to tell the church, as soon as possible, about Mum's favourite hymns and bible passages so they could be added to the order of service.

I can only come up with ones I liked from school, which certainly wouldn't do for a funeral. *For those in peril on the sea,* for example, or *Jerusalem.* Gillian isn't any better, but Emma saves the day again and types *Hymns for funerals* into her tablet. That solves that part, and it comes in handy again for the readings.

Gloom descends when Gillian starts crying and goes off to the kitchen. I follow her, but we don't talk much. Neither of us has much to say. Instead, we peel vegetables and exchange platitudes on the art of the shepherd's pie.

Eventually, we – as in the Sandford contingent – escape. The one bottle of rather acidic red wine for five of us hasn't really had the effect I was hoping for, so we end up in a halfway decent pub near the hotel and have a few more glasses, upon which Emma makes her excuses. Judging from her smile, I suspect it has a lot to do with Luc and online chatting.

***

Tuesday has been designated as Craghill Road day. We arrive there as planned after a hotel breakfast that is as plastic as the surroundings and another night of very little sleep and fighting with the pillows. My request for another one had been met with astonishment, and a polite 'we'll see what we can do'. I presume that was the politically correct way of telling me to get lost.

For the first couple of hours, we start going through Mum's things, which sets Gillian off crying again, and even Emma joins in, particularly when she pulls out some photo albums of Mum when she was much younger.

"She was stunning," Emma says quietly. "I don't think I ever realised."

She was. Tall, slim and well-dressed beside her rather short, definitely portly and prematurely grey husband wearing glasses; the contrast is surprising. It's obvious who I take after although I have at least inherited her height.

There aren't – luckily, I think – too many photos of Gillian or me. My parents' photography tended to be blurry landscapes: from Whitby, or from the first package deal holiday to Switzerland. Later ones show scenes from their first holidays with us, and include Geneva's famous water jet, leaning slightly, or the über-picturesque main street from a trip to Gruyères.

Emma pulls one photo out of the older pile and looks at it quizzically. It's a sort of semi-formal shot and I think it's from Gillian's eighteenth birthday party. I don't remember much about it except it was held in some sort of function room and had mainly involved the boyfriend of the moment and some girls from her office. I can't remember why so much was made of it – wasn't it your twenty-first you celebrated? In any case, I'd never had a function-room birthday party, but I probably would have loathed the idea anyway.

Gillian, in the picture, is standing straight, elegant in a tight-fitting sheath dress. Her hair is an artful concoction of blonde curls, and she's smiling sweetly into the camera. Me? I'm scowling. I'm dressed in some shapeless thing that hides my nine-year-old chubby figure, with white ankle socks and sandals. My dark hair sports a pudding-bowl cut, thick and rebellious like it's always been.

Quietly, Emma puts it back on the pile and I feel tears close to the surface. Not of grief, but of anger, of frustration.

Eventually, we've sorted out the personal things that we don't want to to the house clearance company. Mum's jewellery box has been opened and Emma diffidently chooses her gran's charm bracelet. It includes all sorts of charms we've bought for it on our travels over the years. The hibiscus from the Caribbean, the lion from Africa, and a tiny *babouche* slipper from Morocco.

I must remember to book flights to Marrakech, I tell myself, and peer at the rest, knowing I should choose something, but I don't want to and suggest Gillian just sells it once she's taken what she wants.

This gets me a strange look from my sister, who I think wants to come out and ask my why I'm not bursting into tears all the time. In the end, I pick up a silver brooch I once bought her and that I'd never seen her wear, and mutter something about wearing it at the funeral. That seems to be a relief to both Gillian and Emma.

Next up is the estate agent, and I cruise through that on autopilot. After him comes the vicar, who is a woman. Once she's gone, Gillian wrinkles her nose a bit like my mother often did and says she finds her a bit of a tree-hugger type.

Personally, I don't see why vicars can't wear flowing skirts and big chunky bangles. She's not exactly Dawn French and her accent is definitely somewhere over Liverpool way, but I like her.

She's matter of fact, offers sincere-sounding condolences, and nods thoughtfully at our dutifully composed list of hymns. Mum might, she says thoughtfully, like something a bit more modern as well – the congregation are more and more into that and she's sure they can add it to the order of service.

Well, I say with forced cheer, I'm all for it.

We have now accomplished all the tasks that needed doing, and there's a whole day to go. Steve – who spent most of the morning browsing through books or going into the garden with Clive, looks relieved at the thought of liberation. I celebrate by nipping into the garage for a cigarette because it's raining outside. Steve comes and joins me.

"We need an evening off," he says. "Kevin's due tonight so I said we should leave them to be together. Your mum was fond of him, and maybe it was mutual."

She was, I remember, and told me how he'd helped out with the garden. Grudgingly, I admit he's done a good job on it from the little I've seen.

Good heavens, I've found a positive thought loitering somewhere.

"Well I suppose he has some good points, but I still can't stand him," I mutter ferociously.

"Right now, Shirley, you can't even stand yourself."

Steve has this habit of coming out with the truth, and not wrapped in velvet gloves, either.

"I know, and I'm sorry. So how about we hit a really good Indian restaurant?"

"That's my girl. Then I can have onion bhajis and fart all night."

"I've always admired your elegance," I say, unable to hold back a smile. "At least it's not the night before the funeral."

"Also," Steve adds, "I told Clive you needed a breather tomorrow as well. We can nip into Derbyshire. Poke around antique shops, find a non-tacky pub lunch somewhere?"

"Sounds like a plan," I nod. "Emma might be bored out of her skull, though."

"She's doing fine," Steve says, and I agree. "Knowing Emma, she'll organise an itinerary on that magic slate of hers tonight. As long as she's planning something, she's fine. A bit like you."

He has a point. And there are a couple of fabric shops I wouldn't mind visiting. Steve and Emma can go and find fudge, or whatever their sweet tooth leads them to, I tell him, while I dig around for something for new cushion covers.

"You're doing well, love," he nods approvingly.

I'm not so sure, but I'm giving it my best shot.

***

Emma

Was this group of people anything like a real family, Emma wondered? She looked round the table in the rather fussy, formal restaurant and decided that what with the geographical distance, the great cultural divide that had opened up because of it, and the fact that her mother and sister were only half-sisters anyway, they seemed like two units that were light years apart.

Her mother, a little revived after what had turned out to be a fairly enjoyable day, was being polite but definitely minding her Ps and Qs and nothing like her normal self. Flashes of that had emerged as they strolled around Bakewell and she'd talked about falling into the ankle-deep river as a child, with her father finding it funny and her mother being utterly furious.

Emma had teased them both about the essential visit to Ye Olde Pudding shop, and their enthusiasm about the produce at the Chatsworth farm shop. They'd come out laden with things that could prove challenging for their luggage, and her mother had even succumbed to a fabulous sweater, chosen by Emma, at a very swish shop she'd bullied her into exploring.

She was wearing it now – deep blue with a few ribbons and bits of braid. Offbeat, and a long way from Gillian's snug suit that was already veering towards Gran-type pastels.

Kevin brayed suddenly at one of his own jokes, and she stared at him. She found him loathsome, and always had, on their mercifully few encounters. Full of himself, his job, his bachelor pad – did people actually still call them that – and his new girlfriend, who was 'in cosmetics', meaning she was probably one of those over-painted women who hovered over glitzy stands in department stores.

Clive had been droning on for hours about how the left-wing city council was doing a wonderful job, and Emma suspected her rather right-wing father was having trouble keeping his mouth shut. Thanks to his years of management meetings, no doubt, he'd adopted an attitude of polite interest, and that despite the fact that both Kevin and Clive had interrupted him every time he attempted a topic of conversation that went beyond Sheffield, or cars, or the wonders of Kevin's latest promotion to area manager. Apparently now, he went to places as exotic as Birmingham.

"About tomorrow," Gillian said primly, in the middle of her roast lamb. "We think we should all wear dark clothes."

That, Emma decided, had to be directed at her, considering the only warm winter coat she possessed was bright red, and it was on the back of the chair. It was either that or her mother's vibrant new sweater that was not considered appropriate.

"Tough," she said cheerfully. "This is what I'm wearing. And if you want my opinion, Gran would be quite happy to know I wasn't going to turn up all in black. She was far more tolerant than anybody seems to have given her credit for."

Everybody stared at her, and her father gave her a warning look.

"It's just more appropriate," Gillian said faintly, taken aback.

"I'm sorry, but I don't like being forced to look like something I'm not. I know Gran was pretty set in her ways about how Mum dressed, but I'm not Mum, just as Mum isn't you, Gillian, and I'm hoping she wears something that *she* wants to wear rather than feeling forced into what you think is right."

"Oh, we know your mum isn't like Gillian," Clive shot back unpleasantly. "She makes that abundantly clear."

That was enough. Emma could see her mother about to open her mouth, and stood up.

"Mum – ladies' room. And everybody else, for fuck's sake this is about a funeral and not about family squabbles. I'll be wearing a red coat. Kevin can go dressed as an Elvis impersonator for all I care. End of story."

She steered her mother into the pink-and-gold powder room, and then gave her shoulder a squeeze.

"Just take deep breaths, Mum. They're just…"

"Horrible? Vicious?"

"No. Shell-shocked, like we all are. Apply a bit of war paint and we'll both go back and act like ladies. And sorry for the 'fuck'. It just slipped out."

"Don't apologise. I think if I had opened my mouth, I'd have poured out a lifetime's grievances."

"See? I have my uses. And at least you brought the black bat cape. If I were you, I'd jazz it up with that bright green scarf."

"And die a lock of hair to match?" her mother said, halfway between laughing and crying.

"Only a lock? I'd actually love to see their faces if you did the whole lot. The food in this place is boring, they're boring, and all I want to do is get out of here. You can go and cheer Dad up in that pub up the road from the hotel, and I'm going to see if Luc managed to install Skype, although I'm not holding out for miracles."

"Even I can do Skype."

"He'll get there eventually. For the moment, emails and messenger chats are pretty good."

"Judging from the smile on your face, that's an understatement."

"Well… yeah. Now, go and tell Dad and the others you think you'll skip dessert because you're tired and overwrought – and *don't* apologise, they're not worth it. Then we can reveal the master plan once we're out of there. Knowing Uncle Clive, he'll already have totted up our share of the bill anyway."

"You've certainly got him figured out."

"Not difficult. Also, he has no taste when it comes to restaurants, or food, or clothes. And look at Kevin? He's thick round the middle at 35 and he'll be a greasy slob all his life."

"You know, Emma, anybody'd think you don't like him."

"He's a little shit. Go and get close to that nice ex-rugby player's gut on Dad, and relax."

Her mother nodded, determination back on her face.

"You're a gem, Em. Oh dear, that sounds dreadful."

"I can be a gem when I try. And so can you; and you mostly are. Enough of the pep talks and think of a nice cold glass of decent white wine and not that tepid muck they chose for the meal."

"All that continental influence of yours is showing," her mother said. "At least they don't make Yorkshire wine, or they'd have chosen that."

Emma sailed back to the table, realising she was in full-on organising mode and relishing it. She'd wondered whether tonight could have been the right time for a quiet chat with her mother about some of Gran's confessions, but not yet.

One day soon.

***

It's no good, Emma. This Skype thing isn't working. And yes, I'm an IT dimwit.

We'll deal with it when I get back home then, for when you're at the fair. Or at least if you can get rid of your roommates at that classy joint you're staying at. Will the place have wifi at least?

It probably doesn't even have running water. The exhibition hall does have connections, though so I can at least email or otherwise I'll phone – I'll send you the flyer?

Please! Well, if you know how to attach things.

Cheek. You got my message from earlier?

Emma could picture him so easily, sitting at his desk, typing, and smiled at the thought.

I did and you damn well made me cry again, Mr Smitten Artist Bloke.

I didn't mean to do that.

Nobody ever wrote anything so beautiful to me. Or so sexy, if you want to know.

Thank you. And after a pause: *I mean it, Emma. Everything I said – about you, about the website.*

I know that. I want your arms around me.

They will be, my love. Friday. Not long now.

Got to get through the funeral first. My mother's family is a minefield.

I'll be thinking of you, Em.

I want to hear your voice – can I call you? Are you at home?"

Yes, and yes. Still type too slowly for you, do I?

Not just that!

Emma was already dialling, and the sound of his voice made everything seem far better.

She broke the connection a while later with a contented sigh, glad that at least she could call Luc's landline on Skype.

Even more blissful was rereading his long mail and savouring it. Was it a love letter? Yes, it was, in so many ways and she had the feeling that the L-word was actually going to crop up once they were face to face, even though she'd studiously avoided it while basking in the way he called her *my love*.

Luc had an unexpected flair for writing in a way that was sincere and anything but explicit or tacky, she thought, reading it again and feeling the now-familiar flutter of arousal.

I want to touch every part of you, Emma. To explore you and talk to you and make endless love to you. To hold you tight and feel you respond to me. I ache for you. It's terrifying and it's wonderful if that makes sense.

Tears came again, but good ones, as she imagined him there, naked, his hands straying over her skin.

She read on, smiling through the tears as he'd added something about how his sister would have liked her, and how his parents were going to adore her.

Then, Luc being Luc, he'd become practical and moved on to business matters, telling her that it was high time she did the world's best online advertising campaign for Mr Luc Theyroux, including Twittering (oh, Luc). Particularly if they wanted that private jet before they got too old to enjoy it. He was counting on her business sense, he pointed out, because he didn't have any.

Please, he'd added a PS after signing it simply *Your Luc* – which brought another wave of tears – *bring back some Jelly Babies. A certain person you know has a thing about them. Also, they don't stain sheets.*

That mail, Emma decided, meant so many things. He trusted her. He wanted her. He wanted her for everything, from her body to her business skills to her often-weird sense of humour.

She should sleep, but first she was going to reply. She was probably better at writing work documents than really expressing her inmost thoughts on paper, but that already gave her an idea.

Dear Sir. Further to your communication of today, we wish to inform you of the following, she started, thinking fast. *The recipient of your message has duly noted the points you mentioned and fully intends to demonstrate her wholehearted approval at the earliest possible opportunity for a meeting. This should preferably take place naked, with Jelly Babies available for the parties concerned, and be followed by other, appropriate light refreshments at its conclusion (which may or may not include runny jam). Business sense will not be required during the entire proceedings, but caresses, kisses, and of course some in-depth mutual exploration of anatomical reactions appears essential. We are convinced that the outcome will be to our mutual satisfaction and that any initial terrifying aspects for both parties will be rapidly overcome.*

Did that all sound too stupid? Probably, but she thought he might find it funny.

And having said all that drivel, she went on, *I can't wait to see you, Luc, and thank you a million times for everything. I shall attempt to behave myself until I see you, but I have *no* intention of doing so in your bed, as you bring out the hussy in me even if I'm a bit scared too. Am I shocking you? I want to know everything about you – everything you want to share with me at least (and I'm very glad that includes the part before the runny jam).*

No, she didn't think she would shock him. She added *Off to sleep now* plus a row of xxx and hit Send.

Her phone buzzed a few minutes later. The text just said *Mmmmmxx.* She laughed aloud. That, for Mr I-don't-text was eloquent enough.

She'd sleep well, Emma decided.

Chapter 16

Shirley

We're all being exquisitely polite with one another this morning as we congregate at Craghill Road, waiting for the hearse and the cars.

It's windy and showery, in contrast to the remarkably sunny day we had in Derbyshire, and I stand at Mum's kitchen window looking out over the hill opposite.

Gillian has agreed to store Emma's boxes from the London flat for the time being, which she's putting in Clive's car. Clive and Steve are outside, probably supervising. Kevin hasn't arrived yet but should be here soon.

A gust of wind blows rain onto the window and I jump, despite my determination to remain calm.

"Do you remember," Gillian speaks behind me, which makes me jump again, "when you were little, and the wind made the glass in our bedroom window bend a bit? You used to be scared it'd break."

"It never did, though." I turn to see her and notice the fuchsia scarf tucked into her sensible black suit. As apologies go, that in itself says a lot. "And you kept telling me it would be all right and I should stop worrying."

"Oh, I worried myself," she says. "I had the bed nearest the window, remember? And I was supposed to be the reassuring big sister."

"You were, sometimes," I say. "But sometimes I was as jealous as hell of you and felt you resented me."

"Seriously?" she looks genuinely gobsmacked.

"Seriously. I felt like the kid in the way, particularly when I tried to hang around you and all you wanted was for me to go to bed early when Mum and Dad were out playing cards so you could have a snog with your boyfriends."

"And you spun it out as long as possible."

"I did," I half-chuckle. "I was a brat."

"You were such a little swot," she says, not unkindly. "And a nosy one at that. I used to be jealous of your good marks at school, and got the impression you felt all superior."

It's my turn to look surprised.

Truths can be blurted out at the most inappropriate moments. Even as I open my mouth to try and answer that, I hear another car draw up, followed by Kevin's over-loud greetings.

"We should talk," Gillian says quietly. "Really talk. Not the right time now, though, is it."

"It isn't," I agree, and impulsively give her arm a squeeze. Her eyes are puffy and her mascara's run, and in that moment, I wish we could just sit down, grab a bottle, and talk for hours.

I keep thinking about that short, stilted yet sincere conversation as I engage autopilot again and we climb into one of the cars behind the procession. Clive, ever the fussy organiser, has put their group of three into the first one and us into the second. I think I see him throw a disapproving look at us, but I'm probably being over-sensitive.

No, I'm not. Gillian's taking the bright scarf off and he's gesticulating.

Steve is wearing a dark suit and a light grey overcoat but has contributed to our apparent flashiness by choosing a burgundy tie instead of the black one I brought. He sees the little circus going on as they get in the car and rolls his eyes.

"Should have found an even flashier tie," he says. "And you should have found a bright purple version of your cape."

Emma guffaws. "Rainer used to wear flashy ties until he got all serious, or rather until he tried to climb the corporate ladder by getting into his boss's knickers."

I hope the glass window between us and the driver makes it soundproof in here, although I'm not sure I care.

"Rainer was a prick," Steve says, rather vehemently for him. "And believe me, after this last couple of days, I've seen enough pricks to last me a while."

I raise my eyebrows and nod towards the glass window, but realise that Steve's been remarkably patient over the whole thing and deserves to speak his mind. I always knew he wasn't fond of Clive or Kevin, anyway. He excludes Gillian from that, he adds, after a minute. He quite likes her, and particularly in bright purple scarves.

"Sorry, Steve," I say. "It must have been purgatory for you, all this."

"Nah. It just got a bit much when Clive decided to expound on how B&Bs didn't attract people any more but offered me a few tips on how to run it this morning."

"He *what*?!" I see the driver's shoulders twitch slightly. "Bingo evenings? Good Yorkshire nosh? I mean, for God's sake, what does he know about anything except pushing papers at the council?"

"He told me he knows about cost savings in retirement homes, which he thinks is all about cheap and cheerful. Food, bedding… processed cheese in wholesale packs, that sort of thing."

My jaw drops.

"Just goes to show," Emma finally speaks up, "Gillian doesn't have as good a taste in men as Mum or, more recently, me."

Steve calms down, and I see the funny side of the Clive versus Steve encounter. When I see Emma chuckle, looking at her phone and then handing it to me, I can't help joining her.

goodkuck it says. Emma explains that Luc is not into texting and probably hasn't found the space bar or backspace yet, but he's doing his best.

"I can sympathise," I nod. We might need some good luck before the day's out.

We pull up outside the church in pouring rain. I'm still on autopilot, even as they take the coffin out. I know that my mum's in there but nothing much is registering. We didn't go down and see her at the funeral home, although Gillian agreed with me on that and didn't go either, so that's one criticism less.

It starts. From the muttering behind me, I realise there must be a fair few people in church but turning around and staring is probably not a good idea. When we came in and sat up front, there were already a few there, mostly of Mum's generation.

Gillian's ordered a meal for around fifty people, from a caterer. It's supposedly one who does a 'good spread', from a contact of Clive's, so I expect we'll get processed cheese.

Ms tree-hugger vicar; who looks smart in her surplice, gives an upbeat introduction about celebrating Mum's life. I definitely like her.

We limp through a hymn and then to my surprise, Clive lumbers to his feet. We'd actually said, Gillian and I, that we didn't want any eulogies, so maybe he's just going to do a reading. Emma has volunteered to do one and so has somebody else from church.

No, he isn't reading from a bible, but from what looks like an exercise book. He mixes words up, pauses in all the wrong places, and as for the content, I can feel my hands balling into fists.

It's all about how Mum appreciated the runs in their car to her favourite spots, them taking her to meals at quiet little places or to do her shopping, and how it had been sheer pleasure to do that for her.

In fact, it's a blatant little demonstration of how good he and Gillian think they've been. Her loving family, as he puts it, adding how deeply they are grieving. The Sandfords don't feature in it at all. Even Mum fades into insignificance beside their feats of selfless devotion.

Gillian, a couple of seats across, looks embarrassed and starts crying again. I glare at her and she shrugs hopelessly. Steve tries to uncurl my fingers and Emma takes a short, sharp breath.

Finally, he finishes and it's off to the modern hymn we go. I stand up and don't recognise it at all, but Emma manages to pick up the tune and does a good job of it, while I still fume about Clive.

The vicar then gives a little sermon about how Mum was liked at church. She is a good speaker and injects humour into it. Mum being a little *directive* at meetings of the seniors' club committee and usually getting her way. Her *very* clear ideas on how the church flowers should be organised. But, she says, every community needs somebody directive, with clear ideas, and that Mum was quite a character and will be missed.

I like that. It's not sugary or trite.

Then, Emma stands up. She goes to the lectern, ramrod straight, and looks the congregation in the eye before she reads from 1 Corinthians, which she'd chosen and said that even if she was a heathen, it was sensible stuff.

"Love is patient, love is kind," she starts, her voice clear. "It does not envy, it does not boast, it is not proud. It does not dishonour others, it is not self-seeking, it is not easily angered, it keeps no record of wrongs. Love does not delight in evil but rejoices with the truth. It always protects, always trusts, always hopes, always perseveres."

There's more, but she puts her tablet down and looks at everybody again.

"My grandmother knew about love," she says calmly. "I was very lucky to spend a few days with her recently. We had a lot of fun because I think we were a little alike. I can be directive myself. Plain bossy, to be honest. We ate pizza and drank wine and talked about love. She was helping me over a time when I was having trouble believing it existed, but she taught me a lot about what it really means."

I feel my throat tighten.

"My gran," Emma continues, "loved many people. And that included her two daughters, both" – she stresses the word – "of whom she admired, different as they are. She told me so. She understood that love takes different forms, and sometimes comes out wrong, or poorly, but it can be genuine just the same. I know her family – all of us – Gillian and Clive and Kevin, and my mum and dad and myself, all cared about her deeply in our own way. I'm not going to go into boring anecdotes about the many, many times my parents invited her over for holidays but believe me there are plenty of them –"

Emma pauses, and then shoots me a faint smile before continuing.

"Let's just say I know she appreciated her visits and how my parents made them special. But speaking for myself, I loved her, as I told her not so many days ago, for being a pizza-eating, wine-swigging, game old broad, and for much more than that. And she laughed her head off."

Emma pauses, and suddenly her lips tremble but her head is still up.

"I'll miss you, Gran," she says quietly and returns to her seat calmly and with dignity.

If tears weren't streaming down my face I'd probably applaud. I do hear murmurs of approval from behind me, and Gillian is also weeping openly, pausing to give Emma a pat on the arm as she goes past.

Emma, too, is crying now but she stands up bravely for the last hymn.

As the men from the funeral company take the coffin away – we've opted for it to be taken to the crematorium directly, which both Gillian and I preferred to an ordeal at a graveside – I realise this really is the end.

Steve takes my hand firmly in the church entrance, and Emma reaches around for a hug as we head off for the reception.

"Thank you, Emma," I say, still choked.

"Wasn't planned," she says, a little pale but very much in control. "And you know, if I smoked, it's about now that I'd rush out for a quick one before we go and be polite to people we don't know."

"As a matter of fact," Steve says, "That sounds like an excellent idea. Take your mum outside for a minute, Em. Everybody'll understand. I'll go and hold the fort."

"Don't kill Clive," I mutter, my voice still a bit strangled. "Or the cousin I've not seen for donkey's years." I'd caught sight of him as we left church and said a brief hello.

"I'll try."

It's drizzling now, so I keep the moment of respite short. It helps all the same.

***

We emerge from the gloomy church hall a couple of hours later. I've pasted on a smile, been polite to everybody and eaten two bites of cheese sandwich. The processed variety. But even if it had been the world's best Brie, it would have stuck in my throat.

There were a couple of locals I recognised, mostly Mum's neighbours, and some of them were lovely. I tried to make conversation with them, and then left them to their feast.

Gillian, Clive and Kevin were off in a corner, sitting with the famous cousin and his wife, who greeted me politely enough but not with much enthusiasm. We're virtual strangers. Clive was holding forth about local politics when we went over there, which meant Steve and I were excluded, so we kept things brief.

Emma was charming, and a number of people enthused to us about her wonderful tribute. According to the vicar, she'd been sensational and that she should be proud of herself. I couldn't agree more.

Clive and Gillian are waiting outside. They're being given a lift back to Craghill Road where they left their car. Do we mind walking, if we want a lift back to the hotel? Or maybe Kevin could take us?

It's stopped raining. One more minute of Clive or Kevin and I'm in danger of becoming unpleasant.

'I think we'll go for a walk and then find our own way back, thanks," I say.

In that case, Gillian says, will they see us again before we leave? She looks distinctly uncomfortable.

Steve tells them that no, probably not, but he's sure we'll be in touch. He even thanks Clive again, and politely, for agreeing to pay an advance on the bill for the reception and the deposit for the funeral service until he can deduct it from Mum's estate. My husband has class.

I feel like telling them that the catering was stingy and mediocre, and the coffee was so bad you could see the bottom of the cups through it, but I don't. What's the point?

They drive off. I light another cigarette and Emma asks me gently what I want to do now.

"I want to be sitting in that pub on the corner with a very large glass of white wine in front of me within five minutes," I say firmly. "They should still be open. Some food might even be a plan, but not if it's as tacky as that apology for a buffet in there. Then we can get them to call us a taxi."

"That's my girl," Steve says. "In fact, I'm proud of both my girls at this moment. Still want to give Clive a kick in the balls though."

"That would be you and me both," Emma nods. "What a creep. And Kevin's no better. He told me last night that as I'm unemployed, their pump factory or whatever it is might have openings for office staff."

"How charming," I grimace.

"I tried to see it as him meaning well, but I was probably a bit short with him and told him I didn't do five years at business school to be a typist. I wonder if Clive's little show at the funeral about how wonderful they were stemmed from that. One-upmanship sort of thing."

"Could be," Steve agrees.

"I suppose it might have come across as me being ungrateful or bitchy," Emma adds. "But then he started making a few digs about the B&B as well, along the lines of it being a bit of a come-down."

"Ouch," I say. That probably came from my mother who, for some reason, seemed to like Kevin well enough and had no doubt expounded on the whole boarding house theme and her opinion of it to them.

"Oh, don't worry. I told him the idea of your B&B was to host intelligent, fun people with taste, so I wasn't sure it would appeal to him. That shut him up."

I burst out laughing.

"When did all *that* happen?"

"Before the outburst on appropriate wear for funerals. Gillian was rabbiting on about something and you were listening to her. Not that I mind her much," Emma admits. "Unlike Gran, and me, she's just not directive *enough*."

"Neither was Dad," I say thoughtfully. "He was kind, but never stood up to Mum. Maybe she gets that from him and I'm the difficult one who takes after her."

Emma gives me a long, thoughtful look and then hooks her arm in mine and steers me in the direction of some much-needed alcohol.

Chapter 17

Emma

It was impossible, Emma fumed. The weather was bad, but couldn't planes damn well take off and land in fog and heavy rain now? Apparently not.

She checked the departures board yet again but it hadn't budged. Still another two hours before their estimated take-off time. At this rate they wouldn't be back in Crest until after ten at night.

She'd texted Luc and got *notto worry willwait.*

Yes, she knew he would.

They'd had another short chat the night before, and he'd talked about finishing off some last prints. They were coming out well, he'd added, enthusiasm clear in his voice.

Maybe he thought he didn't have any business sense, but he cared a lot about what he did. Hearing Luc sounding so happy had cheered her up, too.

And now this delay.

"This is ridiculous," she said to nobody in particular. Her father was deep into the *Financial Times*, and her mother had her head in her e-book. When things were difficult, she always plunged into her reading.

"Patience." Her father looked up.

"Not good at that," Emma said grimly. "Good book, Mum?"

"It's actually a really clunky novel about an American couple who open a B&B. And when I say clunky, I mean clunky."

"Ah." Emma tried to be interested. It would be better than watching the departures board.

"They do these 'packs' for pre-dinner drinks and snacks. And I'm not even talking about the crappy plot line."

"Packs? Packs in what way? You know, Mum, that's not such a bad idea if it's a glass of some sparkling wine, like *Clairette de die* and a couple of olives, maybe some of those mini-quiches or that tomato relish on little toasts?"

"Maybe," her mother said, not looking very convinced. "But for crying out loud I don't want to do *packs*."

"Then call it something else. Or even market the place as B&B plus A for aperitif and add a bit to the price."

"Not daft," her father said, from the depths of his newspaper.

"Maybe."

"Mum? About Gillian?"

"Emma." Her mother looked up. "Would you mind if we didn't discuss Gillian. Or Clive. Or even my mother, right now?"

Emma sighed and nodded agreement. Airport lounges weren't ideal for difficult conversations about family history, it was true.

Then she pointed at the departures board.

"Look! They've reduced the delay to an hour and a half."

"Big deal," her father said. "I'll believe that when I see it. And yes, I do know it was my idea to fly. I'd forgotten how bloody frustrating it can be."

"Welcome to the twenty-first century," Emma grumbled. "I'm going to stretch my legs. If they suddenly call the flight, I'll be the one throwing myself at the departure gate."

"Ah, the optimism of youth. The way this is going, we'll be stuck here until tomorrow morning."

No, Emma decided. That just couldn't happen.

"I'll go and look at the shops."

"And buy more Jelly Babies?" her father asked.

Emma rolled her eyes. She'd already found a supply of those at the local shops, so that was one mission accomplished.

"I'm part of the shopping generation, Dad. Want to come with me and look at the lingerie selection?"

That brought another eye roll from both her parents.

***

The main door to Luc's apartment building opened before she'd rung the bell, and she stood there, staring at him.

"I saw your dad's car arrive," he said softly, pulling her inside and pushing the door closed. "And don't babble about being late, or anything else. Just come here and let me kiss you."

Seconds – or maybe minutes – later she broke away, looking at him and smiling.

"Can I babble a bit now?"

"Make it short," he said gruffly, still holding her close.

"Can we go upstairs? Now? Please?"

"God yes. Or we'll end up –"

"I know. Could upset the neighbours if we go on like this," she said, bolting up two flights of stone stairs in front of him.

The door closed; he pulled her tight against him again. This time, his hands strayed under her coat, opening it, running them over her breasts, her stomach.

"Oh Emma – I need this."

"And me."

She shrugged off her coat, still holding him, running a hand down his stomach slowly and then further as he pulled up her sweater and cupped her breasts. Under his loose sweat pants, he was wearing nothing. It made her catch her breath, and he gasped.

"You have too many clothes on," he muttered tightly, and she helped him pull them off, frantic for more contact. His fell to the floor too. They stood there, slightly apart.

"You're beautiful, Emma."

He was too. Slim yet muscled, and his voice rough with need. Suddenly his hands were sliding over her and hers over him.

"Couch," she said, on a breath. She half-fell onto it, pulling him onto her.

"We should – we shouldn't –" he said, his voice shaky. "Here?"

"We should," Emma said firmly. "Here. Now."

His eyes looked straight into hers as he fumbled for a foil packet in a pocket of his discarded clothes with trembling fingers. "Certain?"

"Yes," she said. "Want you, Luc. *Now.*"

***

If that first, frantic coupling had been glorious and fast, it led to an exquisite, far slower encore.

Emma shifted slightly on the bed, still watching him as she slowly got her breath back.

This time, they'd explored. Played, even, before the arousal turned into pure need and he'd slid inside her again, still caressing her, taking her close to the edge and then over it only seconds before he cried out in release.

"I don't know what to say that doesn't sound corny," she said quietly, letting her hand stray across his chest. "But I feel wonderful."

"You look it too," he murmured, leaning up on one elbow. "I was so determined not to rush you tonight – really failed on that front."

"I think you can safely say you didn't fail at all," she chuckled. "You didn't rush me either – I think I was the pushy one. And I don't regret it one little bit."

"I'm glad." He brushed a strand of hair off her face. "I wanted you so much. Years of virtual celibacy has a lot to answer for, I suppose."

Emma stared at him, amazed. Despite her memories of that last time with Rainer and of the misery of faking an orgasm, plus the apprehension that accompanied any first time, Luc's lovemaking had set her body on fire.

"Virtually celibate? For years? Seriously?" she decided to ask, curious beyond measure. "You haven't lost your touch, then. And you didn't even – you know?"

That old *you know* her mother always fell back on.

"There was a bit of *you know* plus the odd one-night adventure, although it's been a while since any of those. When you got here, it was all way faster than I intended. And about a thousand percent better than I could have imagined. I was as nervous as hell."

"Likewise. Maybe it was your fault for being practically naked when I arrived," she said airily.

"That from somebody who has her breakfast in skimpy pyjamas when a poor innocent carpenter happens to come by."

"I was surprised you remembered I spilled jam on me."

"I thought it was sexy. I was disappointed when your mum mentioned something about your partner and you living in London."

"Seriously?"

"Seriously." Luc let a finger stray down to her breasts, and then to her stomach. "But to get back to here and now, that underwear you had on… I know I didn't stop to admire it much at the time, but that was most definitely sexy."

"We aim to please," Emma laughed. "I had a weak moment at East Midlands airport. You know, just in case I had a romantic assignment ahead of me."

"I thought you'd be expecting romantic."

Emma looked around the room, taking in the crisp sheets and the candles, and reached out to hug him again.

"I think there's something extremely romantic about hot, needy sex, followed by even hotter, more lingering sex."

"Anybody would think that you just liked sex."

Emma pondered on that for a bit. It didn't sound like a criticism, but it stung a bit.

"I do. I like it a lot. I'm not going to say I don't. But there is sex for the sake of it and sex that means a lot more."

"Agreed. And I'm not teasing. I like it too, as you may have noticed."

Emma shivered, feeling his fingers slowly arouse her again. She caressed him in turn, kissed him, pulled him to her.

"More?" he whispered.

"Mmm. But you have to be up and on the road in… not many hours from now."

"Sensible lady. And you must be exhausted."

"I don't feel it," she said honestly. "I just can't get enough of touching you. Or that –" she gasped as he teased a nipple.

After a few minutes, though, and despite the sensations running through her, she felt her eyes start to droop.

"Sleep, young lady. I shall be serving you with tea in four hours from now."

"Promise?" she murmured sleepily.

"Count on it. But wake-up time is a good half hour before that."

"Mmhm," she said, registering that with a tiny jolt of excitement. "Nice."

***

It was more than nice waking up to the feel of a hand stroking her thigh slowly, sensuously. Way more than nice when caresses turned into need again.

"Luc?" she glanced at the pack of condoms beside the bed, undecided whether to slide one on him as she'd done the last times or whether to take another major step.

"Mmm?"

She decided on forthright, caressing his hardness and taking a deep breath.

"With Rainer, we always used condoms... I mean I'm glad we did, or I mean he did, but I take the pill as well and we were exclusive or rather I was, so... oh Jesus I'm babbling again but... if you like –"

"I'd like."

"I'm not pushing you. It's just – "

"I'd like very, very much Emma." Smiling, he pulled her astride him and she revelled in it, watching his face as she sank onto his erection and started moving, very slowly.

"Good?" she whispered.

"Very good," he half-moaned. "Oh Jesus, Emma, it's more than good, feeling you like this. It's fucking amazing."

It was, Emma thought. The whole condom generation mindset had been part of her sex life since she'd lost her virginity. But this? This was like discovering her sexuality all over again.

"Remember on the tower?" she said softly. "That silly comment about you liking to be on top? I should have told you that I did, too."

"Oh, I remember it," he said. "I wanted you even then. And in the cinema? It was bloody purgatory. I was having X-rated thoughts all the way through the damned film. And it was so soon after your break-up –"

"You were a complete gentleman," she reassured him, shifting slightly. "But please don't be one now."

She increased the rhythm very gradually, making him gasp and thrust up against her as she moved, sliding his hand between them to caress her. She cried out in pleasure, revelling in the touch of his fingers and the hard silkiness of him.

When she climaxed, she sobbed out his name and kept her eyes open, watching him as he gasped and followed her.

And then, still inside her, looking up at her, he took her face between his hands.

"I love you, Emma Sandford. And thank you, my love. That meant so much."

More tears threatened, but so did a huge, bubbling surge of joy.

"I love you too, Luc."

He laughed again, that amazing, deep laugh of his.

"I was scared about saying it – is that stupid? It is too soon? And now I feel like saying it over and over and over."

"It's not stupid at all. That was the most fantastic way to wake up ever. And you can say it as often as you like."

"I will," he nodded. "Right now, though, I'm going to put the kettle on and have an extra-fast shower. Then I'm going to leave you a key so you can get ready in your own time. And also, because next time you can come straight up, and we don't risk getting arrested for indecency on the stairway."

That sounded good. Then his head popped up at the top of the staircase again.

"Em? It's pouring with rain. Want to get dressed and I'll drop you off on the way, rather than you walking?"

"Nope. I'll order a chauffeur, if that's okay. Mum won't mind."

"Sure?"

"Certain. She and Dad are all soppy about the idea of us anyway. They like you."

"Useful. It's mutual."

Emma leaned back on the pillows, feeling deliciously sated and full of energy at the same time.

Her clothes, she remembered, were in a heap downstairs. Luc had pulled on a bathrobe, which left her the choice of a sheet or nothing at all. Where were baggy t-shirts when you needed them? Preferably one of Luc's, but his bedroom was tidy and poking around wasn't really a good idea.

She yelled down to him and requested he toss the shirt he'd worn the night before upstairs, and her underwear, and it arrived rapidly except there was only the bottom half of the set she'd bought at the airport. She grinned and left a couple of buttons of the shirt open.

By the time he got out of the shower and emerged dressed, she had filled the teacups, unpacked the Jelly Babies and found a carton of orange juice. Grinning, she admired what she saw and decided he looked equally good in semi-smart clothes, his working gear, or in nothing at all.

"Not ideal, but it's going to be yesterday's baguettes, toasted," Luc said matter-of-factly. "Butter and jam in the fridge. Snap to it, wench. I know I said it before but those are *very* nice panties. The bra would have been a shame, though. A man likes a decent view over breakfast."

"Yessir," she smiled, feeling like singing.

Chapter 18

Shirley

Seeing Emma this happy is definitely a good thing.

I refused to ask any questions when I picked her up at Luc's, but the answer was written on her face.

She attacked her dissertation with awful music playing and I've been attempting to ignore it most of the day, while tackling some tedious translation.

By mid-afternoon, a document called 'Emma's masterpiece' appears in my inbox with a message saying, 'Over to you, head editor'. Apparently, I have a whole week to do it, and looking at the first couple of paragraphs it's going to need a few bits of punctuation-wrangling and sorting out in general. It's also interesting.

When Emma comes down to make tea, I tell her it looks fine. That gets me a huge hug, and an unwelcome rerun of the music from hell.

I get disturbed again later, before I've made much headway. Emma rushes downstairs, hugs me again, and tells me she has an interview on Wednesday in Lyon. I congratulate her and she beams.

I'm still in a weird place where I don't know what I'm feeling. Steve is still being careful, and not getting irritable when I burn a batch of whole-wheat bread or mix up a load of laundry and shrink a woollen sweater he loves. Tonight, I fail to appreciate a particularly fine Burgundy he's brought out of the cellar in the evening to go with a mediocre beef stroganoff that I dug out of the freezer, unwilling to make the effort to cook something fresh. I tell myself that the few containers in there are for unforeseen situations, and I think this qualifies.

Emma's cheerfulness saves the evening from disaster. So does Steve's snap decision to hit a source of fine wines next week, and Helen and Joe's invitation to go over on Sunday evening for a meal. Emma is invited too, after she gets back from the craft fair, but she says she needs to make inroads on a website for Luc and to do a bit more with the one for Olive Blue.

I can't sleep. Maybe I didn't have enough of the Burgundy.

After a while, I leave Steve snoring and get up.

Earplugs help usually. Having my own pillow rather than the one in the hotel should help too. Tonight, nothing works. I have too much going through my mind.

I sit at the table where I often work, stroking the richly-waxed old wood. If eight guests opt for my cooking one night, it can seat them all plus Steve and me.

Right now, I'd have trouble serving up baked beans on toast without burning both, let alone being a smiling, helpful hostess.

Idly, I turn my laptop on and bring up some mindless games. They don't like me either. By the time I've seen FAILED a dozen times, I close the window and give the cats a stroke. They always think it's a great idea to have company during the night, and probably expect me to conjure up some daylight or, failing that, some cat treats.

As I can't control daylight yet, I bring out the cat treats and I'm rewarded by two purring bodies flanking the laptop and one draped over a chair. One day, one of them is going to bung up the air vents and it'll overheat. Steve has warned me more than once.

If they do, then they do. I stroke them, remembering that somebody, somewhere, said that a cat's head was made to fit a human hand.

I let my mind wander to Mum, even though my logical side tells me that this isn't going to make me sleepy or ready to make another attempt at the conjugal nest.

My messenger bleeps suddenly, and it's Emma, a few metres upstairs.

Mum? Why aren't you in bed?

I could ask you the same question.

I was just chatting to somebody I know. Going to bed in a mo – still okay for Tweetie tomorrow, to go to the craft fair?

Of course. What time will you leave? And am I disturbing if you've got Luc online?

No, it wasn't him – it was Sophie, the girl who recommended me for the job in Lyon. He doesn't have a connection where he's staying, but I'm leaving about nine tomorrow. See you for breakfast before you go off to buy booze?

Deal, I type. This reminds me of Emma as a teenager, sending me messages from her room to avoid bringing up things she didn't want her dad to hear. Like whether she can go to a sleepover at friends or whether Dad was going to cough up for a moped (probably, but don't push your luck).

Her typing speed soon grew to match my own, but I think that's true of her entire net-crazy generation.

I think fondly of Steve pecking away laboriously at a keyboard and wonder if Luc's equally slow, considering how much he dislikes the whole thing. Probably not a good idea to ask in case it sounds negative.

You OK, Mum? Or just going to say you're fine, as always?

Not so fine, but I'm surviving. Don't worry about me.

But I do. Want me to come down and talk?

I think about that for a bit.

No, going back to bed in a minute or two.

Sure?

Certain. Emma? Don't ever let me get as critical as your gran.

Oh Mum, you wouldn't. And she honestly wasn't that bad.

If you say so. Can we change the subject?

Well, I do say so. And if you don't want to talk about Gran, I need some advice.

?

Jeans and sweater or skirt and heels for a craft exhibition?

LOL

Muuummmm stop trying to be geeky with all the netspeak.

Well I am actually laughing. Depends if he's a jeans and sweater bloke or a heels bloke or if he really couldn't care less. Note I am saying nothing about how he probably rather likes you in nothing at all.

MUM!!!!!

I wasn't born yesterday. And no, I am not going to ask awkward questions.

Good!!!!!

But, if you want an answer, the weather's supposed to be getting worse and worse. If you don't want to go down with a filthy cold, dress accordingly.

Good motherly advice.

A speciality.

Go to bed, Mum. Love you lots.

You too.

I click off the messenger tab and absently stroke a feline head again.

It could be time for a quick cigarette in the garage. Then I should look for flights to Morocco, which I should have done well before this.

There, that's better. Nothing like a blast of nicotine at one in the morning. I go back to the laptop.

We won't be going up to Sheffield now, so we could go away at Christmas, or New Year. But what will Emma be doing? Should I talk to her about it first?

Considering the wealth of craftsmen working with wood in Morocco, it might attract Luc, but should I be presumptuous? Would they rather be left on their own? Would they be embarrassed if we offered them the flights?

I click off the *Royal Air Maroc* site before I even start checking availabilities.

Now I've run out of things to do.

And then I sit, staring into space. Even the cats seem to think this is not a great opportunity after all and disappear, probably to take over my half of the bed.

I'm about to go back upstairs, knowing I'll probably toss and turn again when Steve appears, hair tousled and looking half asleep.

"Did I wake you? I'm sorry," I say miserably. I've tried to be quiet, but he probably saw the light on downstairs.

"Sort of, but doesn't matter." He sits down next to me and takes my hand.

"I honestly don't know how to help, Shirley, except to say it's all right to feel relieved, or angry, or whatever you like."

"If I could just decide what I do actually feel, that would be a start. I loathe myself, basically. I just never got through to her."

"It takes two," Steve says thoughtfully. "Always remember that. And you can't change it now so there's not much point in letting it get to you."

"More of that water off a duck's back you always mention at times like this?" I probably sound bitter. "How do you really move on, Steve? You always did."

He thinks about this a bit, and then delves in the bar and grabs two glasses.

"I think it's all about realising you can't win on every front. Sometimes people simply don't like each other much."

"I know. I know all about the times we've told Em we'll always love her but when she's a spoiled brat having a tantrum, we don't like her a lot."

"So, go with that. Somehow, for your mum, you rubbed her up the wrong way, and it was mutual. She had her reasons, and you just have to accept that you may never know why. It was the same with my dad."

"Are you trying to tell me she loved me?"

"That," Steve sighs, pouring me a generous measure of Armagnac, "you may never know but it's fair to say she must have done, in her own way. Just as in your own way, you at the very least respected her."

"For some things, yes. Others not so much." I take a most unladylike swig. "I'm sorry, Steve."

"Don't be. Just stop hating yourself. You're human. And you're a lovable human at that. Em and I think so, remember?"

"I know. That helps."

"Good. No more beating yourself up over your mum. You were good to her in your own way and you just took everything she said the wrong way."

"Maybe."

"Definitely. But that's how you are. Over-sensitive and inclined to find fault with yourself. I can live with that as long as you don't go completely off the rails."

"Like shrinking your sweater?" I grimace. "Burning the bread?"

"That's no big deal. But losing sleep and feeling worthless is wasting your battery, Shirley. We've got so much to look forward to, no? And for heaven's sake, think of Gillian and Clive. They're hardly a shining example of very much. One thing you can never say about us is that we're boring."

"You're right," I say firmly. "I mean, look at Emma? And everything's gone so well with the building. We'd never go on a tacky cruise or order processed cheese either."

"Exactly. Now drink up, Mrs Sandford. I have a secret recipe for helping you sleep."

"This?" I hold up the glass.

"Not quite. Think more on the lines of me showing you just how lovable you are."

"Good heavens," I feign amazement. "Are you intending to seduce me?"

"I am. Now, drink up and get up those stairs."

***

Emma

The hall was crowded, Emma noted with satisfaction. And a whole lot of people were stopping at Luc's stand.

She felt ridiculously proud of him every time somebody leafed through the prints, all on thick, luxurious paper and beautifully presented in transparent envelopes and displayed against dark backgrounds – meticulous, careful work. He'd made some prints for framing, and some greetings cards with simple, beautiful Christmas themes. There were packs of bookplates, too, with Provençal motifs. She ran a finger over one of the cards that he'd left out for people to pick up, and enjoyed the silky, rich feel of it.

Each print was signed. Luc's handwriting was attractive, but she would have swooned over his shopping lists. What he did need to do was slip a visiting card in with his website address, once he had one. She made a mental note. He'd need flyers, too.

The cash box was filling up nicely, and Luc wasn't getting much time to engrave even though he'd brought along a wood block and his magnifying glasses. He wasn't sure, he'd said, whether anybody would actually buy anything so it would be better than being bored. Modesty was another of his qualities. Even when he spoke to the visitors, he talked about the work, the processes involved, but never pushed them to buy.

She loved to see him work. Long fingers, total concentration. She'd pushed him to work at least a little so that people could watch him while she charmed the public.

Eventually, in the early afternoon, there was a lull and he looked up and stretched.

"Breather?"

"But you might miss a sale!"

"I might also miss a few kisses with a wonderful woman out in the park. And we need to eat – we can grab something at one of the food stalls."

"But what about –"

"I'll ask the lady at the next stand who does painting on silk."

They'd watched that stand for half an hour while the artist grabbed a sandwich. Emma had even managed to sell two scarves for her.

Carrying some respectable-looking sandwiches they went out into the courtyard. The exhibition and craft fair were in a dignified old building in Grignan, well down into the real Provençal part of the Drôme, and the public seemed not only enthusiastic but happy to spend their Euros. Christmas was only weeks away.

"It's going well," Luc said between mouthfuls. "The other people here seem all right as well. Better than the digs."

He'd already told her a little about that, but there hadn't been much time in between customers.

"It's fun," she said, meaning it.

"And you're the saleswoman of the century. Also, I love you."

Emma leaned over for a kiss. "Love you too. I have good news as well. Something I didn't tell you in the mail I sent you this morning or while we were in there, because I wanted to tell you face to face."

"Tell me?"

"Job interview in Lyon Wednesday, and they need somebody to start in the New Year."

"Fantastic!" That got her another long, sensual kiss. "I'm proud of you."

"I haven't got it yet. And I'm proud of what you do too."

"In the engraving department, or in the pleasures of the flesh department?"

"Both, silly," Emma said, smiling at him. "I keep thinking about that."

"So do I. All the time. Last night I was wondering whether to skip the dinner for exhibitors and the demonstration for schools tomorrow, and come home straight away tonight, once it's over."

"No." Emma was so vehement she spilled some sauce out of her sandwich. "Much as I want to be back in your place and carry on where we left off –"

"I know. You're right. There are lots of contacts here. And I quite like the idea of letting schoolkids come and ask questions about different crafts."

"It's a good idea," she nodded. "And I'm glad you signed up."

"I should be back by mid-afternoon. You have mustard on your chin."

Emma swiped at it with a napkin, and he batted her hands away, using his own.

"You really are a messy eater."

"I'm messy in general. I do try. Mess just sort of happens around me."

"I can live with that, Emma."

Emma looked at him, feeling happiness starting to bubble over again.

"You can?"

"I can. We'll figure all sorts of things out. But only once I've had my wicked way with you again when I get back. Bring your toothbrush this time. That dissertation's finished, right?"

"Right."

"Good. I'm taking a week off building work. I have to do the logo for your parents, but I also need some time with you. So, you can work on the website while I'm doing that. We can do more personal anatomical research as well, as I think you put it."

"Oh, we can," Emma said, her mind going back to the feel of him again. "Research is a good thing. I think I can handle that. Except for Wednesday in Lyon."

"Approved. And before Christmas we'll go up there together."

"For me to go flat hunting? What if I don't get the job?"

"We'll discuss that Monday. Or Tuesday. Or when you find out if you get it. But the idea is mainly to meet my parents. I emailed them today to say we would be coming up. Can you handle that?"

"I think so," Emma said. "What if they don't like me?"

"You can be very stupid for an intelligent, sexy woman. Of course they'll like you. My mum says she likes you already, considering you are apparently having a good influence on me."

Emma took a final bite of the sandwich. "I'll take your word for it. Time to go back and get famous, Mr Theyroux."

"Another kiss first, please. To tide me over for twenty-four hours. Less if I'm lucky."

Emma held her face up and revelled in it. So did he, she realised, holding him close and feeling his arousal.

"Do they have cold showers in the exhibition hall?" she gasped. "Or I'll be searching for a quiet storeroom with a lock on the door."

"God, I wish. But soon, my darling."

"Maybe I should get to your place before you get home and wait there with not many clothes on?"

"Don't," he half-groaned. "Or maybe do."

"As long as you keep your mind on the road, I just might, but let me know when you'll arrive?"

They held hands as they went back inside, and she wondered if life could get any better than this.

***

Driving, Emma thought, was a better way to let your mind roam free than ironing, whatever her mother thought. She pushed a CD in. On the drive down, it had been Elton John ballads and Rod Stewart. This time, she chose Mozart – her mother said that the flute and harp concerto was great driving music.

The country roads of the Drôme weren't without their tricky parts, but nothing quite like driving in Lyon, where she'd learned. For the couple of years that she'd had a car there, she'd had to learn to be aggressive, pushy. It was different further south. At first, she'd hated the country roads and their elderly drivers in clapped-out cars, the tractors, the narrow lanes and ditches, but it wasn't so bad once you got used to it.

Had she got used to country life since she'd been in Crest?

Emma wasn't sure. Partly. It was pretty, although she'd never gone into raptures about scenery like her parents did. Did you grow into that?

Maybe, she thought. She'd not missed the overcrowded tube, the constant traffic, and she hadn't even missed the shopping or the funky restaurants that much.

No, that wasn't true. The shopping, she really did miss, although it had been good for her bank balance. If she ended up back in Lyon, there would be plenty of opportunities.

And a regular supply of sushi. She didn't know if Luc liked it. There were still hundreds – thousands – of things to find out about him, and vice versa.

Like when he realised just how messy she was. His place had always been tidy. Could she reform on that score? She'd made an effort with Rainer, on and off, but he'd been untidy as well, at least until he'd found a mistress. Had Luc made an effort with his flat to impress her?

The whole tidy or messy business was one of the things to work out. Like not pushing Luc too hard about the website and social media. Or being too bossy.

Was she really bossy? Had she been too pushy with the visitors to the exhibition?

She didn't think so. Just enthusiastic about Luc's work, and it had certainly paid off. If you believed in a product, it showed.

For a brief second, she remembered Reg Small and his coat hangers, and laughed.

Emma negotiated a crossroads and wondered if she'd taken the right turning. She pulled over for a minute, wishing her mother at least had a support for a phone so she could prop the GPS up where she could see it.

Yes, that was the right direction. The Mozart was pretty cool as well. Probably more suited to mountains, or really apocalyptic weather, considering it was pretty majestic in parts, but not bad.

It started to rain and she turned the wipers on. The regular swish felt a bit like yes – no, yes – no.

Directive, that vicar in Sheffield had called it. What a lovely word, and much better sounding than bossy. That was a word you could even use in an interview.

All things considered, she definitely had a directive streak. And a stubborn one. A bit like her gran, as she'd said so spontaneously at the funeral. Her thoughts often strayed back to Sheffield and that remarkable conversation they'd had.

On the other hand, Luc wasn't exactly the type to let people walk over him either.

Good. They'd have to talk about things like that, but without it getting into a shouting match like it had done all too often with Rainer.

She could even think about Rainer without feeling humiliated or angry now, which was quite an achievement. He'd had his moments, except he was always trying to change her, and neither of them had been prepared to budge an inch.

That, she decided in a nutshell, was probably why it hadn't worked. She hadn't fit into his mould, and he hadn't made much of an effort to make any compromises either.

She turned the windscreen wipers onto fast, watching them thud out the four syllables and nodding along to Mozart.

Compromises, compromises.

That was the secret, and with Luc, she thought she was ready to make them. With him, she would make a huge effort to round off a few corners.

She'd email Luc tonight with a few thoughts, so he could read it when he opened up tomorrow.

She rolled up at her parents' house to a particularly impressive crescendo. She'd have to put that CD onto Spotify, and possibly teach Luc how to use that.

***

Shirley

"Kids," Joe sighs. Our meals together often tend to have this as a theme. "Well, kids and houses. Just when you think everything's going well, they turn around and surprise you."

Steve and I nod sympathetically. Their daughter and family are hesitating about coming over at Christmas because they have so few days off, and called to say so just before we arrived. I can tell Helen's upset – she usually half kills herself with all the preparations but wouldn't dream of missing a single element of it. Her son and his wife are probably not coming either, but planning to go away somewhere exotic.

"You decided what you're doing?" Helen asks me.

"No idea. We may need to see what Emma wants to do, but we were considering Morocco. Maybe with her and Luc, maybe not. It's early days with them."

I've already given them a short run-down of the latest developments, trying not to sound too mother-hen'ish. Now I need to not sound too enthusiastic about Marrakesh.

"Sounds nice," Helen says wistfully. "This damned weather is getting me down."

"I'll soon run out of buckets – the sun lounge roof's leaking," Jim sighs. Then their phone rings, and Helen goes off to answer it.

She rushes back a few minutes later, pink and breathless.

"They're coming anyway. All of them. They've even booked. It'll be short, but they said they couldn't imagine not being here."

I cheer. Helen sits down and grabs her glass.

"Kids," Joe says again, but he's grinning too. "I tell you, they just about kill you. Just wait until you have to start with Santa again, including being woken up by grandchildren at four in the morning on Christmas day."

"I bet you love it," I say. "Come on, Joe, admit it."

"He does," Helen nods. "Every last minute of it. Right, let's eat."

We do, and chat amicably as always. Helen collars me as Joe steers Steve into the sun lounge for him to smoke a pipe and probably to grumble more about the leaking roof, plus the fact that every firm he's called to fix it is booked up solid.

"Dessert can wait a bit," Helen says. "They'll be doing man-gossip for a while, not that they'd ever admit it."

"Perish the thought," I agree.

"So, how are things really? Was Sheffield a nightmare?"

"In some ways," I say thoughtfully. "And I still feel a bit odd, but I'm doing fine on the whole. Steve's been great, and Emma's in seventh heaven – it's infectious."

"Good. It's not a crime to feel relieved, Shirley. Or mixed up. We're only human, you know."

"I know. I'm just doing a lot of thinking about why we never got on, Mum and I."

"It happens. I'm never, ever going to be a fan of my son's wife. Hard, but true. I do my best with her but there's just no connection. You just can't make yourself love people, even if they are your own kids or whoever they end up with."

Very true, I think. If Emma had still been with Rainer, I suspect it would have been a bit like that.

"What is it about her? Your daughter-in-law?"

"I can't even tell you. Something all deep and Freudian about her stealing my first-born from me?" she says wryly. "She's pleasant enough, and relatively normal. I just can't talk to her, and it's frustrating. She's a lot less weird than some of the girls he used to bring home."

I chuckle, and describe a few of Emma's past conquests, and the one with pierced eyebrows, shaved head and no ambition in particular. Helen laughs when I tell her about him and how Steve glowered menacingly everytime he saw him.

"Seriously though, Shirley," she says, "your mother may have been difficult but it's over now. Time to get on and enjoy life."

"Maybe you're right. I'm even trying to accept it was probably partly my fault as well – as time went on, I couldn't see anything positive about her."

"That's human as well. Self-defence. She really did pull you down, but you always tried to see it coming and where you'd need to justify yourself, and it left you worn out. I could see that, just in the space of one evening."

Helen can be very perceptive. She's right, I admit. I add that Steve says I should move on and that I feel I owe it to him.

"No, Shirley," she says firmly. "You owe it to yourself. Letting it hang over you any longer isn't going to achieve anything. Think about the good things ahead."

"I do. Often. I was thinking of grandchildren today, as a matter of fact."

"Probably not wise to mention that to Emma quite yet," she says. "Although you do every time you see me."

"You're just a good advert for it. I wasn't thinking of dropping hints to her, don't worry, but it's a nice thought."

"You mean including being woken up in the wee small hours at Christmas?"

"That too," I chuckle. "And lots of other things."

"It's fun," Helen nods happily. "Keep me posted on her job interview? And on things with Luc?"

"Count on it. Also, about your roof? I'll ask Luc to have a word with the masonry firm – see if they have some free time, or if he can persuade them to find some."

"Now that would be a miracle. And gosh, I'll need to get going on my candied fruits. And mincemeat."

"There's a thought," I say cheerfully. "Considering the amount Luc can eat, I'd better get going myself."

We grab the dessert, and I think about a turkey and trying to hunt down some fresh cranberries. Maybe we should try to have a really family Christmas. Could I invite Luc's parents down? Is that being way too presumptuous?

I'll have to talk to Steve. And to Emma, about their plans.

As we drive home, Steve shoots me a quizzical look.

"Lost in thought?"

"Christmas cake or pudding?" I say, because that's the last place my mind flitted to.

"Silly question," he snorts. "Both. And mince pies. And we should look at flights to Morocco for the New Year, maybe? Try and do Christmas with the kids?"

"Stop reading my mind."

"I've had a lot of practice."

He has a point.

"A white Christmas would be nice," I muse.

"You mean we move south to escape snow and now you want some? You do remember a couple of years back when everything ground to a standstill because the French don't know what snow tyres even are?"

I do. It doesn't snow often here but it's chaos when it does. After so many years in Switzerland, where it snowed often but road clearing worked, and where people knew how to drive in it, it had been quite a revelation.

"A little romance never goes amiss, though," I say. "Just think of grandchildren, and snowmen. And sledging?"

"Takes nine months, remember. A bit late for this year. And let them have some fun first?" Steve's smiling too, though.

I chuckle happily and watch the rain. It seems to have rained forever, even though it's only been a day. According to the forecast, there's more to come.

***

I feel better this morning. Not back to fighting speed, but definitely better. I tell myself that Steve's right and it's time to move on. Things are going smoothly with the B&B preparations, Emma's happy, and I should be in full-on positive mode.

I'm trying. I produce a superb plaited loaf for today's breakfast and listen to Emma's account of her day in Grignan yesterday and her plans to get Luc on the map. She's up early, but says she's got lots to do on his website and social media presence. Sounds familiar.

So, what's missing? Why aren't I completely back on track?

I'm in a hurry now. I want the place to be finished, the website up, the bookings in. I even want Emma to get back to her career and settled with Luc – not that I mind her being here, and right now it's great, but it's time she got on with her life. And it would be a relief not to have every available surface filled with whatever she puts on it and then forgets.

Why isn't she tidy? My mother was and I always have been, apart from a first crazy year at university when I lived in a small room that looked as though a bomb had hit it. After a while, though, I'd got sick of it and weeded out the posters, the general clutter, and felt much better.

It's not my problem, I decide. Tidiness isn't that important in the great scheme of things. It's a bit like Steve and colours – it's not on his list of priorities to have the right shade of blue. Neither is putting things away when he's used them. Emma obviously inherited his messy gene as well as his matter-of-fact gene, but he and I have found a cruising speed somewhere in the middle. It works. Emma and Luc will have to find their own way ahead.

I'm feeling optimistic all round. This is a good thing.

I've offered to take dessert to Helen's, so I'd better get moving. I mix lemon curd with Greek yoghurt and set off the ice cream maker. Some brandy snaps might be nice to go with that, so I start on those.

Emma turns up as if by magic.

"Biscuits!"

"To take to Helen's, but I could make a few extra to take to that man of yours tomorrow?"

"Please. Can you show me how to make them? I need a break."

We work together for a while. I show her how to curl the oven-warm biscuits over a rolling pin, and she soon gets the hang of it, and eats those that break plus a few more.

"Amazing, Mum. I need to improve on biscuits."

"Can't think why."

"I'll have to be careful about my weight, though."

"Sex uses up two hundred calories a time," I say casually, putting another tray of biscuits in.

"I'll be fine then," she giggles. "Honestly, Mum, you sounded just like Gran there."

"Like *Gran?*"

"Sorry, I didn't mean to bring the subject up, but she could really be pretty forthright."

"If you say so," I answer her stiffly, and she sighs.

"I think it was just easier for me, being one generation removed. I'll stop bothering you now – better get on."

She picks up two still-warm brandy snaps and rushes upstairs again.

Remembering my conversation with Helen, I start wondering about being a grandmother again. I used to do that when Emma was with Rainer but not that often. Somehow, I couldn't ever see it happening, but with Luc… that has crept into my thoughts a time or two these last couple of days. Maybe it's wishful thinking.

Stop it, I tell myself. They're not there yet, but they would be an interesting combination; a bit like Steve and I, except it's Luc the arty one and Emma who is the down to earth type. He brings out the best in her, whereas Rainer made her constantly tense.

I nearly burn the last tray of biscuits, imagining curly-haired moppets and a swing over by the orchard.

Chapter 19

Emma

Monday morning dawned grey, and it was still raining. It didn't dampen Emma's mood.

She'd had a couple of rapid emails from Luc at the exhibition, and after his closing dinner there. One to say it was going well but he missed his chief saleswoman (and loved her) and another in reply to her long, rambling one that she'd written when she reached Crest. She'd talked about rounding edges and messiness, about being directive, about their lovemaking, and about anything else that came into her head. Brandy snaps, flyers for his work. She'd also told him again how happy she was that he was open to using the internet despite his fears.

The answer to that had made her smile and made her feel a bit tearful too.

Dear Ms Directive (or should that be bossy?)

Would you please stop worrying? Plenty of time to sort all that out and nothing we can't overcome – unless you post naked photos of me on the web (joke). Also, I love you and have to run – need to keep charming the shoppers, having had a good teacher. Good thing they can't read my mind though as many thoughts definitely not fit for public knowledge but make me v. happy.

She'd replied simply. *I don't want photos of you naked, Cher Monsieur. Prefer the real thing.*

And before long she would have the real thing, she thought to herself, idly wondering what to wear for the interview, and whether she could charm the company in Lyon. The job would have to be interesting – moving back to Lyon seemed like a plan, but not just for any job.

What would happen if she had to travel a lot? Would it complicate matters with Luc?

Her career was part of her, just as his two professions suited him. He'd talked about the pleasure of working on the 'big stuff', on a construction site, as well as the slow, meticulous engraving. The physical side of building work kept him fit, which was no bad thing.

The doorbell rang and she wondered if it was the dress she'd ordered, or just somebody delivering something for the new rooms. The mattresses were due.

Humming, she pulled on an old tracksuit.

"Emma? Could you come downstairs, please?"

Good. It must be the dress. She skipped down the stairs and then froze in her tracks.

Rainer was standing in the kitchen.

"What the hell are you doing here?"

"Hello, Emma," he said, with a half-smile.

She stared at him, taking in Rainer in smart-casual mode: Burberry's raincoat, Lacoste sweater.

"Terrible weather." *Vezzer.*

"I presume you didn't come to talk about the *vezzer.* " Emma mimicked him unkindly, but she couldn't help it.

"Can we talk?"

"I'll go," her mother said, obviously not sure what to think. "I'll just be in the office."

"We won't be long," Emma said tightly. "I don't think we have much to say."

Her mother disappeared anyway, looking worried.

Emma continued looking at him, trying to decide what this was all about. His face was impassive – his banker's face.

She pointed to one of the chairs around the dining table, hoping he'd sit down. She had no intention of doing the same, but being the one standing up always gave you an advantage.

He didn't move, but rain dripped off his coat.

"So, talk."

"Emma, please. I came all this way."

"So? I didn't ask you to come."

"I know." Rainer spread his hands out in a gesture of helplessness. "But I had to. And you are still very special, and beautiful when you're angry."

"What do you expect me to do? Greet you with open arms?"

"Of course not. I do know you are angry with me."

Was that an attempt at penitence? Emma found it hard to decide. His features seemed to be suggesting that, but she wasn't sure it was genuine.

"Shall we sit down?"

"Go ahead," she said tightly. "Not that it makes any difference."

"Let me explain," he said, calmly. Was that how he talked to people at the bank? All Swiss restraint, neutral expression.

"Rainer there really isn't –"

"There is," he insisted, but with only a slight extra emphasis on the words. "First, it is over with Alex."

"Really? She ditched you?"

"It was a mutual decision. For the best. I told you in London it was a mistake, and that I was sorry. Besides, Alex is staying in London and I am moving to Zurich."

"So, she'll need another toy boy?"

"Please, Emma. It is not like that. I spoke to my parents about you leaving – my father told me I was a fool."

"Good for him. I like your father, Rainer."

She wondered if he'd told his father the whole story, or just that they'd split up.

Rainer nodded. "You do, I know. I asked him for a favour. He has many contacts, as you know."

"And he got you the job in Zurich," Emma said wearily.

"No." Rainer looked offended. "It is a promotion."

"A reward for services rendered?" That was mean, but he deserved it.

He ignored that, and stood, up. Started pacing.

"My father has friends at Saatchi and Saatchi in Geneva. They are prepared to hire you on his recommendation. You know how much he likes you."

Emma felt her eyebrows raise. If there were household names in marketing, that was at the top of the list.

"A junior product manager to begin with, but you are brilliant. Very soon you would get ahead."

Her head spun. A job like that, handed to her on a plate?

"And why would he do that?" Good sense kicked in. There had to be a catch.

"There are trains every hour from Geneva to Zurich," Rainer said, attempting a smile. "I was hoping we could see us a little. I won't give you up easily, Emma."

See us a little? Why had he never got the hang of 'each other'? That was Emma's first thought, followed in a split second by the fact his father was trying to buy her for his son. Was that it?

"And that's the condition? I never thought he liked me quite that much. And what if I don't want to see you?"

"That is not the condition, Emma. But I would like us to be friends."

She looked at him. Studied the even features, remembered him groggy from sleep, or those first few, giddy months when London had seemed so exciting, so *foreign*. Was this a gesture of apology?

"I don't know, Rainer. I honestly don't know if we can be friends."

"That is up to you. I had hoped it was possible. I am just asking you to give it a try."

Emma was silent for a moment, mentally calculating how long it would take her from Geneva to Crest – and Luc – at weekends. Would it be possible? Or they could meet in Lyon, sometimes, at Luc's parents? No way was she interested in going to Zurich, or to give Rainer another chance, but wouldn't Luc be proud of her if she landed an opportunity like that?

Her mind worked fast. Did she want another long-distance relationship, like hers had been with Rainer at first? Lyon had seemed so perfect, and so close to Crest but Geneva couldn't be more than three hours, door to door, could it?

The temptation was massive. There was absolutely no guarantee she'd get the job in Lyon. And even a year in Geneva, with that company on her CV would be a wonderful reference.

"I think… I think I would have to go to Geneva and talk to them. And as for us being friends, not immediately."

Probably not ever, she thought, but why slam doors if this was really as stupendous as it sounded.

Rainer smiled. It was a strange sort of smile, though.

"It could be arranged. There is one small thing I need to ask you in return, however."

So, there was a condition after all. How naïve, how stupid of her to think there would be no strings attached. Her mind raced. What in heaven's name could it be?

"Those emails. The ones you stole from my tablet."

Emma gaped at him, her heart suddenly beating wildly. So that was it.

"All I want, Emma, is your promise that you will delete the copies and never use them against me. Or ever mention what happened with Alex. It is such a small thing to ask. A very small thing."

"You're scared somebody will find out your little secret, is that it? Like your father, or his friends? The bank?"

His face hardened. Her fists clenched.

"You are despicable, Rainer. You know that? All you care about is your reputation. Not about me. This was never about helping me, was it? How did you get your father to do all this? Did you lie to him, as well? Tell him you still cared about me?"

"Emma – please. I do still care. It's just…"

"No, you don't care. You actually thought I would blackmail you? Or Alex?"

Suddenly, she realised she had never answered his question about whether she'd copied anything off his tablet, but he'd obviously made his own mind up about that.

"When you are angry, Emma, you do crazy things." The half-smile was back. It was probably meant to appease, she thought, her fury increasing by the second.

"You never did know me, did you Rainer? Not ever. Because everything was all about *you*. What *you* wanted. *Your* friends. *Your* reputation. Making an impression on your family."

"That is not true, Emma."

"Bullshit." Emma shook her head. "You just wanted it all, didn't you? A girlfriend, your job – it wasn't enough. You wanted a housemaid and a bit on the side as well. You even wanted to tell me how to dress."

"It was for your sake – to show off your elegance."

Oh, please.

"Bullshit again. I don't like being bullied, and I respect people who are honest. People who don't use other people."

"We can all make mistakes."

"Yes, we can. But you just made the biggest one of all, thinking you could blackmail *me*."

"It is a fair exchange, no? I would say more than fair."

"It is not. Because once the water is under the bridge a bit, or if I don't accept to see you again, your dad gets me fired? Is that it?"

"How could you think that?"

"Because it's how you are, Rainer. You plan everything. You always like to have contingency solutions – you once told me that was the secret of getting ahead. Damage control, right?"

"Oh, it is," he nodded. "As is a reputation. It is so easy to destroy one."

"Is that a threat? I refuse the job and you do what? I have nothing to be ashamed of."

Rainer looked at her coldly.

"You have never apologised, nor promised not to use those emails against me. I asked you in London. I would have asked you again, but you have been blocking me from your phone, your mail."

"You are just unbelievable," she snapped. "So, you reached the conclusion I was out to destroy your precious life – you do a good enough job of that on your own. Sloppy over the corkscrew. Even sloppier to screw your boss in our apartment. You deserve all you get."

"I did think you were an honest person, Emma. Are you now threatening *me*?"

"Oh, for fuck's sake, Rainer," Emma signed, more disgusted by the second. "Just go away. Tell your dad to stuff the job. No, in fact don't – I liked him. Tell him thanks, but no thanks."

"You are making a very big mistake, Emma. I had hoped you would be pleased, and willing to see things reasonably." *Wery. Villing.*

How in the name of God had she ever thought she cared about this excuse for a human being?

"I am seeing things reasonably. Yourself included."

"You have somebody else," Rainer said, almost casually, after a slight pause. "And I don't like to lose, Emma."

"You lost the right to ask me questions when we split up."

"It wasn't a question." Rainer got to his feet. "And you should think about some damage control of your own."

"And what is that supposed to mean?"

"It means just that. Is that your final word, about the job?"

"We aren't playing 'Who wants to be a millionaire', are we? But yes. I think you can find the way out."

Without another word, Rainer got to his feet.

***

"I don't like it," her father said, once they'd heard Emma describe the conversation. She was still shaking slightly, but slowly getting a grip.

"He's out of his mind," her mother said firmly. "Barking, if you ask me."

"I can only hope so. But, Emma, the most important thing of all is whether you did copy those emails."

"I know that, Dad. And no, I didn't. But he seems to have got it into his head that I must have done – judging me on his own standards. I should have told him back in London that I didn't, but I was too angry. I thought I'd make him worry a bit. And you know," she shook her head sadly, "even if I did copy them, I would have deleted them by now."

"It's also very hard to prove you didn't do something in this particular case."

"I know *that* as well, Mum. I should never have told him I even saw them. I was just so angry."

Her father nodded. "Well, I hope it's all just empty talk, but watch your step, Emma. Never say anything about Rainer in public. Or even too much about yourself."

"Dad, *please.* If anybody's careful about what they put on the internet, it's me. I haven't been on Twitter for weeks. Or Facebook. And considering the way Luc feels about gossip, if I ever use them again it'd be for work."

"Good. I hardly think he's the type to get sucked into social media."

No, Emma shook her head, he wasn't. When she looked back at all the hype with Rainer over who was on whose list of friends, it made her shudder. She'd been included on Alex's private Twitter but for what purpose? So that Alex could look at hers.

"Now and then I used to tweet about stuff I did with Rainer, but nothing tacky," Emma said, certain of it. "No photos of us, ever. And no, he doesn't have incriminating photos of me, either."

"So, it was just dented pride," her mother said with obvious relief. "And as you said, he doesn't like to lose."

"He has an ego the size of Florida," Emma said tightly. "And his dad must have way more clout than I ever realised."

"That, or his dad owes him a favour. Maybe Rainer knows something about his dad that he doesn't want made public?"

"Oh please, Shirley – let's not get into conspiracy theories," her father frowned. "We'll never know, and do we really want to?"

"We might. What if he writes filthy comments about the B&B without visiting it?"

Emma knew that this was one of her mother's concerns in general, even without Rainer on the scene, so she squeezed her arm. "Not that likely, and people get wise to really nasty Trip Advisor reports from a person with a single review to their name. It's obviously just spite, or something personal. Or the competition."

"I hope so."

"I think the best thing to do is just let him go away and get it out of his system. But I think at some point you have to tell him you never copied those mails. Just a one-line email. And maybe sooner rather than later."

"Maybe," Emma signed. "For a minute or two I wished I had copied them. It even crossed my mind, but I didn't see the point. I'd have just agonised over them, quite apart from it being wrong. I shouldn't have even looked."

"I can understand why you did, love."

"Thanks, Mum. All I can say is good riddance."

Emma sighed, feeling a little more settled, but it didn't stop her wondering again about the comment about her having somebody else, and it not being a question.

He couldn't possibly know anything about Luc, but she'd make sure Luc had a few lectures on internet safety.

"Good God, listen to that wind," her father said, glancing outside. "They've forecast storms, as well. And to think your mum was fancying snow – this could be a blizzard and a half if it was cold enough. What time's Luc due?"

"Sometime this afternoon. He'll let me know and I'll go down to his place and meet him."

"That'll do you good," her mother nodded. "Steve, we should go and pull the garden chairs in before they get blown away. I think there's already one fallen over by the deck."

"Is that the royal we? But yes, going, love. As this is comfort food weather, what's for lunch?"

"Heavens yes – that bloody idiot threw all my planning off. I'll make some veggie soup and ham sandwiches. Soup will take a while unless you want the packet variety, but it's only just after eleven. If by any chance Luc gets in early, I'll put some in a thermos – he might be glad of it."

"You're brilliant," Emma said. "And no, Mum, we do not want blizzards. This is quite bad enough. I thought you came here for the sun?"

"Exactly what your dad said yesterday at Helen's. This is unusual for here. I thought the climate was supposed to be getting hotter and drier?"

Steve Sandford snorted as he went outside.

"Fluctuations, Mum. It's all about gradually increasing extremes. Just be glad you don't live in an earthquake zone."

"Gee thanks."

"And thanks for listening. What on earth did I see in that jerk anyway? I must be a lousy judge of character."

"I don't think so, but if you were, you're improving. Vastly. Luc is a completely different cup of tea."

"And not a tattoo or piercing in sight. Or even out of sight," Emma giggled suddenly.

"That is what they call TMI on the net, isn't it? Too much information?"

"Full marks, Mum. And don't go all embarrassed on me. You know how nosy you get. I'm just telling you, in a nice daughterly way that things are going well on every single front – including the famous *you know,* and would you stop blushing?"

"I would never have asked. Credit me with that much tact."

"I know you wouldn't. I do love you, Mum."

"You too, Emma. Now go and get peeling vegetables. And you might want to take note of how to do this."

Emma saluted smartly and went off to the kitchen.

***

Shirley

Emma keeps looking at the clock and checking her email, and finally, just after lunch, she heaves a sigh of relief.

"He's setting off in a few minutes. The weather's really lousy down there but he'll call me when he gets near to home."

She stares out the window and so do I. The sky is an unbroken dark grey and the rain isn't letting up. I expect she's worrying about him driving, which is all too familiar to me. When Steve used to be late, long before mobile phones were around, I did the same, and particularly in bad weather. Even when he did have a mobile, I didn't worry much less, because half the time he forgot to turn it on.

I decide it's a woman thing, all this senseless worrying about men and arrival times, and head off to the cellar to bring a bottle of wine upstairs.

When I open the door to Steve's pride and joy, I suck in a deep breath and yell for him. It's ankle deep in water, and a couple of centimetres below the wine on the lowest racks.

Steve lets out a few expletives. We had a drain put in there when the building work was being done, so why the hell isn't the water going down it?

A few minutes later, in his rubber boots, Steve wades in, locates the drain cover and sighs.

"It must be blocked – can you and Emma move some of this wine out into the main cellar while I go and look at the other end? Maybe there's a stone in the way."

I remember that the end of the pipe is out near the fruit trees. He'll get soaked.

Steve rushes out, and I grab my own rubber boots.

"Emma, you stand there, and I'll pass the bottles to you."

I'm not certain, but I think the water's rising. I really don't like this. The wine cellar floor is a foot below the level of the cellar, which also houses a big freezer and all kinds of pipes and tubes and wiring.

I grab armfuls of bottles near floor level and realise I'm right. The water's virtually touching them now.

We clear several dozen bottles by the time Steve comes back, not happy. There's a dribble of water coming out of the pipe near the bottom of the garden, but not much. So, where's the damned water coming from?

Steve grabs the big yellow pressure washer, which has a drain de-blocking head on it, and connects it up rapidly as Emma and I start on another level of bottles.

He works quickly, and the hose starts making its way down the drain. I hold my breath. It snakes its way along and doesn't seem to encounter any obstacles, but there isn't any sign of the water level dropping either. Or is there?

No, it's not dropping. I think it's higher still.

Steve lets out even more expletives. Judging by the length of the hose now inside the drain, it's definitely reached the outflow.

"What now?" I ask, still passing bottles.

"The old owners left a gizmo for draining cellars," Steve says. "Let's at least try and get some of the water out and see if we have a leak from outside."

We find the gizmo in question, and I grumble bitterly that maybe the old owners had been through this, particularly if they had what I discover is called a 'cellar emptier'.

By the time we get it in place and shove the outflow hose outside the kitchen door, I'm wet and muddy, and there's now thunder and lightning. My heart is hammering. It looks cataclysmic out there.

"Welcome to France," Steve says, throwing the switch. Water starts to stream out of the hose immediately, and I dash back inside. We all stand there watching the level go down slowly, very slowly.

"Even if we empty it, if there's a leak in the foundations somewhere…" Steve says grimly.

"Cheer me up, why don't you."

There isn't much point moving more bottles. If the water rises again, it'll spill over into the main cellar before it reaches more wine. I'm more worried about short circuits than anything else, and I think Steve is too. I'm also terrified that there's a major structural issue with the house.

So much for thinking all the building work went like a dream.

Gradually, the level sinks a fraction more, but it's taking forever. The wine cellar isn't huge, so why isn't it going faster?

"If we can drain it out," Steve says, "and see where the water's coming in, we can try and block it up with something."

"Like what? I don't have any sandbags on hand."

"I probably have a sack of sand left over from the building work. I'll go and get it."

Steve rushes out, and there's a massive peal of thunder. And the lights go out.

"Fuck," Emma and I say in unison.

Emma – to my astonishment – hauls out her mobile phone and taps it, and a beam of light shows us the door in the pitch black.

"Torch app," she says. "Knew it would come in handy one day."

With something resembling calm, I grab a couple of normal torches, give one to her, and go upstairs again. Steve's dragging a sack of sand towards us, rain streaming off him.

"Now what?" I say as we troop back downstairs.

"Water's rising again," Emma says calmly. "I'm going to call the fire brigade."

"Do it," Steve says, dragging the sack across the kitchen tiles and down the cellar steps.

Emma lets out a whoop after a few minutes.

"They're on their way right now. Shall we thank our lucky stars that all of Crest doesn't have flooded cellars yet and we're on a waiting list?"

"Right," I say. "Steve, out of those wet clothes or you'll catch your death. Just dump the wet ones over by the washing machine."

I dash upstairs, trailing mud as I go, even though I've pulled the rubber boots off. Grabbing some old sweat pants and a sweater, I thrust those at Steve, together with a big towel.

Then we wait. I mutter about it taking forever and Emma tells me it's only been five minutes and that they'll be here any second.

And they are. Never have I been so glad to see flashing lights coming up the hill. In the meantime, I've found a raincoat of my own, as has Emma, and we raise the big garage door to let them in the fastest route possible.

There are three of them, and they're devastatingly efficient. Their own cellar-emptying pump is the big brother of ours, and it's connected to a massive hose.

This time, the water level starts to go down rapidly, as Steve explains his concerns about a leak.

Bit by bit, and thanks to the firemen's powerful torches, we start scanning the walls.

"There," one of them says. "There's water coming in through what looks like an aeration hole, near floor level but there's not that much, and the drain should evacuate it."

"It should," Steve frowns, and they frown too, because although a lot of the water is gone, when they switch off the machine for a second, we can see it coming up through the drain.

"Something's filling up the drain," I say stupidly. You don't say, Shirley.

"Where's your down pipe?"

"Outside," I say even more stupidly. That gets me one of those 'women' grunts from Steve, who says he'll show them. I pass him my coat, and they all head outside.

Again, it feels like we're waiting forever, and then Emma points.

"No more water coming up the drain. Or through the aeration hole."

I'm not quite ready to drink champagne yet, but I stand by the kitchen door to see what's happening.

A lot of male self-congratulation and back-slapping is going on. Steve beckons the guys inside, and they all look pleased with themselves. They're also spreading mud over the floor and apologising profusely about it. I shake my head that they shouldn't worry.

"You're not going to believe this," Steve says.

One of the firemen nods cheerfully and explains. The chair that flew off the deck hit the cap of the aeration hole, and some rain was coming through that. The main culprit, though, was the down pipe. The chair falling over on the terrace had dislodged the joint, so all the water coming off the roof – and there was a lot of it – was streaming not into the outside drain, but down the one into the cellar.

Or something like that. It's not the French language I don't understand, even with the gently southern *drômois* accent, but the intricacies of plumbing. From what I gather, the *stupide* builders put some sort of a *stupide* pipe in with a bend where there shouldn't be one, or at the wrong angle, so the water was flowing in the wrong direction.

"So," the tallest of the firemen says, "You just need a *machin* for the pipe with a *truc* to connect it."

I expect Steve will understand what the 'whatsits' in question are, because he's nodding.

The main thing is that the problem is provisionally fixed, and short of more flying chairs it should hold until Steve hits the DIY store and fixes it properly.

Steve continues in DIY-speak for a few seconds about the tubes and they nod approvingly.

"So," I say, relief sinking in. "Let me pay you. And can I offer you a drink? Not that I can offer you anything hot, but –"

Non, non, they have to get back – more people are starting to call – but there's no charge either. With luck, the power will be back before long. Or not.

I blink. No charge?

They explain patiently that the fire services are all in the deal with the local taxes. I don't think even Steve knew that, but I did know they're mainly volunteers.

"But," the youngest of the three pipes up – he looks about sixteen, "You do buy our calendars, right?"

Well yes, we do, I assure him. They come around once a year, near Christmas, and flog them – I think it's used to train up recruits, or for their parties. Whatever it is, they deserve it.

I hope none of this lot are among those I teased last year that I'd give them twice as much if they did one with good-looking firemen without the top half of their uniforms rather than pictures of their vehicles and equipment.

"Oh, I thought I'd seen you before," says the middle one of the three. I think I recognise him, too, despite the heavy gear. "And no, still no exciting calendars this year. Sorry."

I chuckle anyway and promise them a generous donation when they roll up with them, naked torsos or not. Emma, arriving on the scene, rolls her eyes at me. I expect she's put two and two together as usual.

So off they go, each of them hugging a bottle that Steve dashes back to fetch from those lined up on the cellar floor. That goes down well. The mud track through the kitchen and down to the cellar is a sight to behold. So is the trail from the sack of sand, which has split open and is adding to the effect.

They drive off, and I realise it isn't raining as much. Steve slings an arm around both myself and Emma.

"I always said we should buy a generator."

"You did? What you mean is that it's just another excuse to hit Disneyland for men, otherwise known as that huge DIY place you haunt. And –" I say firmly, "aren't the *pompiers* more fun? They sorted the problem out, right?"

"They did," Steve nods. "God, that was quite something. I just hope none of the bottles got damaged or lost their labels."

"The *bottles?* What about all the wiring? Everything in the normal cellar that would have got damp?"

"Well, that too. What time is it?" Steve peers at the clock. It's nearly dark. That little adventure lasted longer than I realised.

"Time flies when you're having fun," I say wearily, trying not to think about mud and sand. I catch sight of both the cats, sitting calmly on the couch upstairs, where they retreated once things got exciting.

Emma is tapping on her phone, and I hear her give a short, impatient sigh.

"Weird. Nothing from Luc. I sent him a message earlier to say we were having a bit of trouble and I'd call him. But he's not answering."

"He's probably just left his mobile somewhere he can't hear it," I say reassuringly. "If he's home, which he should be by now."

"Yeah," Emma says, looking a bit worried.

"Try him again in a few minutes. Let me find some candles, and we'll get a fire going."

Steve obliges and throws in a couple of logs. Our wonderful Danish-style stove is soon pouring out heat.

"No lights on across the valley," Steve says. "Must be quite a big failure. Bring on the candles, forget about the bloody floor until we get the power back, and let's open a bottle.

"No, thanks", Emma shakes her head. "I still can't get Luc and I can't understand why."

"Maybe he's out of range? Battery out of juice?"

"Could be. Let me try his fixed line?"

"The power might be off in town as well."

Emma tries, and says it's ringing.

"He's probably just popped out for something and left his phone behind," I say, but I admit this is strange.

"Yeah. I am really not going to get paranoid," Emma says, but it's not very convincing. "Maybe just one glass, then. And Mum? You have rising damp on your jeans."

Chapter 20

Emma

She was clutching the wheel too tightly, Emma realised.

The rain had stopped, but there were branches down all over the lane into town, and massive puddles and patches of mud.

She should have been helping her mother clear up. The power had come back soon after they'd all rummaged for clean, dry clothes and the house looked pretty disastrous, but her mother had simply sighed and decided to leave the cleaning up for the following day. When she left, they'd been sitting amid the mud and mess in the kitchen, sharing the rest of the bottle of wine with some pâté and toast.

They were worried about Luc too, she knew, but doing that parent thing about finding all kinds of reasons why he hadn't called or even driven over to their place.

Her only theory at the moment – if he hadn't driven into a ditch, which didn't bear thinking about – was that he'd broken down somewhere and hadn't been able to call for some unknown reason. Maybe his mobile was out of battery and he couldn't remember her number if he wanted to call from somewhere else?

Maybe, maybe, maybe.

Much as going to his place didn't make much sense, she needed to do something, anything.

Tweetie hit a particularly deep puddle, sending arcs of water flying. There were flashing lights over by the main intersection: police or ambulances, she wasn't sure, but it set her heart beating faster again.

Before leaving, she'd checked the road conditions from Grignan, and local accident reports.

Town was deserted, and there were few cars on the road. She opted for the small parking area nearest to Luc's place, hoping for a space, and found one immediately.

From there, it was only a few metres up the steep cobbled street.

Should she ring the bell? Or just go up?

Deciding on a compromise, she opened the main door with the key he'd given her and stared at the staircase. A thick trail of mud and footsteps went all the way up, past the apartment on the first floor.

That had to be Luc, didn't it? Surely burglars wouldn't be tramping around with mud and grit on their shoes?

Her heart was beating furiously, and she sped upstairs, hammering on the door, key ready, and found it was open when she tried the handle.

Luc was sitting by a lit fire. He looked up when he saw her, with an expression that stopped her in her tracks. It looked very much like disgust.

"Luc –"

"I thought you might turn up," he said coldly.

She stared at him, taking in the mud caked on his jeans, the boots discarded by the fire, and a massive pile of boxes on the floor. His stock of paper and inks, she realised immediately. A couple of them looked damp.

For a split second she thought everything was going to be fine. He'd got in, found water in his own cellar, where he did the printing, and had had to rescue that like her parents had rapidly moved the wine.

But that didn't explain why he hadn't called, or the look on his face.

"What happened?" she said stupidly, knowing her voice sounded shaky.

"Your ex happened." The three words were curt, cold.

"Rainer? He came *here?* I mean how did he – he doesn't even know where you live!"

"Not so hard to find somebody in a phone book once their name and the town where they live get plastered all over the internet, I suppose. He was waiting for me when I got back."

"Plastered all over the net how? Where?" Emma stammered.

"Oh, come on, Emma. Or should I say Temptress Em?"

She stared back at him. "Who?"

"The one with a Facebook page talking about Luc, the sexy artist from Crest. *That* Temptress Em."

"I don't understand…" Emma said. "What Facebook page?"

Suddenly, her mind started to whirl. Rainer was behind this, but behind *what?*

"I must say he was polite," Luc said. "And worried about you."

"*Worried* about me?" Emma was completely at a loss.

"Your attempts at blackmail to start with, and your need to gossip to the whole fucking world. He said he came down here to talk to you about it, and to your parents."

"Gossip? I have absolutely no idea what you're talking about. Rainer didn't even speak to my parents – he came to try and make up."

"Sure," Luc said bitterly. "I don't like lies, Emma. And I don't like having my private emails to you rehashed in public, including my name, stuff about my sister and my oh-so-tragic life."

"You – I –" Emma grasped for words. "He told you I'd done that? Made a Facebook page about *us?* The jerk who screwed his boss in our flat? And you think *I'm* a liar? He is a complete manipulator and you fell for it hook, line and sinker."

"I told him to get lost at first. But he just asked me to look at the evidence. He thought it was only fair to warn me."

"To warn you?" Her mouth was dry. "To warn you about what? And what evidence?"

Luc reached over to a handful of sheets of paper and thrust them at her. She could see the Facebook logo straight away. The picture of a woman in profile, but from the neck downwards only. Naked. And then the name: Temptress Em.

Her hands shook uncontrollably as she skimmed it. Entries quoting their emails. Her private, most intimate thoughts – and his. Even the exhibition flyer and his name.

"This isn't me," she said, once she got her voice to work. "Luc – Rainer did this."

"Oh sure. And you hacking into his private email never happened either?"

"I did *not* hack into his emails. He left his mail client open when I found him in bed with that woman. So I read them."

"But you threatened to use them against him."

"No," Emma whispered. "No, I didn't. How could I, because I didn't copy them. I just don't understand…" she looked down at the revolting pages again.

"I think I understand quite enough," Luc said, reaching out and grabbing them from her shaking hands. With one swift gesture, he threw them into the fire.

"Luc – you seriously believe all this?"

"He was actually concerned about your obsession with the social media and with sex – had been for a while, apparently. He told me that you'd made that site to make him jealous, and even sent him the link to it. Also, he says it's not the first time you've made websites about your conquests just for the hell of it, even when you were with him."

"Lies," Emma said, incredulously, feeling tears come. "It's all lies."

He looked down, not saying a word.

Emma felt the key cutting into her palm, suddenly, and let it go, dropping it on the floor.

"All I can say, Luc Theyroux, is that you are wrong. So very, very wrong but even when I prove it wasn't me who made that Facebook page – which I will – that doesn't change a thing now. If you don't believe me that I would never do anything like this, if you don't trust me, then there is nothing more to say."

"Emma –" he gave a tiny shake of his head but still didn't look up. "He also said you don't know the meaning of the word 'faithful', but he was trying to change you."

"For what it's worth, I was never *ever* unfaithful to Rainer and I do *not* sleep around and I would *never* have unprotected sex unless I really, really trust somebody..." Emma took a huge, gulping breath, and then decided there was nothing else to say.

"You're a bastard, Luc. An absolute *bastard.*"

She slammed the door on her way out.

***

She didn't remember the drive home. She did remember walking into the house calmly and telling her parents that they might need somebody else to make them a logo, because Luc Theyroux could rot in hell for all she cared and may not want to work for anyone to do with her.

Her parents, obviously stunned, had asked her to explain but she'd shaken her head and bolted for her room.

It didn't take her long to find Temptress Em's Facebook page, but it was set to private. It promised 'tempting, real-life revelations of a love affair' if you requested friendship. The total number of 'friends' was two, but knowing Luc he'd not even seen that.

Her finger hovered over the request button, but she stopped herself.

Rainer, she swallowed. And, perhaps – or almost certainly – his hacker friend Jakey. They'd know if she accessed the page and she wasn't going to give them that satisfaction.

Rapidly, she messaged Sophie – Jakey's ex-girlfriend and now somebody she chatted with regularly.

Sophie was online within seconds.

Had Jakey ever tried to hack her mail, Emma asked her?

"*Oh oui,*" Sophie shot back immediately. He'd taunted her about some emails she'd sent to friends when she was trying to break up with him. She'd changed all her passwords since then and her email address.

Dear God. Emma leaned back in her chair, mouth dry. Then she typed again.

Did you report him?

No. First, Sophie explained, it was hard to investigate and Jakey was clever. Also, it would have meant revealing some very intimate things to the authorities. And why the questions?

Emma explained briefly, and then told Sophie she had to go.

I am a coward, Sophie told her. *I am so sorry, Emma. But good luck with the interview.*

Emma signed off and sat there, staring at the wall.

When she heard the light tap, she sighed.

"Not now, Mum."

"Not your mum." Her father put his head around the door. "She sent in the B team. According to her, less girly tears on both sides if you talk to me, which you might prefer. I'll have to report back, though."

"Thanks, Dad," she said softly. "No, I'll come down and explain."

She did.

Her father pushed a large measure of something strong into her hand – probably brandy.

"It strikes me," he said, after hearing her out, "that it could possibly be proved it wasn't you. But it would take time."

"But why?" Her mother looked close to tears. "Why would Rainer do that? Jealousy?"

"Maybe. But that was his contingency plan, don't you see? His damage control. If I *had* copied his emails to that woman, and if I'd sent them to anyone – the bank, Alex's husband, he could come back with so-called proof that I was a paranoid social media addict who made Facebook pages about my love life. For all I know, there's stuff on that vile Temptress Em page that says I made all that up – about him and Alex – just for fun."

Emma had given it a lot of thought in a very short time.

"It's revolting," her mother said. "But explain to Luc. Explain properly. Tell him about Rainer's hacker friend and tell him we *will* prove it's all fake somehow. And that Rainer never spoke to us about it when he came."

"You know, Mum, that wouldn't change anything. I know it's fake and so do you. Maybe we could prove it to Luc after months of fighting Facebook, but – so what?"

"What do you mean, Emma? You love the man."

"Call it being naïve and on the rebound or something, but how could I ever love anybody who doesn't believe me? Who doesn't trust me? I told him he was a bastard for that. And thinking about it, he's a gullible idiot."

"But Emma –"

"It's over, Mum. He believed my lying, cheating ex rather than me. That says it all, I think."

Emma said it calmly enough, but inside she was furious. It was a cold, hard, all-consuming rage of sheer betrayal by somebody she'd been foolish enough to trust, blindly.

"I don't think you should make any rash decisions now, love." Steve Sandford spoke quietly.

"I've already made a decision, Dad. Luc deciding to believe Rainer was pretty well thought out. He had hours to ask me about it. But no – he let me believe something awful had happened to him and then called me a liar."

Her father shook his head. Her mother was crying.

"Don't, Mum. Please. Let's say it was a wake-up call. And speaking of calls, I don't expect any from Luc. If you want to carry on working with him, that's up to you, but I never want to set eyes on him again. If he comes here, please warn me and I shall keep out of sight."

"You can't leave it like this, Emma." Her mother sounded choked.

"Try me."

***

Emma poured a bucketful of muddy water down the sink, and looked around.

"Nearly there," she said, watching her mother putting another load of filthy clothes into the washer.

"It does look a bit more normal, eh? And thanks for helping."

"In my own interests, Mum. You're supposed to be working on my dissertation. Also, and as Gran told me once when I was little, there's nothing like hard work for forming the character."

"Oh, I've heard that one often enough. Look, Emma –"

"Mum, I do not want to talk about Luc. Yes, it hurts, yes, I hardly slept, but no, I haven't changed my mind."

"This isn't like you, Emma. Being so categorical. I really think you need to talk to Luc."

"No bloody way. I can be stubborn as well. Just like you. And Gran was too, remember?"

Her mother sighed.

"You could say that about us all, I suppose. It doesn't alter the fact that she never found anything good to say about me."

"Mum, you are so wrong. Did you even listen to what I said at the funeral? She admired you. She said so. And you've been avoiding the subject of her ever since we got back."

"We all have our coping mechanisms, Emma."

"True. But what I've been trying to tell you and I'm going to explain, right now, is what she was going to talk to you about at Christmas."

That, Emma realised, got her mother's attention.

"Right. Sit down, and I'm going to tell you about somebody called Brad."

Emma did just that, to her mother's obvious astonishment.

"So, my prudish, critical mother had a fling and even an illegitimate daughter? Good God."

"If you want to put it like that. But just think about her life, Mum? Married to somebody who was kind and lovely, but who she didn't *love,* at least not like she loved Brad*?*"

"And with a second daughter she didn't love much either."

"Not true. She just found you very different from Gillian, which is hardly surprising. So yeah, I'm not saying she didn't make a lousy job of being a mother, or even that she didn't hurt you, but Mum, life couldn't have been that much fun for her either."

"Particularly when she ended up with a daughter who was odd, fathered by somebody she was married to but didn't want," her mother retorted bitterly. "And neither did she want another child at all."

"She didn't deny any of that, Mum. Just that she'd made a massive, stupid mistake with that American and he ditched her, when she was pregnant. And sixty years ago, or more. Can you even imagine?"

Her mother gave a small, tight sigh.

"Well, it answers a lot of questions I suppose. And you really thought she was going to tell me?"

"I'm pretty sure she would have told both of you. I even think she really wanted to get it off her chest before she died. Maybe telling me was just insurance? I don't know. All I know is that Brad was a bastard. Like Rainer. Like –"

"Not like Luc, Emma."

"Like Luc," Emma said, attempting to make it sound firm, but her voice wobbled a little. "Exactly like Luc."

"Oh, Em –"

"Do. Not. Cry."

Too late. Her mother stood there, fighting back tears. Instinctively, Emma reached out and hugged her and remembered the first, equally impulsive hug from Luc the night he'd met her train.

Then she cried, too.

***

By the time her father walked in, arms full of large, grey tubes, Emma felt slightly better. She'd managed to get her mother talking, openly, about many things: her childhood, her dreams, her feelings of insecurity.

In turn, Emma had opened up about her fear of being misjudged. She reassured her mother that her parents hadn't been too bad on that score, but no single man had ever seemed to accept her for what she was. And to be misjudged by somebody who seemed as honest and caring as Luc had just made her lash out and slam the door.

Fortunately, her mother hadn't pressed the point about getting in touch with Luc again, because she was damned if she would.

A little voice reminded her that she'd half expected him to call, or to turn up, but he hadn't. All further proof he was a bastard.

"So, ladies," Steve Sandford looked at them quizzically. Emma supposed their eyes were red and puffy, but they were in the process of rolling out pizza dough and chopping ham.

"More comfort food, Steve. Not that I expect you'll mind?"

"Never. The place looks great."

"Any more sacks of sand inside the house and you will be the one clearing it up. Emma's been a great help though."

"What wouldn't a girl do for the only man I've ever met who isn't a jerk," Emma said, trying to make it sound light-hearted.

"Do men who aren't jerks get a beer? That builders' supply place is a labyrinth, and half of Crest seemed to be in there ordering gravel. A few people had earth slides. Lots of floods, drives washed away or turned into lakes."

"Not that there was any man-gossip involved while the poor Cinderellas were clearing up," her mother said, but without malice.

Emma went to fetch a beer, watching her parents and feeling envious at their ease with each other, particularly when her father casually planted a kiss on his wife's cheek and wandered off with his tubing – leaving muddy footprints behind.

"*Steve!*"

"Sorry, love."

"What?" Her mother caught Emma staring.

"You two are just, well – you go so well together."

"We do. Even if he's obsessed with DIY and I'm a born worrier." It was said with a smile.

"What was that?" Her father came back into the kitchen.

"Nothing," they said in unison. He rolled his eyes.

"Well, on with the cooking then ladies. Do I have time to go and fill up with diesel?"

"You do. But not if you gossip with half of Crest while you're at it."

"Which reminds me," Emma said. "It's okay if I take Tweetie to Lyon, right? Or shall I look at train times?"

"I'm taking you," her father said matter-of-factly.

"No, you're not. I may feel like crap emotionally but I'm a good driver."

"No arguments. Your mum says she wants to get on with editing your dissertation, and I want to pick your brains about digital media strategy."

"Pull the other one, Dad, it's got bells on. Mum put you up to this, right?"

"Actually, no I didn't. Don't jump to conclusions Emma." Her mother's tone was sharp.

"Sorry."

"Accepted. But where's my beer?"

Chapter 21

Shirley

They leave in a flurry typical of Emma, who remembers at the last minute that she's forgotten one of the documents she wanted to take with her. Remarkably, she finds it rapidly because Steve has been champing at the bit for a while, fearing the morning rush into Lyon.

She has done a great job with her make-up, but she looks pale and tired. I really hope a couple of hours in the car with her father's calm presence will help on that score. Last night she escaped to her room and told us in no uncertain terms that all she wanted was to be left alone.

We respected that.

She's been trying – and failing – to keep the tears at bay; that much is clear. I've been close several times myself, including during the night. The emotions of the last 36 hours have left me feeling like a limp rag. First the flood, then the mess with Luc, then the revelations about my mother.

So much for moving on and being strong, I think, sniffing over my third cup of coffee and fourth cigarette. It's barely seven in the morning.

I keep watching the clock and wondering if I have the nerve to do what I intend to, but by ten to eight – and another two cigarettes – I go and get my coat.

This could be the most stupid idea I've ever had, but quite honestly, things can't get much worse.

In fact, there are two things I need to do today, but this one takes precedence.

I drive down the hill rehearsing what I'm going to say, but it always sounds ridiculous. I'll have to play it by ear, I suppose.

Nothing goes as planned anyway. Emma told me that Luc was taking a week off building to work on the logo, but he doesn't answer the doorbell.

Maybe he can see the door from his window and doesn't want Emma's interfering mother there.

I give up after a couple of minutes, feeling deflated, and start to walk away. Then I see a garage door half-open, and a figure in there.

I peer through the gloom, wondering if it really is Luc or if it's just wishful thinking.

"You'd better come in," Luc says wearily from somewhere inside. "I suppose you came to see me."

"I did."

I take a couple of steps forward and see him standing there, dressed in filthy working gear and cleaning mud off the floor and his printing press.

If Emma looked below par, he looks terrible. It's not just that he's not shaved – it's more.

He turns slightly to see me against the light and bites back a yelp.

"You're hurt." I see his lips in a grim line, and he's chalky white. "Did that bas-"

"Self-inflicted," he says tightly. "I fell down the stairs. It's nothing much.
What can I do for you, Mrs Sandford?"

He's polite and neutral, but I have the feeling he just wants me out of there as soon as possible.

"I think you know."

"If it's about the logo, I made you a promise and I'll do it. If you still want it."

"Oh, don't be so bloody obtuse, Luc. And yes, I did notice you're doing the Mrs Sandford thing again." We'd been on first name terms practically since the outset.

"I'm sorry, but I don't want to discuss your daughter."

This could be even more difficult than I thought, if he can't even call her by name.

"For heaven's sake, Luc. Sit down on that stool over there before you fall down."

I go over and lean on the printing press, mud and all. Eventually, he sits down, wincing again.

I'm not sure whether I feel like hugging him or yelling at him. I take a few seconds to gather my thoughts, and then take a deep breath.

"She never made that Facebook page. We can prove it eventually, but it takes time and patience. And lawyers, probably. But frankly, I'm amazed you could be so damned easy to convince by that… that jerk."

"You know, Mrs Sandford, my sister took drugs. She would swear over and over that she'd finished with it – and she'd convince anybody, including my parents and me, that it was genuine. I always wanted to believe her. I always *did* believe her. I was gullible."

I nod, but he hasn't finished.

"But you see, sooner or later she'd come home as high as a kite or call me to pick her up. So it's not quite as easy to pull the wool over my eyes these days."

"Emma is not your sister," I snap. I can't help it. "Neither is she addicted to drugs, or anything else, including bloody social media. What she *did* do was to look at some Rainer's emails to that woman. It was stupid, but he'd cheated on her. And she *only* looked at them. She didn't download them. He'd left his tablet on, so… she looked."

Luc seems surprised.

"I didn't know about any of that that. He talked about her threatening to blackmail him."

I roll my eyes and explain that it was nothing like Rainer had said.

He says nothing. He's not comfortable on the stool, from the way he's shifting but I'm not finished yet.

"Luc, she's impulsive sometimes – like me. And stubborn. On the other hand, she has her father's absolute, complete sense of right and wrong. She also likes to fight her own battles – even when she was bullied at school as a kid, she'd never let us intervene, so she has no idea I'm here, as I expect you're wondering."

"I was." He looks at me with a different sort of pain on his face now.

"She is not a liar, Luc. Whatever you want to think."

"He had evidence," he retorts, but a little less emphatically than when he talked about his sister. "Including parts of our private emails, published on Facebook."

"Luc, I like you a lot. I respect how you feel about your privacy and about social media, and I expect your emails to each other talked about that too, which probably gave Rainer the idea of this whole thing in the first place. For God's sake *anybody* can make a Facebook page. Emma even showed me how to do one – I think

I tried it for about a week and it bored me to death until I realised it'd be useful for the B&B."

"And anybody can get hold of my – our – private mails?" he says harshly. "Hardly."

"Anybody with certain skills could, yes. One of Rainer's closest friends has those skills and apparently used to brag about them. Surely you've heard of hackers?"

Luc nods thoughtfully.

I explain a bit more about Rainer and his visit, and what exactly happened. Somehow, I think it's very different from Rainer's version. I go on to explain what Emma told us about the job offer in Geneva, Rainer's obsession with damage control, and his threats to her.

Eventually, I stop. My voice trails off and I just shake my head.

"Oh, and one last thing. I could bash your heads together, you and Emma. Quite frankly, you're as bad as each other at this moment."

At that, he gives what could be a slight chuckle, or a snort.

"I mean it, Luc," I say, unable to keep myself from feeling choked. "I'd have told her exactly that by now – you're both acting like cowards and seeing the worst in each other – but to be perfectly honest I wanted her to get through that interview first rather than her getting into a state all over again. I've kept my mouth shut for the time being but *only* the time being."

"I think it's too late to change anything now," Luc says quietly, miserably.

"Well, I'll make damned sure you get the proof about that Facebook page, whatever happens between the two of you, because I think it's important."

Luc stares at his feet. I haven't quite finished.

"Emma is a lot of things, Luc, and not all good – I admit that and probably so would she. But you're not exactly coming out of this smelling of roses right now either."

Luc says nothing for a minute but then looks up and runs a hand over his face.

"I agree I fucked up. If that's what you want me to say."

"You have. You both have. Emma didn't help matters by just storming out either, from what I gather. The thing is though, if you *are* going to talk, one of you has to make the first move."

"So, is that why you came here, Shirley?" he asks. "You want me to make the first move?"

"I wanted to talk to you. Not to put pressure on you, and I won't put pressure on Emma to call you either. Yes, I was prepared to give you a hard time over believing Rainer, but I admit you're bringing out the mother hen in me. You look like something the cat brought in."

"The bruises don't help," he says wryly, a tiny flash of the old Luc in there. "And to be honest neither does the hangover or the feeling like a jerk."

"If you overdid the alcohol and you're on painkillers, then I should have no sympathy whatsoever."

"You sound like my mother. I daren't even tell her about any of it. I suppose I really am a coward. You know my dad's an ex-cop, right?"

"He is? No, I didn't know."

"He'd probably know what to do to help, about the hacking. Or find people who can. It could be tricky, though – they're in England, the ones who did it."

"Now you're actually thinking. But yes, why not. Emma didn't want to do anything about reporting him because of the private aspect of your emails. But Steve would like nothing better that to see Rainer get his come-uppance."

"And you?" Luc actually manages a tiny smile.

"Pretty much the same. And it's time I went but I do have one favour to ask you. I would rather Emma didn't know I've been here."

"Fair enough. What time's her interview?" he says gruffly, as I start to walk out. "Mind, she might have blocked my calls. She knows how to do just about everything like that."

"I have no idea whether she did or not. She should be out by eleven or so. Then they have to drive back. Steve took her."

Luc nods.

"Well, better get moving. Good luck with the mud," I say, looking at the mess in there. "We had a fair bit of it ourselves."

"You did?"

I give him the short version of the wine cellar and the fire brigade and he raises his eyebrows.

"So *that's* the trouble Emma sent me a message about."

"Well yes. What did you think?"

"The wrong thing," he sighs. "I could win prizes for it. That was another reason I believed Rainer. He said he liked you and Steve, and that you were disappointed in Emma once he'd explained. I thought that was why she wasn't here until later – that there'd been a big argument at home."

"That's light years from the truth," I sigh. "She was going frantic when she couldn't get hold of you."

"Jesus, Shirley, what a mess. And I just ignored all her calls. What with all this –" he gestures to the floor, "and then going arse over tit on the stairs…"

"Messes can be fixed," I say. "Sometimes."

I hope I'm right.

***

I get back home, trying not to get my hopes back up and look at the clock. Emma's interview is at ten and it's only nine-thirty.

I'd like to talk to Steve about my visit to Luc's, but I'm not sure whether I should. I don't like keeping secrets from him, but I'm also a firm believer in men not needing to know quite everything, and particularly when it comes to some of my more hair-brained ideas.

The next item on my agenda is probably another of them.

I've been better at putting some things in writing than doing them on the phone ever since I was small, so I log onto my email.

Ideally, I'd prefer to talk to my sister face to face but this can't wait, or I'll just put it off like I've been doing for a couple of decades at least.

Somewhere during yet another long, sleepless night punctuated by thoughts of Emma, my sister, my mother and several dozen other things, I decided that saying anything about Brad, her real father, would be a bad idea. What right do I have to do that, and probably give her a massive shock? We both loved the man my mother married.

I just want to say a few things to her to continue our couple of aborted attempts at a conversation in Sheffield.

Does Clive read her mail? I hope not, but it does have just Gillian's name only. If he reads it and tells her it's a load of rubbish and she doesn't reply, so be it.

I start writing.

Just after ten, Steve calls. Emma's at the interview. She's sort of fine, he says carefully.

"Only sort of?"

"She's focused on this interview. I just think it's a bit of a case of flood gates that might burst afterwards."

"They never really burst with Rainer, Steve."

"That was Rainer. Luc is different."

"And if he called, you think she'd talk to him?"

"I don't know. I think she's blocked his calls", Steve said. "But that's just a guess. For once, she hasn't been looking at her phone every two minutes."

I heave a huge sigh. This could be harder than I thought.

***

Emma

Emma fixed a smile on her face as she walked into the interview room.

Her interviewer seemed pleasant, and surprised she'd obviously read up on the company. Emma thought that was a no-brainer.

He also seemed interested in her dissertation and asked several questions about it. It was only when she mentioned start-up work for small businesses that, for a second, she felt her concentration waver.

"Is everything all right?" The guy was frowning slightly, and Emma realised that she'd come to an abrupt halt.

She had to think fast.

"I'm so sorry. I should probably tell you that my grandmother died a few days ago, and it's been hard. On my parents, too. They're just starting up their own business and a couple of days back their house got flooded. It's been a tough week… and although I know private life should stop as you walk into work, it's been a bit of a series."

"They live down in the Drôme, you said? I read about the floods. And think nothing of it. We like to work with human beings here, not robots."

"Thanks."

It seemed that Myles, her old boss in London, had given her a glowing reference, as had the one from her previous job in Lyon. The fact she was completely bilingual with English was another point in her favour, as were her superb grades from business school.

Before long, her interviewer called in somebody from HR, for a few more questions.

There was the traditional awkward question about her faults, and she answered it honestly.

"I might be a little directive. As in downright bossy at times. And perhaps a little stubborn when I'm pretty sure I'm right about something."

That brought a chuckle from her interviewer, who would, as it became clear, be her new boss. She wondered if his policy was to have long rounds of interviews, even if she passed this first one.

Not much later, they asked her to wait outside for a few minutes. She'd done so, and managed to make polite conversation with a girl who was clearly supposed to look after her.

The place looked modern but not sterile. The salary range they'd quoted was fine – even generous. People she saw coming in and out of the lobby area next to the interview room seemed cheerful; casually dressed but not scruffy. Her dark jacket and bright shirt didn't seem either overdone or not smart enough.

They called her back in and Julien, as he'd introduced himself, offered her the job.

Seeing her surprise, he grinned and told her he didn't like to draw things out, so if she had no commitments, could she start straight after Christmas, a little over four weeks hence?

She could. And noted that the contract would reach her later that day.

Emma managed to thank him politely and even convey the enthusiasm she was sure she should feel and probably would, eventually. She wondered whether to suggest starting earlier, but that could seem odd. She'd need to find somewhere to live, and with luck that would happen fast – anything would do, really.

Going out of the office building into the sunshine, she took a huge, shaky sigh.

Everything had worked out perfectly, hadn't it? She should feel like doing cartwheels in the street or whooping with joy.

She should, in fact, be calling Luc right now to babble on about it all, thrilled about the prospects it had opened up in her career, and it being so close to Crest.

But that wasn't going to happen. He hadn't made the slightest attempt to call her, at least by the time she'd gone to bed last night, at which point she'd simply blocked him.

And neither had she contacted him, she reminded herself. What would she say anyway?

She walked on, looking at the shops she'd told Luc she missed. Even a sushi bar. All she could think of, though, was that tiny restaurant where he'd told her about his sister, and about how the internet repulsed him because of it.

A stationery shop displayed arty cards on expensive paper and brought another wash of memories.

How could something so good be destroyed so quickly, all thanks to Rainer and his ego?

And to Luc's stupidity, she reminded herself. He was just as much at fault.

Wasn't he? Or had she been too quick to judge him?

No. He'd sat there and said straight out that he believed her ex. Which made him a bastard. Simple as that.

And that was quite enough turning the whole thing over in her mind, for at least the hundredth time since it had happened. It was time to move on.

She reached the café where she'd agreed to meet her father, clinging on to that thought.

Her father had his nose in a newspaper, as ever, and an empty cup of coffee beside him.

"Dad?" She sat down abruptly, which he interpreted as bad news.

"Didn't go so well?"

"They gave me the job. I accepted." Then she burst into tears.

Her father produced a large handkerchief, put some money on the table, and steered her outside.

"Sorry, Dad."

"Don't be." He pointed at a bench. "Sit down."

"Shouldn't we just go home?"

"Two solutions. I told you I'd take you for lunch either here or on the way back. Or we can go home, and you can deal with this."

Her father handed her his phone and clicked on a message.

Please tell Emma I am a jerk and should have belieeved her and need to bpologise for everytjng because I love here Luc.

Emma stared at it.

"That must have taken him hours," she said, and then, unexpectedly, started laughing and crying at the same time.

"I'd say that's called love," her father said gruffly. "Don't get me all sentimental, miss. Somebody's got to drive."

"Without speeding – well, without speeding much – we should be back in, what, an hour and a half," she muttered, almost to herself and pulled out her phone. Her stupid fingers made unblocking Luc's number harder than it should have been, but she got there.

Neutral ground, café beside your flat at between 13.30 – 14.00? Still in Lyon but on way home.

She hesitated for just a second before sending it, her finger over the x.

Should she? Shouldn't she?

One x. Then she hit "send".

The reply came in seconds.

"Thanks xxxxx"

"Let's hit the road, Dad. And don't go thinking it's all going to be fine just yet. We have a lot of talking to do."

"Better call your mum and tell her about the job."

Emma did, and this time let herself sound pleased. Oh, she added casually, she'd arranged to meet Luc for a talk on neutral ground and under *no* circumstances should her mother read anything into that.

Of course not, her mother said. Definitely not.

Mothers, Emma thought affectionately.

***

Luc was sitting looking out at the street as she approached the café. It was just after two – she'd cursed every bit of slow traffic on the way down the A7 and every tractor along the country roads, but in between, she'd been thinking.

She paused, looking at him for a minute, seeing the strain on his face. He caught sight of her and stood up quickly as she came through the door, but then seemed to bite back a gasp and nearly double over.

"What's wrong?" Something definitely was. Come to think of it, he hadn't even got out of his chair when she'd seen him on the Monday. "You didn't have a fight with Rainer, did you?"

"No. I fell down the stairs after he left, when I was saving my stuff from the cellar," he said. "Nothing much."

Emma pointed at the chair and he sat down again, carefully. Being sympathetic to him wasn't how she'd intended to start this encounter, although she'd gone through a dozen possible ways to do so. She still wasn't going to let him off that lightly, though.

"By the time I got to your place on Monday I'd been thinking you were lying dead in a ditch."

"I realise that. I know I was a coward not to answer your calls. But I meant every word of that text to your dad. I didn't know if he'd show it to you."

"My dad's a secret softie. And I'd been contemplating sending you a message after the interview."

Well, that was true even if she'd decided against it at the time.

"You were?" Luc's eyes flashed hope.

"I was, except it would have had things like punctuation and correct spelling. But the thing is, Luc, you didn't believe me on Monday and I'm still having great trouble digesting that."

He nodded, silently and shifted awkwardly.

"But," Emma added, still aiming for matter of fact "I didn't know you'd half killed yourself either when I was at your place. I suppose that acts in your favour when you were being a complete jerk. Is anything broken?"

"No. Just bruises."

Emma glared over at the waiter who was heading their way and shook her head. He retreated.

"Rainer is a manipulative bastard and you fell for it."

"I know."

"He has a friend who got into our emails, and that meant he knew exactly how you felt about the social media. A hacker. I even know him. He's horrible."

"What am I supposed to say? I'll admit that I was taken in at first and I'll admit that it was stupid. And yes, he's clever."

"He is. Particularly at lying."

"When I'd seen you, at my place, I did start to wonder who was playing who."

"Well thank goodness for that," Emma said, a little curtly "Not that you felt like acting on it until now."

"Pride again. Nobody likes being called a bastard, Emma."

"Well, you were one. Although I do admit that I probably gave him the whole idea for this horrible little game of his by looking at his emails to that damned Alex woman. I shouldn't have, but I did."

Emma explained about the still-open email client.

"I didn't know about that, but I don't blame you for it. He hurt you. And I should have trusted you."

"He did. You should. All the time we were dealing with the flood at home, I kept thinking I was finally rid of him."

"Flood?"

"Flood. To the point we called the fire brigade to pump out the cellar. And I'd been worried sick about you not answering my calls, so I wasn't exactly feeling calm and logical either. I might even have been a bit… hasty."

"Just a bit," Luc managed a half-grin. "So, I've been a bastard and you've been a bit hasty. What happens next, Emma?"

"Well," she said, glaring the waiter into retreat yet again. "I have a way of proving it was Rainer behind it all."

"Like I just said, I should have trusted you."

"Like *I* just said, you should have, but that's not the point. I do need to do it, including for my own satisfaction. And this way, it won't take weeks or months. I can do it now. Right now, this afternoon. But I don't particularly want to do it in this damned café."

"I don't understand."

"You will," she said. "Can you make it up those stairs of yours?"

"I can. But just to warn you, my place is still a mess."

"Won't shock me. I'm not known for being tidy – and what did you have to save from the cellar? Did it get flooded? Was there a lot of damage?"

"Some water and mud got in. I only lost one box of paper. I fell down just before I got to that – too much mud on the stairs. But there's one more thing you should know, now you've mentioned looking at his emails. Rainer said he'd been to see you to ask you to stop threatening to blackmail him over them because you'd copied them. So when you sent me that message about having some trouble at home, so I reached all the wrong conclusions and thought he'd told your parents about that."

"Talk about misunderstandings," she said. "We're all too good at it. Rainer probably didn't realise you were close to my parents and that some of his lies would come out fairly easily. That's where he went wrong."

"True," Luc said thoughtfully. "Emma – I'm so sorry."

"I'm sorry too. For the record, and like I just said, I didn't copy the mails so there was nothing to blackmail him about. But I did tell him I'd seen them when he turned up in London and he assumed I'd kept copies. I didn't deny it because I was so angry with him. I should have done."

"Let's go," Luc said, and took her hand. "No more saying sorry."

***

"You don't have to do this," Luc said once again as she finished explaining what she wanted to do.

"I do. I just do, Luc."

He grabbed her hand, and it felt good. So had the kisses when they'd reached his apartment.

"That helps", she said shakily, squeezing his hand in return. "Just don't let go, please. I'd give anything right now to kiss you forever or even to drag you upstairs but – I think this is necessary."

"Do it then, Em."

She dialled, clicking on the speaker as she did. The familiar British ring tone went on and on.

Please, please let him answer. Please don't let him ignore it, or let it go to voice mail.

"Yes, Emma?" Rainer's voice actually made her jump.

"Rainer. Listen – can you talk?"

"I can talk, but what do you have to say to me?" *Vot.*

"Look, I think I've been pretty stupid. And I think we're quits now, right?"

"In what way?" his voice was cold, wary.

"Oh, come on, Rainer. Let's not beat about the bush. I caught you cheating, and you dreamed up Temptress Em to get your own back – and very clever damage control it was. I thought that was actually a stroke of genius."

"I beg your pardon?"

"Let's say I found that a whole lot funnier than Mr Sexy Artist going into a meltdown over something as trivial as a bit of fun on social media. He said you'd talked to him."

"Briefly," Rainer said.

"Right. So anyway, he went ballistic but all I could think of was – well – you. I couldn't help it."

Emma gripped Luc's hand like a vice.

"Really?" Rainer was still being cautious, she realised.

"I told him it was just you having a bit of a laugh but he seemed to think it was a really big deal, when it was just a stupid fake Facebook page. And quite honestly, the way he reacted was a huge turnoff."

Emma swallowed. Was this going to work?

"Anyway," she went on. "Like I said, I was stupid. You had a fling, I had a fling these last few weeks to pay you back."

"You hurt me a lot, Emma. And you did seem very fond of your artist."

"I know, Rainer. You hurt me too, with that Alex woman. But all the time I kept thinking and thinking. You know, about the old crowd and the fun we had with them. Specially Jakey – good old Jakey. He helped you with Temptress Em, I suppose. He's really brilliant. I always knew it. It really was all so clever."

"Emma are you saying you are not any longer angry?"

"Oh, I was. I was furious at first – even when you came down here. And then I remembered how we'd argue and then make up in bed." Emma felt herself blushing. "And just how amazing that was. I'm even thinking about that right now. And some nice cosy little place in Zurich."

"I remember those times also." This time Rainer sounded a little less cold. "Ach, Emma – you always were a temptress. And impulsive."

"I know, I know. But like I said, that Facebook page was just amazing – made me realise just how much we are alike. We plan. We get things done. We use our networks."

"You think?" He sounded almost amused, relieved. Now she had to go for the kill.

"Oh definitely. I must say it felt a bit odd, Jakey getting into my emails, though – I'd rather you both stopped that now, and particularly if we – you and me start, you know...?"

"You only have to say the word and we'll stop it all," Rainer said, and Emma's heart leapt – there it was, the proof. "Jakey said that was easy to do also. I did not do this lightly, Emma. But you started it by copying my emails – so it was, how do you say, all is fair in love and war." *Vor.*
"And it was fair to actually *hack* even though I didn't even do that?" She couldn't keep the edge out of her voice. Only the feel of Luc's hand and the look in those grey eyes kept her going. "I never did copy those emails, Rainer."

"Really? Well, good. But don't get angry again, Emma. Really, you should not. Maybe we should put all this down to a little adventure, ja?"

"Actually," Emma said, "it all started when *you* cheated on me. And there's something you should know, now we've had this conversation."

"Tell me? Or perhaps I should invite you to Zurich for the weekend – I shall be there – and you can tell me there. A nice bed, some champagne..."

"Oh, I don't think you'll want to speak to me again after this call. I should have told you straight away that I didn't copy those emails, I admit that, but I wanted you to suffer, Rainer. And today, I wanted proof that you and Jakey had been behind that horrible site. Mission accomplished."

"Emma –?"

"And what's more, I never want to hear another word from you. Go back to your twisted little world and your pathetic hacker friends. Maybe your next victim will be more open to being bribed with a job to make sure your little ways never come to light."

"What –"

"See, Rainer, I'm sitting here with Luc. You know – the sexy artist whose privacy you invaded too. The one you put through hell. The person who didn't deserve any of this because he happens to love me, and it's mutual."

"I don't believe you. Is this another game?" Rainer's voice was actually unsteady.

"It's not a game." Luc spoke directly into the phone, and to her immense satisfaction, Rainer gasped audibly. "And you might be interested in the fact that this conversation has been recorded. We finished here, Em?"

"We're finished with Rainer," she said, "or nearly. Rainer – that Facebook page had better be gone within hours. And I mean gone, using all Jakey's talent to remove it and every damned trace of it, or I'll report both of you. Is that clear?"

"Emma -"

"Is that *clear?*"

"Yes." It was barely audible.

Emma clicked the phone off. Her hands were shaking again, suddenly, and tears were close.

"Come here," Luc said gently. "My brave Emma."

"Recorded the conversation?" she said, her voice strangled, holding him tight.

"Permit me my moment of drama. It would never hold up in court, I don't think, even if I'd had the first idea how to do it. But if you want to try to bring charges, it might make him scared enough to admit all he's done. I did tell you my dad was an ex-cop."

"You did. But I don't know if I want to drag your parents into this."

"That's up to you, my love. I just know he'd help."

"I just want it to be over. And I never, ever, want to go through anything like this again, Luc. I couldn't."

He stroked her hair, soothing. "Me neither. I love you, Emma. I was stupid. Too proud –"

"We were both stupid. I'm impulsive, over-sensitive…"

"And I'm paranoid and have a temper. What a pair, eh?"

Emma chuckled.

"You want some good news? I didn't even tell you. I have a job as of the beginning of January."

"You do?" Luc grabbed her and gave her a swift, urgent kiss. "Have you told your mother? Well, your parents?"

"Dad drove me. He'll have told Mum."

"Call her anyway. Tell her not to wait up for you, maybe?"

Emma grumbled mildly, anxious for more kisses, but she dialled.

"Mum? It's me. I'm with Luc."

"So your dad said. Is everything –"

"Everything's fine, Mum. I won't be home for dinner. Or breakfast."

Her mother gave a long, drawn-out sigh. "Well thank God for that. Is Luc feeling any better after that fall… oh dear."

Emma thought about that for a second.

"Mum. The only way you could possibly know that Luc fell down the stairs is because you talked to him, didn't you." Emma tried hard to sound stern and flicked the microphone back on. "And you, Mr Theyroux, just happened to omit that little fact, right?"

"What can I say?" Luc spread his hands in mock exasperation, but he was smiling. "But for the record, she used words on the lines of 'acting like spoiled children' and threatened to knock our heads together. You were up for the same lecture, Em, once you'd gone out and got that job."

"*What?*"

"I'm sorry, Emma," her mother said, not sounding particularly sorry at all. "But I didn't want you to end up unhappy. Either of you. So yes, I popped in to see him this morning."

"Still fighting my battles. I should probably strangle you, Mum."

"It wasn't a put-up job, me sending you that text message" Luc interrupted. "Not by any means, so don't go thinking she twisted my arm to do anything."

"Hah. And dad was in on this little setup?" Emma was still attempting to sound angry and failing miserably.

"Hell no. And don't *either* of you tell him. He's outside happily digging new tubing in to prevent any more floods."

"Oh Mum, you're impossible," Emma said, unable to stop herself from laughing. "But we'll discuss that later. When I've dealt with this injured artist of mine."

She broke the connection and stared at the injured artist.

"She's amazing, your mum," he said quietly. "I think she would probably have boxed my ears if I hadn't been a bit battered. She swore me to secrecy about her coming to see me. I had to pretend I didn't know about your flood."

"I see."

"And for what it's worth, she only told me what I think I already knew. That I should never have doubted you. But her coming was all in a good cause, no?"

"Hmm. I suppose I might let her off then. Particularly as you're a bit battered, as you put it, and she has a huge soft spot for you."

"It's mutual. And I'm not so battered I can't have my evil way with Temptress Em – or let her ravish me at least," he said wickedly, silencing her with a kiss that left her breathless.

"You ever, *ever* use that name again and I'll…"

"Have to get the undies to match? I was thinking black lace, maybe."

"You are –" words failed her.

Chapter 22

Shirley

"Steve? Steve, wake up."

"Not morning yet."

"It is. I have to get the turkey on. And there's a million things to do."

Steve sighs heavily.

"Shirley, it's not even seven. Luc's parents said they'd be here around midday. How long does a bloody turkey take?"

"Forever. Did you bring plenty of logs in? And did you check the heating is on in their room?"

"Yes, and yes." He rolls over. "Before you ask, the right room. The first one, with the sludge-coloured wall."

"Taupe," I correct automatically.

"Sludge."

I sniff. It's the nicest and sunniest room with the biggest private patio. Like the others, it's going to have a name once I've sorted out name plates with Luc, which should make things easier. That one will be *Olivier,* as it has a splendid view of the olive tree. The others will be *Tournesol* – sunflower – and *Lavande.* As for the upstairs suite in the main house, I'm toying with the idea of *Romarin* or *Thym.* I'm looking forward to all the finishing touches, and to buying fabrics and a few other things in Marrakesh.

"Shirley? Earth to Shirley?"

"Sorry, just dreaming a bit. And thinking of name plates."

"Take a break, Shirley."

"I am. I will. Really. I just want everything to be ready for them. You know what I'm like."

Steve grins and rolls onto his back.

Luc's parents are coming for Christmas lunch and will be staying overnight, both to see us and for his father to see his brother, who owns the building company that first recommended Luc to us.

I feel a bit as though I'm doing a test for the B&B. Fortunately, we've already met Sarah and Patrick Theyroux in Lyon a couple of weeks back.

I like them. Luc is the image of his mother, who is funny and charming, even if there's sadness in her eyes sometimes. We talked a little about her daughter during a walk through Lyon's massive *Tête d'Or* park. Marie's birthday and Christmas are hard, she admits, but she gets through them, and seeing Emma and Luc together is doing her good.

I'm glad. I'm also glad that Luc's dad is a very no-nonsense Frenchman and has a stupendous sense of humour. I have the feeling that before long, we'll need to get them together with Helen and Joe, so the two men can swap cop stories.

"Coffee?" I suggest hopefully. "Steve?"

"Could be arranged. As long as you don't start worrying about food quite yet."

"I'm not worrying about anything," I retort. "Well, only whether we will actually get any bookings. The site's been live for hours now."

"Shirley – people don't usually browse B&B sites after midnight on Christmas eve. In the New Year, maybe. If we get a booking today, I'll break out the champagne."

"I want champagne anyway. It's Christmas. And I just –"

"Look, Emma's done wonders. The site looks fantastic, the logo's superb, and she's the right person to make sure the word gets out there. Be patient."

He's right. Emma's been working hard. She's also finished a website for Luc, which looks equally smart. It's linked to ours, which gives him credit for the logo.

His own site went up a couple of days ago, and it's getting views. Emma gets a little jumpy when she looks where visitors come from, but I heard the whole story of her showdown with Rainer soon after it happened. I don't think he – or the unsavoury Jakey – will give them any more trouble.

"You think Rainer will ever try anything again?" I ask as Steve pulls a bathrobe on.

"I knew you'd find something to worry about. And the answer is no. I thought both Emma and Luc might want to take it further, but I can understand why they don't. As for Rainer, I think he knows when he's beaten."

"I hope so."

"So, any more things stored away in that endless well of things that bug you?" Steve's voice is kind, but I sigh.

"Gillian. She never answered my mail."

"How many times –"

"I know, I know. I can't force it. I just wish we were in touch, Steve."

"I know you do, love, but try and just let it go? Think about the lovebirds instead."

"Give me coffee. Then I might be able to think more positive thoughts. Emma said they'd be here to help after breakfast."

"That could mean any time before lunch," Steve chuckles. "And certainly not before nine or ten. How about I bring you a coffee upstairs and we take a leaf out of their book?"

"Can't think what you mean," I grin at him.

***

Following a relaxed meal, which included a perfectly cooked turkey and a short walk, we're all back inside, listening to Luc and Emma chatting easily about their plans, both long-term and immediate.

Emma, after a lot of thinking, has accepted Luc's parents' offer of a room in their apartment in Lyon, at least while she sees how the job works out. They'll spend some weekends there and some in Crest. That suits me fine, just as it seems to suit everybody. The Theyroux obviously like her and it's mutual. I just wonder if they'll handle her untidiness, but that's out of my hands.

So, I think to myself, happy endings all round for Luc and Emma.

I hear a faint ping, and Emma grabs her tablet. She punches the air with her fist.

"Mum, you have a booking for two couples in March."

As my webmistress, she can see all that but it's up to me to do all the confirmations. I peer at her screen and can't help smiling.

"And Luc had more views today."

"That's wonderful," Luc's mother says sincerely. "I'm so pleased."

"Me too," Steve says contentedly. "I did promise champagne if it happened."

"Right now, Dad?" Emma asks sweetly.

"Could do." He nods agreement. "As long as we don't have to decide immediately on which rooms they get."

"The photographs of the rooms look great, by the way," Emma enthuses. Sarah Theyroux knows her way around editing images, and I thank her again. Luc is good with a camera, but as a professional, she has tremendous talent and vastly improved the photos he sent her. I'll ask Luc to do some more of them when I'm happy with the décor.

"Thank you. Your place will be a success, Shirley," she smiles at me. "You have such a flair for design. I'm looking forward to seeing it all finished, and those extra notes of colour you wanted."

Steve snorts.

"I think I could handle that champagne now," I say, glaring at him.

"Girls' drink," Luc's father, Patrick, grumbles amiably. "I could probably sacrifice myself, all the same."

"I should go and confirm that booking," I say, still staring at the screen. Two people, three nights. They're from Lille, up north.

"Mum," Emma rolls her eyes. "It's Christmas day."

"I know, I know. It's just symbolic, somehow."

"You –" Emma points to Luc, "had better not start packing up prints within minutes of orders. Particularly at inappropriate moments."

Luc laughs and slings an arm around Emma. Steve's description of them as lovebirds isn't far wrong.

"First, I actually need to sell something using that fancy online order form."

"You will." Sarah and I say it in unison.

"Besides," I add, "you made a killing at the Christmas fairs, right?"

"I did," he nods. "Thanks to the saleswoman of the century here. I need to get down to work on some new pieces next week, before I go back to construction sites."

"Within reason," Emma chides him gently. "Another week and I'll be working for a living again. The phrase 'holiday period' is supposed to count for something."

Steve goes off to the fridge to fetch the champagne, and I slip out quietly and into the office. The email from Lille is there, in the B&B mailbox. I confirm the booking, trying not to sound either surprised or effusive.

Then, out of habit, I check my normal email account and see one from Gillian.

I'm so sorry to take so long to reply. We went on our cruise and then I kept putting it off, but thank you so, so much for that wonderful mail and please also thank Emma for Skyping me yesterday – she suggested I should contact you for Christmas and she was right.

I skim it rapidly, amazed.

Emma called? They Skyped? My sister uses Skype?

Yes, the mail continues, she wants to keep in touch. Yes, she is even working on Clive to come and visit. And she ends by saying that we must talk properly – maybe on Skype, as she's discovered it and uses it with Kevin. Could we chat on Boxing Day or soon after?

The temptation is to answer it immediately, but I don't. I will later today.

When I get back into the living room, Steve's working on the champagne cork, and I pass around the glasses once the bottle is opened. We all raise them.

"To Olive Blue," Sarah says. "And to a wonderful Christmas. Thank you, all of you."

"Another toast?" Emma says cheerfully. "To your holidays, Mum and Dad. You deserve them."

"Thank you," I say quietly. "And I need a word with you about Gillian, and Skype. She emailed me."

"Oh?" Emma attempts nonchalant, and then comes over to give me a hug. "It was Luc's idea as well. He's been practising Skype for when I'm in Lyon, and we found her Skype address. And you know, Gillian's okay. She told me she's not that good at writing things down, unlike you, you scary editor woman."

"Me, scary?"

"Terrifying," Luc says amiably. "I think it's a mother thing. You do remember you wanted to box my ears not so long ago, Shirley?"

His own mother raises her eyebrows, but she's grinning. His father chuckles delightedly.

"You deserved it. Both of you," I retort.

"Luc told us about it," his mother admits, which is something of a relief as we carefully avoided that subject on our first meeting. "The whole thing. Patrick would have been on his way across the channel to string the little bastard up given half a chance, but Luc and Emma prefer just to let it go."

"If I'd known, we could have made it a joint expedition, Patrick," says Steve.

"Why doesn't that surprise me." Sarah speaks again, draining her glass. "Mind you, both you and Emma were a little hasty to judge each other, Luc. Let this be a lesson to you both."

She says it firmly. I'm starting to like her more and more.

"I think," I say cheerfully, "they seem to be learning. I do hope so."

Emma grimaces. "In the end, Rainer did us a favour of sorts. Can we change the subject now please, Mum? Who found you those tickets for Morocco for New Year? Who even grabbed a room at your favourite place when somebody cancelled? I'm not all bad!"

"Okay, okay," I concede. "You and Patrick should go some time, Sarah. You'd love it. It's great for photography. And before anybody asks, I do intend buying up half the souk."

"Knowing my wife," Patrick says, "she will buy up the other half."

"Well done, love," Steve says to me, as he pours us all a refill.

"What for? The booking? But whatever it is, is it worth another dozen plates as hand luggage?"

"I'd say a container's worth of freight, for sorting those two out," Sarah says cheerfully.

"At least," Emma nods. "Would there be another bottle of those bubbles lying around?"

There is, and we make another few toasts. To families, to the future, and all kinds of sentimental things that not even the men seem to mind. That's Christmas for you.

I look out of the window. I haven't closed the shutters because the tiny white lights I've woven around the handrail going down to the pool look festive. The spotlight shining up through the branches of the olive tree make it look majestic against the dark water.

I love your olive tree and how it reflects in the pool. That was one of the last things she said to me.

I raise my glass once more.

"To my mum."

Shirley's Recipes

As Emma says, I have an irritating knack of saying things will be cooked 'when they're done', and the quantities of ingredients should be 'the right amount'. This is why I think that writing a cookbook would be daunting.

All the same, here are a couple of my personal favourite recipes, which even have quantities and cooking times (Emma and Steve insisted, and even helped with the testing).

Obviously, using local produce is ideal, and we are fortunate enough to have superb fruit, vegetables, honey, goat cheese, and olive oil on our doorstep, but most ingredients can be found easily enough elsewhere.

Roast Pepper and Goat Cheese Extravaganza

For decades, I was rather unimpressed by bell peppers, whether in salads or stir-fried. Then, only a few years ago, I tried them grilled, and it was an instant love affair. Roasting them and peeling them makes them smoky and sweet. Combined with goat cheese, they're stunning. Here are a couple of suggestions. Arrange these prettily with goat cheese wedges and olives to make individual starters, or serve them as a tasty pre-dinner finger-food platter.

It's all super-easy, quick to make, and looks and tastes great.

Ingredients for 6 people
4-6 large bell peppers, in whatever colours you like: red, green, or yellow (but keep the red and yellow for the *ktipiti* below, which might not look as attractive with green ones!).
1 small tub of spreadable goat cheese (about 150 g)
1 pack of Feta (about 200 g)
Oregano, small bunch if fresh, a generous tsp if dried
2 French loaves: one for the *ktipiti,* the rest to go with the cheese wedges
A selection of goat cheeses
Olives (optional), preferably Greek style and pitted
Olive oil (optional)
Liquid honey (optional)

1. Roasting the peppers
   Line an oven shelf with baking paper, and heat oven to at least 220° C. Remove the stalks, seeds and white flesh of the peppers and cut them into 4 lengthways.
   Cook for 15-20 minutes, skin facing up, until the skin is blistered and blackening (yes, *really* blistered).
   Let them cool, and it's easy to slide the skin off. Set the pieces aside: keep any strips that are difficult to peel and are less regular-shaped for the *ktipiti* (see below).

2. Pepper 'cigars"
   Place a generous teaspoon of soft goat cheese on one end of a strip of pepper and roll. That's all. We find these don't need salt, pepper, oil or anything else.

Best served at room temperature.
If you're serving them as part of a finger-food platter, provide cocktail sticks.

3. *Ktipiti*
   This is a Greek recipe and in some versions of it, the herb used is mint or even parsley. We grow lots of oregano, and that's the way we like it best. If you've tried this in a tub from a supermarket, this is way, *way* better and incredibly simple.
   Place two-thirds of the pack of Feta, crumbled, and about the same weight in peeled, cooled peppers in a bowl, plus a tablespoonful of fresh oregano, and mix (I use a plunge mixer).
   Taste. You might want to add more Feta, or more peppers, or both (because you can never have enough of this). No salt is needed. Chill until serving.
   Serve on thin slices of French bread, toasted or not, but add it at the last moment before serving. Add a couple of tiny oregano leaves on top.
   This also works well as a dip, served with breadsticks, celery sticks and cucumber wedges with the seeds removed.

4. Goat cheese wedges
   If possible, use a couple of different semi-soft goat cheeses. Many of them in southern France are small and flat, and around the size of an ice hockey puck.
   If you're serving this as part of a platter, use tiny slivers of discarded roast pepper or a sliver of olive and use cocktail sticks to decorate the wedges.
   If it's part of a plated appetiser, be a little more adventurous: add a tiny drizzle of olive oil and a little freshly-ground pepper, or a drizzle of liquid honey (both options are rather dangerous for finger food, as they're a little messy).
   A final alternative is to sprinkle a few buds of dried lavender on top of those with honey. It's unusual, but rather glorious.

Chilled Courgette (Zucchini) Soup

Ingredients for 6–8 servings
2 medium-sized courgettes, in cubes
100 g spreadable goat cheese (or Philadelphia)
2 cl crème fraiche (preferably) or liquid cream
2 fat cloves of garlic or 3–4 smaller ones
2–3 tbs lemon juice
Grated rind of one lemon
Olive oil for frying
Herbs (basil, oregano, parsley, or a mix), preferably fresh, to taste.
Salt
Black pepper
3–4 very thin slices of Parma ham or other cured ham (optional)

Fry the cubed courgettes gently in a small quantity of olive oil. Keep stirring until it's soft but not mushy. Add a couple of tablespoons of water towards the end if it starts looking too brown before it's soft. Allow to cool a little.

Place the courgettes in a blender with the goat cheese, garlic, cream, lemon juice, lemon rind and herbs and blend until smooth.

Add salt and possibly more lemon juice to taste.

Chill for at least a couple of hours and taste again. It's a fairly thick soup, so add a little chilled water (or more cream) if you prefer it less so.

I serve this in small bowls, with a little blob of sour cream and a sprinkling or herbs on top, and a twist of freshly-ground pepper. It goes well with olive bread or garlic bread.

For a more sophisticated version, cut or tear the slices of cured ham into bite-sized pieces, place them flat on an oven sheet and cook them at 200° C. Depending on how thin the ham is, it will be crunchy in anything from 5–10 minutes. Keep checking!

Add the hot flakes of ham to the soup at the very last moment.

Veal with Lemon (also possible with pork)

This is a Swiss recipe from a publisher of recipe books and monthly recipe leaflets called *Betti Bossi*, which is something of a national institution. This is from the book *Fleischküche* (cooking meat), published in 1982. The recipes were, and no doubt still are, *always* fool proof and *always* good. I've been making this regularly for so long that I no longer need to check the quantities. Here's a translation, which includes some of my small adaptations. A couple of the ingredients aren't readily available outside Switzerland, like the brand-name sauce base, but I've found alternatives.
It's a fabulous and easy thing to serve for a special meal.

Ingredients to serve 4–6 (halve the quantities for 2–3)
Veal fillet (around 800 g) or two pork fillets (around 800 g in total)
1 large untreated lemon

Marinade
1 tbs neutral-flavoured oil
1 tbs mild mustard (grainy is fine if you like it)
1 fat garlic clove or 2 small ones, pressed
1 tbs lemon juice
Large pinch of white pepper
½ tsp salt

Sauce
20 cl chicken stock
15 cl liquid cream

Remove the lemon peel in strips, avoiding any pith. Cut these into tiny rectangles (about 25–30 of them). Make small incisions on the meat (except underneath) and push the lemon peel well down into them, for a 'hedgehog' effect.

Mix all the marinade ingredients together and paint the meat generously. Ideally, leave this in the fridge (covered) for up to 4 hours, and remove it to get to room temperature about an hour before cooking.

Cook at 180° C for about an hour for the veal, and at 210° C for about 30 minutes for the pork. Add any remaining marinade at regular intervals. Cover the top with foil if it gets a little too brown: the lemon will sear a little anyway.

Take the meat out when cooked and keep it warm. Keep the roasting tin and juices ready for the sauce.

Make up 20 cl of chicken stock. I use French 'fond' which is self-thickening, but if you use chicken broth cubes, warm the broth and thicken slightly with a little cornflower (cornstarch). Add a tsp of lemon juice.

Pour the thickened stock into the roasting pan with any remaining marinade and juices and stir well, reducing it a little. If the meat residue in it disturbs you, sieve it. Add the cream and heat gently, without boiling.

Serve either with the sauce poured over it, or with the sauce separately. Gran (and *Betti Bossi*) thought it should be served whole and carved at the table, and I disagreed and prefer to plate it. Please suit yourself. Add a couple of slices of fresh lemon as a garnish if you like the idea. We don't think it needs it.

We serve this with rice or fettucine (Steve's favourite, and bring on the extra sauce), plus some green vegetables such as broccoli or haricot beans.

Lemon Curd Ice Cream

If you have an ice-cream maker, this has to be one of the easiest recipes ever. I've tried various versions of it that I found on the internet, and this is the one that never fails. The first time I tried it was a commercial brand and delicious, but our local shops discontinued it. So I thought I'd better try it for myself.

Ingredients
1 jar of lemon curd (usually 400 g). If you make your own (bravo!) this is a way of keeping it longer than its normal shelf life, too.
Equivalent weight in liquid cream. Full-fat is ideal but you can use low-fat too.
Grated rind of half an untreated lemon
Cubes of candied lemon peel (optional)

Make sure that the lemon curd and cream are both well chilled in the fridge. Whisk them together, add the lemon rind, and again make sure the mixture is well chilled.

Haul out the ice-cream maker and pour in the mixture. Churn. If you're using cubes of candied lemon peel, add them just before it reaches the ideal texture.

Pop it in the freezer. Eat. Enjoy both the ice cream and the compliments.

I serve it with almond biscuits, or with a little bowl of strawberry soup (see below) on the side.

Strawberry Soup

Yes, strawberry soup. Steve got a little carried away when planting rather a lot of *Garigettes*, which are the wonderfully aromatic local ones. Even after eating them daily in season, giving them away, and making endless pots of jam, we couldn't keep up. Then I tried this dessert in a local restaurant and knew what to do.

Ingredients
Strawberries
Sugar (a little, maybe)
For serving:
Balsamico cream (reduced balsamico vinegar, fairly easy to find these days)
Mint leaves, blueberries, blackcurrants or redcurrants
Whipped cream

The thing about strawberries is that they don't freeze that well whole. However, blend them into a thick 'soup', pour the mixture into muffin tins and freeze, and the result is astonishing.

Depending on how flavoursome the berries are, add a little sugar as you blend.

Once frozen, take out the muffin-shaped blocks of purée and freeze them in bags. Thaw before serving and serve with a drizzle of balsamico cream on top, plus a couple of mint leaves, and sliced fresh strawberries stirred in if they're in season. Out of season, I add some other fruit.

Cream is always an option, of course.

I've used the same technique with gooseberries, to make a purée (or 'coulis') for other desserts.

Quince, Lemon and Almond Jam

This is a recipe I found at some point on the internet, years ago, and have never found again, but it's fairly basic. It's a change from quince jelly (and less work). It makes a rather thick, cloudy jam depending on how much you reduce it and how much ground almonds you add, but it has a unique flavour. It keeps for at least a couple of years without refrigeration, if it lasts that long. We have a friend from Chile who goes into raptures about it as he was brought up on a similar version to this. He emptied my jam cupboard of it in a week.

We like it on toasted baguettes, with warm *brioche*, with Greek yoghurt as an instant dessert or, in Emma's case, straight from the pot!

In Provence, quince paste (a heavily reduced quince jelly) is a traditional speciality, doused in sugar. This isn't quite as solid or chewy but it's delicious. Thanks to Helen for beautiful, downy quinces by the bucketful!

Ingredients
1 kg quince, peeled, cored, and chopped roughly, quickly dipped into water with lemon juice to stop it going brown
1 kg sugar
20 cl water
2–4 tbs lemon juice (we like it lemony)
100 g ground almonds (or a little more, depending on your taste)
A handful of flaked almonds

Boil the quince in a jam pan or other large pan with the water until soft, adding more water if necessary. Once soft, add the sugar, and boil until it's at setting temperature (test on cold plates or with a thermometer). Add the ground almonds and flaked almonds, stir again, and fill your jam jars.

Yum.

Acknowledgements

Books need readers, and they need editors. I'm both when I'm not writing. I strongly believe that writing anything worth publishing is the result of a lot of support, whether it be helpful insights from family and friends, the competent, critical eye of an editor, and a glass of wine and encouragement on days when it just isn't coming together.

I'm lucky to have had that support. This includes those who read earlier drafts: Mo, my lovely sister-in-law in California, and friends (Pete, Frances, Vic, and Dinah). They nagged me to do something with it. A fellow writer on a forum, Nathalie, provided some extremely down-to-earth criticism that helped a lot, but I then sat on the manuscript for a couple of years while starting the sequel and going through a lot of self-doubt. And then I encountered Rebel Magic Books and Sue Fitzmaurice, because I'd been reading Sue's book recommendations for years. Her editing is outstanding, and her professionalism in seeing Olive Blues published has been fantastic. It's a real pleasure working with her.

My chief naggers and first readers – my husband and daughter, the 'two Cs' – have provided pep talks, wine, and patience. I love them both to bits and I couldn't have written this or got it out into the world without them. Please stop nagging now.

Last, thanks in advance for those reading this novel. I hope you enjoy it, and that it makes you want to explore my little corner of the world (and, of course, the next book in the series).

About the Author

Bren Atkinson has been a 'liner-upper of words for other people', as she puts it, for over 30 years. She worked in bars, cleaned hotel rooms and was miserable in a tax office during her studies, which included stays in Germany and the USSR. She then moved from the UK to Switzerland for one year and stayed for 30. She has worked in publishing, international organisations and as a freelance translator and academic editor, and while doing so has travelled to over 60 countries. Now lining up her own words, Atkinson moved to southern France in 2007 and put down roots there. She and her husband now enjoy a peaceful existence amid olive trees and rolling hills, and are dictated to by their three extremely spoiled cats.

Watch out for Book 2 in *The Edge of Provence* series, to be published in late 2019.

www.brenatkinson.com

21642719R00203

Printed in Great Britain
by Amazon